# untethered

## KATIE HAYOZ

*For my mom,*
*from whom I inherited a love of books*
*(and popcorn and bright colored coats).*

part one

## October 28th

*I'm stuck in this body. And I can't get out.*

*I stare at my arms. These arms. They're not mine, but I'm wearing them. They're thick and muscular and covered in hair. The veins run like rope down the insides.*

*I squeeze my eyes shut for the hundredth time, hoping that when I open them, I'll look down and see my own thin arms. My own delicate veins.*

*I don't.*

*Oh, God, do I need help. I need help. Now.*

*I stand and my head spins. Grabbing onto the desk, I wait for the dizziness to pass. Wait for my head to clear. It doesn't happen.*

*I look from the desk to the bed to the floor to the walls and see where I am. Clarity won't come. Can't come. Because I'm not where I'm supposed to be.*

*My eyes travel to the mirror and the face staring back in terror. "Please," I say. The face says it back, but sloppily. Like a drunk. "Please," I beg again. "Where are you?" This time the words feel formed. This time my lips, his lips, work the way I expect them to. Or close to it.*

*But there's no response.*

*I lift a hand. Take a step. My movements are staccato. Jerky. Clumsy. Like electrodes are flexing these muscles. Not me. Everything about this body is heavy and long. I take another step forward and it's smoother, but I'm not used to the bulk of this body.*

*And I don't want to get used to it.*

*I want out. Of him. Of here.*

# one

## August: Life As Usual (yeah, right)

"Rise and shine, Sylvie," Dr. Hong says, his voice full of forced cheer. "PSG's done. You have a couple hours of free time before the MSLT. Go crazy." I open my eyes and the first thing I see is the bramble of silver hairs sticking out of his nose. Note to self: Buy Dr. Hong nose hair clippers for Christmas.

He helps me sit up and I look down at myself, feeling like something out of a horror movie. Sticky pads with wires dot my legs and chest. I can't see the ones above shoulder height, but their glue makes my chin, forehead and the areas around my ears and eyes itch. A heavy ponytail of wires cascades down my back and leads to a machine on my left. Probes tickle my nostrils.

Doc rearranges things and unhooks me so I'm able to walk around. I almost thank him, but catch myself before I do. I'm here because he doesn't believe me. He's brought me here to prove himself right. As with all the other tests I've taken.

But so far, he hasn't proven anything. It drives him nuts.

It drives me nuts, too.

I go to the window and open the blinds. Outside, the sun is bright. Another stifling summer day in Wisconsin. Outside, I know the air sticks to your skin like Saran-Wrap and feels thick as cotton wool. I can almost smell the fresh-cut grass, the acrid scent of blacktop burning.

But here, in the lab, it stinks like antiseptic. And it's dry and cool. The perfect sleeping temperature. That's what I'm here to do: sleep. It's the last weekend before school starts, and while everyone else is tanning on the sand, I'm snoozing in a sleep lab.

Talk about social suicide.

Dr. Hong writes something on my chart. "I'm turning you over to the team," he says. "I think these tests will help us figure it out, Sylvie." When I don't respond, he goes on. "You know, the cataplexy—that's where you have the sudden loss of muscle tone. Then the sleep paralysis…" Here he looks up from the chart and directly into my eyes. "And, of course, the hallucinations."

*Of course.* The hallucinations. I stare back at him without blinking. He breaks the gaze first and I feel a ridiculous sense of victory.

They're *not* hallucinations. That's what bothers me the most, what scares me and pisses me off: Dr. Hong insists it's all make-believe.

"Your mother's worried about you." Dr. Hong's voice is accusing. Like I've been giving my mom problems on purpose. If there's one thing I don't want, it's to make my mom worry *more*.

"There haven't been any more incidents," I say.

Dr. Hong narrows his dark eyes at me. I know he doesn't believe me. He never believes me. I might actually be offended—if I were telling the truth.

"Well, that's wonderful, then. But with all that's going on–"

"I'm doing fine. Really." No need for him to play shrink any longer.

He's silent a moment. Then he says, "Okay, Sylvie."

"Everything's set for school?" It's a yearly ritual. Tests, tests, and more tests. Then the paper that declares me fit to fester in the classrooms of my high school.

"Sure. We don't need these results to know that. I'll contact St. Anthony's and let them know everything's in order for your –" he picks up my chart and looks at it again "—junior year." He sticks out his hand and I shake it unenthusiastically.

"I'm sure school will be a lot of fun. You must have the boys lined up." His eyes crinkle as he tries a smile.

"The only boys lining up are those who are trying to get away," I say.

It wasn't a joke, but Dr. Hong looks at me and laughs loudly. He throws his head back and I get a direct view up his nostrils.

*Note to self: Forget the nose hair clippers. Buy the guy a weed whacker.*

After a day full of forced napping, I sit in the waiting room paging through old copies of *Good Housekeeping* while Mom fills out paperwork. Despite hating the lab, I suddenly don't want to leave it. I don't want to go back home.

I throw the copy of *Good Housekeeping* onto the coffee table.

When Mom is ready, her eyes are glistening but she doesn't seem overly concerned. Relieved, maybe. We walk to the car in silence. Once the doors are shut she reaches over and pets my head. "You okay, Sylvie?" she asks. "I know you didn't want to do this."

I shrug. "I never want to do any of it. I feel like a lab rat."

"I know, sweetie." She takes a breath. "Dr. Hong said to keep an eye on you—"

"It's good, Mom, okay? Can we just not talk about it?"

We both sit staring out the windshield at the concrete wall in front of us. Neither of us wants to go. But we don't want to stay, either.

Mom starts the car and leaves the parking garage. She takes the long way home. I notice as we get closer she starts swiping at her eyes. She never used to cry.

My own sadness strangles me enough that I know it's going to happen. I can feel it in the way my limbs go all tingly.

*No. Not now.* I slouch down as far as I can in the seat, hoping it's over quick so that Mom won't notice what's happening. If she sees, she'll freak.

My entire body hums and buzzes with electricity. There's an insane ache in my head. It's like I'm being shoved out of a tiny hole in my skull.

Then suddenly, I'm above us both, against the roof of the car. I watch as my body stays still a moment, then crumples in upon itself, my head dropping forward.

Luckily, we turn onto our road and Mom is too engrossed in what's going on ahead of us to even glance at me. My Dad is hauling boxes into his Volvo. And Sam, being Sam, is looking miserable, but helping. There's a pile of Green Bay

Packer paraphernalia in the driveway, along with Dad's beat-up desk chair.

I hover near our heads, but I don't stay there for more than a few seconds because Mom slams on the brakes so hard my body is jolted forward and I'm yanked right back into it. There's a crack of pain all down my spine and bile rises into my mouth. I swallow it and spread my fingers out on my thighs to make sure I'm solid.

"Last stop," says Mom, her voice hesitant.

Dad's just shoving his pillow into the trunk of the Volvo.

Home sweet home.

# two

## August: The Girl on the Other Side of the Hedge

It's midnight and I can't sleep. I'm at the desk in my room, drowning watercolors, watching them saturate the paper and seep into one another. Sometimes one color dominates, sometimes they stay separate, a jagged line providing the barrier between the shades. But mostly the different colors blend to create something changed. Unrecognizable. Burnt Umber becomes sludgy brown, Rose Lake morphs into pinky gray, and Sepia changes to greenish black. I wet my brush and let water pool in the middle of the page. The textured paper buckles and bubbles as if tortured.

I try not to think about my dad's leaving. I try not to think about how tonight he's sleeping in some apartment he's rented, because he's decided he prefers that over living with us. I try not to think about how if I were normal, he may never have left. I try not to think about it, but I do.

The pain of it is sharp and thorny. I want to hold back tears, but one escapes and falls onto my paper. It bleeds into the mess of paint. I push the palms of my hands against my eye-sockets, concentrating hard on forgetting.

A low and steady sputtering from outside my window breaks my concentration. I look out to see a guy on a motorcycle pull up next door and Cassie hop off the back of it. Her date. She doesn't kiss him—she barely even waves—just heads straight up her front steps and into her house. He guns the motor and skids a bit, then disappears down the street.

Thirty seconds later my cell phone beeps. The text is from Cassie: "*Outside.*"

I pull my sweatshirt off the back of my chair and quietly open the door to my room. The house is dark. Mom rarely stays up later than eleven, so I'm not too worried. I tiptoe down the stairs, through the kitchen, and out the back door.

As I cross the cool concrete patio and step onto the lawn with bare feet, I hear the squeak of Cassie's screen door. The moon is a tiny slit, and in the darkness I can't make out Cassie's features right away, but I see a flash of pale and know she smiled at me.

We both move towards the hedge that separates our yards. The hedge where we met eleven years ago.

I can still remember Cassie then. Her hair was shiny, almost sparkling, and my five-year-old self thought it looked somewhere between my Crayola colors of Copper and Fuzzy Wuzzy Brown. In it were perched two silver butterfly barrettes, catching the bright winter sun. There was a lot of activity going on behind her, people carrying boxes and, every once in a while, two or three men puffing under some large piece of furniture. My dad was one of them.

The second he'd seen the moving van pull up next door earlier that morning, he'd shrugged on his coat and said, "I'll see if they need help."

"I'll make them some soup, you know, to welcome them to the neighborhood." My mom was already taking out a large pot.

"I don't—" Dad started, but Mom shut him up with a look. I didn't know it then, but Mom doesn't cook like other people. We don't eat like other people. Words like *scorched, congealed* and euphemisms for *gross* are a daily part of our vocabulary. *Delicious* isn't. I only found out from Cassie a couple of years ago that she and her parents had taken one taste of my mom's soup then poured it into the toilet.

Mom moved in front of the table with a handful of vegetables and glanced out the window. "That girl should have a hat on. It's January, for God's sake." But before I could see who she was talking about, she said, "Outside, you two," and stuffed my brother Sam and me into our snowsuits, yanking woolen hats hard onto our heads.

That's when I saw her. She wore a heavy sweater and a scarf, but no coat.

My Moon Boots punched holes into the snow as I made my way to the hedge. The girl's green eyes followed my progress, her skin pale under a dark smattering of freckles. "Hi," she said when I was standing across from her.

I wanted to be her. I knew it deep in my gut and tight in my heart. I wanted nothing more than to see her eyes and freckles in the mirror. To have that mane of hair free to catch snowflakes blown in the winter breeze.

A snowball whapped me smack in the back. I pointed over my shoulder and behind me, rolling my eyes: "That's my brother."

Cassie's gaze slid over to Sam, then back to me. "Can I play?"

The three of us built a lopsided snowman with pinecones for eyes. Of course, Sam decapitated it the second we were finished. When he went in for hot chocolate, Cassie and I stayed outside to make snow angels.

We didn't want to mess up the angels with our footprints, so we stayed lying on the ground. The minutes passed as we lazed there, sinking into the snow, staring at a wisp of a cloud in the cerulean sky. As the cloud disintegrated into nothing, my entire body prickled and there was a huge squeeze from my feet up to the top of my head, like all of me was suffocating.

Suddenly, I was floating outside myself, above myself, for the first time ever. Everything showed up brighter and in more minute detail than normal, from the poppy red Cardinal clinging to the bristly top branches of our tall pine tree, to the snappy twitching of a squirrel's tail as he ran across the telephone wire, to the diamond surface of the snow in the yards all down the block. And I could see two girls below— me, bundled up and stiff in my pink snowsuit, hat pulled tight over my head and Cassie, loose as laughter in her fuzzy wool sweater and scarf. Her long hair was spread out around her, a shock of color against the white snow.

I wasn't scared to be out of my body. Maybe because I was too young to grasp what was going on. Or maybe because it was so peaceful that first time—after all, it's only recently the shadows have shown up.

Regardless, I didn't freak out.

I came back to my body, not with the jolt I usually feel now, but I slid back in, almost imperceptibly. A strand of Cassie's hair tickled my cheek.

She turned to me then, her smile radiant. "Hey," she said. "Wanna be friends?"

Now eleven years later, our friendship is…well, perfect. Except that nothing's perfect. You just have to look a little closer and a little longer to find that out. Even supermodels are photo-shopped.

I lean against the hedge and can now see Cassie clearly, despite the darkness. A pinprick of envy pierces my chest; Cassie has really gotten gorgeous. Even with her hair in a messy ponytail, even in a T-shirt and well-worn jeans, beauty clings to her like fairy dust.

What I wouldn't give for a pinch of that dust.

I give her an exaggerated smile and say, "So. Your place or mine?"

She laughs and motions for me to go there. I move close to the house where there is a tiny break in the hedge and squeeze through, passing fluorescent patio furniture and an industrial-sized grill. Cassie is already lying on her back in the grass. I lie down in the opposite direction, the top of my head almost touching hers.

How many times have we done this—met in the middle of the night, in her or my backyard, looked at the stars and talked? I don't remember how young we were when it started—when we met at night instead of day—because like most everything with Cassie, it's always just been that way. I do remember how old I was when my mom freaked out about it, though: thirteen. Cassie and I had fallen asleep out in my backyard, and in the morning when my mom saw us there she completely lost it (for a yoga nut she can get pretty wound up). She started screeching at us never to go out alone at night (even in our own backyards) because who knew what kind of murderers or kidnappers or rapists lurked waiting to get their hands on us. Who knew what would happen to me if I were out of her sight. Of course, Cassie's parents thought the whole thing was hilarious. They would let Cassie sleep on the lawn every night if she wanted to. So now Cassie comes out with no worries, while I always have to sneak around as if I'm doing something criminal like selling drugs.

The grass is cool but dry. I bend my legs, knees in the air, and grip the lawn with my toes.

"Tonight was the worst, Sylvie. I swear that Ted is deranged." Cassie lifts a long leg up into the air as she talks. From where I am it looks like her toes are pointing to the Big Dipper. "Get this: he bought two big servings of pasta from Infusino's—not to eat—but to show me how they splattered all over the place when he ran over the boxes with his Harley!"

I laugh and lift my own legs into the air. But next to hers, they look like short twigs.

Cassie sighs. "I can't believe I spent the last night before school starts with him. I should've spent it with you."

"Yeah, well. I was pulverizing pasta tonight, too," I joke. "Messy, but fun."

Cassie giggles, but she knows what I did tonight. Same as I usually do while she's out with boys: absolutely nothing. We stay quiet a minute, listening to the crickets and gathering our thoughts.

I take a breath, hold it, then let it out long and slow. "My dad moved out today," I whisper.

I feel a whoosh of air behind me as Cassie sits up and looks down at me. "I don't believe it."

"It's true."

"While you were at the sleep lab?"

I nod.

"He really did it. I thought he was bluffing. But he really did it." Cassie bites her lip and puts her hand on my arm. "Oh, no. I'm sorry, Sylvie."

The pain I'm feeling must be the same pain the lady in the box would feel if the magician ever actually sawed her in half. I sit up. Cassie's hand falls from my arm, but she stays closer to me than usual. "Yeah," I say. "Well, you're not as sorry as I am. With Dad gone, Mom's taking Dr. Hong's orders to feed me healthy food a little too seriously. We had millet pilaf for supper. With a beet Bundt cake for dessert."

"Beets for dessert?"

"According to Mom, they're sweet." I pause. "Actually, the Bundt cake was almost edible. It was the pilaf that didn't turn out. Not for lack of trying, though."

"She does love cooking," Cassie says, cringing.

"Yeah. Too bad none of us have the heart to tell her how badly she sucks at it." The thought of my Mom standing in front of the stove stirring something black and sticky brings a smile to my face. She thinks she's a food alchemist. That she can carbonize dinner and still somehow turn it into something delectable. It never works, but she never gives up. It's one thing I love about her.

I guess it's one thing Dad doesn't love anymore.

My smile fades.

Cassie gives me a hug. She smells like chocolate and Aviance Night Musk. I want to cling to her and cry, but instead I give her a squeeze and pull away. "Ugh. Let's talk about something other than family."

"Okay," Cassie says. She smirks at me, raising one eyebrow (she can do that, raise one eyebrow at a time). "Gonna ask Kevin out this year?"

Kevin Phillips is a god. He is the sun and the rest of us are planets circling around him. He is the hottest, most popular guy in school: the pitcher on our high school baseball team and one of the best on the swim team. But I fell in love with him before his popularity—way back in fifth grade when he still had braces and thick Coke bottle glasses that got knocked off every time he played a sport.

Now that Kevin's got straight teeth and contacts, he only looks at girls like Ashley Green or Kayla Conroy. Pretty, snotty, and easy.

"Shut up, Cass. You know I'm not going to ask him out. He's been with what's-her-name since March, anyways. They're gonna have their lips grafted together soon."

"So what?"

I cross my arms and study her. Cassie and I have always hung together, two loners against the world. Me, the medical misfit. Her, the caretaking kind that's never left my side. Of the two of us, she's the cute one. Even in first grade, people would comment on her thick hair, the sprinkle of freckles on her nose. However, by age ten, Cassie's cuteness got eclipsed by her gawky limbs. We were a perfect pair then—me, the short, skinny one, her, the tall, gangly one. "Late bloomers," my mom always said about both of us—although all I have to do is look at my mom and see that I'll never "bloom" into something curvy. But just this summer Cassie did. She turned beautiful, really beautiful. Like some exotic creature, not my best friend. And here I am—barely skirting average on a really good day—right next to her like a nasty zit on a perfectly made-up face. There's no way a zit like me is asking Kevin out.

"Just forget it, okay?"

Cassie finds a dandelion and picks it. Then she takes a breath and says, "Don't get me wrong, Sylvie. But don't you ever want to maybe…look at other guys, too? He's not the only one out there, you know."

Fear trickles through me. "You like him, don't you."

"No, that's not it." She shakes her head. "I just think that either you talk to him or you…branch out. That's all."

Thing is, there's no "branching out" for me. Because maybe Cassie doesn't remember, but I can't forget how in fifth grade I would go to school nauseous with fear, knowing that Randy Lang would get me at some point during the day. How he'd call me *skinny* and *creepy* and, how no matter how hard I gripped my lunch money in my sweaty hand, he'd manage to pry my fingers back while grinding my spine into the rough tan bricks of the school wall. How I'd always end up a quivering mass of jelly on the ground. How Randy made me feel so small and worthless and scared, I never told on him. And how Kevin stopped it. Kevin, in his crooked glasses and bright orange braces, should have looked ridiculous standing up to Randy to defend the class weirdo. But instead he looked like a hero.

"Leave her alone, you stupid ape," he said one day.

"Yeah, whaddya gonna do 'bout it metal mouth?" Randy growled and pushed Kevin into the same brick wall.

And then Kevin did it. He bit Randy. Not a clean bite. A nasty one, one that left ripped skin stuck in the wires on his teeth. One that got Randy screaming like a baby. One that got Kevin a month of sitting in the principal's office after school. And one that saved me from any more torture all the way through to the end of eighth grade.

Even now I can't think of Kevin and that day without tears clawing their way out. I swallow and say to Cassie, "No other boys. No one but Kevin. I'm just not ready to talk to him yet." *Yeah. Not until I suddenly grow a new face.*

"You know you're obsessed, right? "

"Cass, you don't understand. You've never been saved by someone."

She looks at me. "Yes, I have. You've saved me lots of times, Sylvie."

"I've never *saved* you."

"In a way. My parents...I'm just glad you've been around. You're there when I need you. Kevin may not know it, but I know you're the best ever."

"Oh, don't start *that* B.S. It's—"

But Cassie reaches over and pokes me in the side, my most ticklish spot.

"Hey!" I laugh and slap her lightly on the forehead. We poke and smack each other, giggling until I see the light go on upstairs in my mom's bedroom window.

"Crap! It's my mom. Gotta head." I stand up, brush the grass off myself and race toward my house.

"See you tomorrow," Cassie says in a loud whisper.

I slip into the kitchen silently and open the refrigerator, yanking out the cranberry juice. I turn on the stove light to see better and get a glass. Just as I'm filling it, Mom appears in the doorway.

"Ah!" She jumps and puts her hand to her chest. "What are you doing here? You almost gave me a heart attack."

"Thirsty."

"Can't sleep either?"

I shrug and sigh, relieved she didn't get up because of me and Cassie. Coming down for a midnight snack is acceptable in her eyes. Going into the yard isn't.

She sits down at the table across from me. She looks like she's been electrocuted, her hair is such a mess. And her eyes are all puffy, like she's been crying.

I hesitate. We haven't said much to each other today and I'm afraid a question might open up a dam. But I ask anyways. "Why are you up?"

"Oh, too much on my mind. With your father gone, I keep rehashing our lives, wondering what I could have done differently. What *we* could have done differently. Just looking at the bathroom sink, where his toothbrush should be—" She stops abruptly. "Oh, Lord. You don't want to hear this, Sylvie."

She's right. I don't want to hear this. It makes me too sad. I try to smile at her but it comes out lopsided. I get up and pour my juice in the sink. "Well, I think I'd better get some sleep."

She nods and gives me a pat on the arm. I hurry up the stairs, but before I reach the top, I hear her sob. In my room, I close the door, shutting out the noise, wishing I could shut out so much more.

# three

## August: Shadow Plays

I toss and turn in bed. The pain and anger of seeing my dad pack up his car and leave hasn't gone away. In fact, it crushes me so hard, I'm squeezed out of my body. Literally. I try to clutch my bedcovers, to stop it from happening, but I have no control.

*Oh, come on. Give me a freakin' break. Like I don't have enough going on?*

I'm out in a matter of seconds. I feel solid, but insubstantial. Like Cool Whip.

I hear them before I see them: the shadows. An icy tongue of fear stabs through me. The noise is a high-pitched hissing. I know it's a language, even if I can't make out the words.

Dark inky pools enter the periphery of my vision. Long, liquid fingers curling around the room. Then around me. Their touch is frigid and insidious.

*Don't panic. They can't hurt you.*

I know what to do. I have to ignore them and concentrate on being heavy. On getting back into my body. On leaving them behind.

*I'm an anchor. I'm a two-ton weight.*
*I'm made of molten metal.*

Wham! Back in my body, my breath leaves me in one loud whoosh. I feel as flattened as a Capri Sun sucked dry.

It takes all my energy to sit up. I search blindly for the switch on my lamp and try to scrape the bad taste off my tongue with my teeth. *Ugh. I hate it when that happens.*

The shadows don't come every time. Thank God. If they did I'd go crazy (if I'm not already). The shadows are like leeches. I don't know what they drain me of, but I feel half-empty after they've come.

And then there's the aftertaste. Sharp and metallic. It coats my mouth for hours.

The only solution to keeping the shadows away forever is to think happy thoughts. Which is pretty hard to manage all the time.

But I try it anyways. So I go to sleep thinking: *Happy, happy, joy, joy...*

## October 28th

*Get out.*

*I stumble to the door, fumble with the lock and pull it open. The hallway is dark and silent. Sleep blankets the whole house.*

*Feeling the textured wallpaper in the hall, I let my touch lead me to the top of the stairs. I hover, unsure how to go down with such big feet. I cling to the railing and move down each step foot-together-foot-together like a toddler learning to walk. Sweat drips down the sides of my face, this face, when I think for a second about what's really happening. So I don't think about it. I can't.*

*Finally, I make it down the stairs and to the front door. I heave it open. The October air is so cold it's prickly. My new legs are awkward, but their stride is long. It only takes a moment of right, left, right, left before I'm sprinting down the street in full force. I take the shortcut through the park and stop at the back of it. The grade school gate is closed. And locked.*

*I should have known.*

*Tears sting my eyes and the back of my throat. The fence is too high. I'm too small. I've never been able to climb that thing. Going around will take forever. Too long. And I don't have enough time. Because I've got to get home before…*

*I've just got to get home.*

*I look down at this body. Then back at the fence. And when I reach up towards the smooth planks of wood, I realize I'm tall enough that my fingers are able to grasp the top.*

*I wrap both hands around the edge and hold on tight. My feet slide and push against the fence, and my shoulders, his shoulders, strain against the weight, but they don't even hurt. And then I'm up and over. Just like that.*

*Get home.*

*I run until my lungs are burning raw and I still run some more. When I make it to my street, red lights are flashing in front of my house. Oh God. An ambulance is leaving, its siren loud and urgent.*

*"No!" I scream. But it speeds on.*

# four

August: St. Anthony's (Patron saint of lost things—like the four years of your life spent at this school)

"Eat. Breakfast is the most important meal of the day." Mom slides a box of All-Bran across the table in front of me and Sam. We're probably the only people in the nation under the age of 50 who actually eat it. Not that we want to, but Mom forces us to keep our digestive systems healthy.

At Cassie's, they eat Pop Tarts.

Breakfast is eerily silent without Dad swearing over the newspaper. It's so quiet I can hear the crunching as Sam eats his cereal.

Mom sits down and pulls a Kleenex out of a pocket of her polka-dotted bathrobe. She wipes her nose. "Your father forgot the coffee machine. I'll bet he's having a tough morning."

All of us glance at Dad's empty chair.

"He said he'd come see you two off. But I don't know where he is. You'd think he could have stomached another night in this house, but—" Mom makes a mewing sound from behind her Kleenex. People say she's attractive, and she is. She's willowy and graceful with deep gray eyes and high cheekbones. Except sometimes I don't get it, because people also say we look alike. And what I see when I look in the mirror is far from pretty: putty brown hair, a pointed chin, a too skinny frame. Plus, both Mom and I get allergic reactions to all sorts of things as well as bouts of eczema—all potential for serious hideousness. Well, at least on my end. Mom's learned to manage it. Mostly.

"You two better get going," she says, shoving the Kleenex back into her pocket and suddenly clapping her hands in fake enthusiasm. "Your first day of high school, Sam! Aren't you excited?"

Of course Sam is thrilled. Not.

She gives us our lunch money and sends us outside.

I push open the back gate and stand looking at the red-brick house next door. Cassie's window is open, so I call out, "Cass!"

Her face appears behind the screen. "One minute."

That means ten.

Sam and I walk to the front and hang out on the sidewalk. I scratch a patch of dry skin and check my watch. That's when Dad pulls up and parks in the driveway like he still has the right. He gets out and comes toward us. He looks like hell—his dark hair is mussed up, there are dark circles under his hazel eyes and his cleft chin is all stubbly. He did miss his coffee; he's usually good-looking. Really good-looking. So much so that if I didn't have his mouth and his weird overlapping second toe (I know, so gross, and Sam's got it too), I'd suggest a paternity test.

"Want a ride to school?" He's all breezy, half-smiling.

Neither Sam nor I say anything.

"I can take you," he insists. When I shake my head no, he coughs and nods. "I just wanted to wish you both luck on your first day."

"Jeez, strange," I say. "I don't feel so lucky right now, do you Sam?"

Sam looks down at the sidewalk and chews on his thumb.

"Fine, I get it." Dad runs his hands down his face then rubs them roughly against his cheeks. "And I love you two."

He walks up the driveway and goes to the back of the house. Sam and I look at each other, and something in my chest widens. Sam looks pale and scared. I want to hug him, tell him it'll be okay. But I don't know that it will. And hugging is something we just...don't do. I muss up his hair instead.

Cassie comes through the door, wearing a purple dress that shows off how much she's changed over the summer. I hear Sam suck in his breath.

"Your dad's here?" Cassie nods to Dad's car as we start walking.

"To wish us luck," Sam says.

I roll my eyes. "Yeah. Lots of luck."

Sam pulls his iPod out of his pocket, and falls behind, keeping out of the girl-talk.

"Well, your parents aren't the only losers," Cassie says. "God, I hate mine. I had to shake them awake for work. Again. I wouldn't mind so much if they just woke up. But they're always pulling the covers over their heads and whining. I'm always playing babysitter."

I wrap my arm around her waist and squeeze. "They're adults, Cass. They shouldn't need a babysitter. They're just lucky they've got you around. "

Her parents have a habit of downing martini after martini practically every night. Which means Cassie ends up having to wake them in the morning, because apparently their alarm clock can wake the dead but not the hung-over.

We shuffle on without saying anything for a while. It's only 7:00 in the morning, but it's already hot and way too humid. A trickle of sweat shimmies its way between my shoulder blades and for a second it soothes my eczema. It's just wrong, starting school before the end of summer. Wisconsin gives you only so many decent days in the year as it is. Nobody wants to spend them in St. Anthony's High School.

Sam drags behind us. I wonder if he's thinking about Dad. No, I'm sure he is.

"How's he taking it?" Cassie whispers.

I shrug. Sam's the sensitive one in the family. But he hasn't broken down. Neither of us have. Not yet. Mom's the only one who's falling apart.

We turn down the lake road and Lake Michigan stretches before us, a perfect aquamarine. That fake-looking blue. Like the pictures you see in vacation brochures for places on the ocean. I should adore Lake Michigan, so like an ocean—so big, so blue. And I guess I do, for the way it looks. But don't force me into water. I panic around anything wet. No baths for me. I'm a shower girl, all the way—and even then, I scrub up fast.

The last time I swam was when I was twelve. Cassie and I were down at North Beach on a really windy summer day. The kind that makes high, white-capped waves perfect for surfing or sailing. Or drowning. We'd been jumping them most of the afternoon when suddenly we found ourselves in too deep and too tired to swim back. The undertow kept yanking us out further and further. We'd try to make a break for shore but the water just sucked us back.

"Sylvie!" Cassie's pale face was gray with fear. She clawed at me. She grasped my swimsuit straps, my neck, her nails digging into my skin, pulling me under with her. Water filled my nose. I sputtered around, any toehold in the sand lost with the next whitecap. We were in over our heads. I was sure the lifeguard couldn't even see us. If we were going to make it out, one of us had to be able to call for help. "Get on my shoulders," I screamed to Cass when I was able to get my head above water for a second. "And yell."

Cassie climbed onto me, her feet grinding into my hips, her hand gripping my hair. Her whole body was shaking.

I can still feel the weight of her thighs pushing against my neck, can still taste the panic every time a wave hit and I swallowed lake water instead of air. And I can still remember losing grip on my body, just as the undertow got the best of me. I watched from above as we started to drown.

I was yanked back to my body as the lifeguard dropped us down onto the sand.

"Summer in Racine can fool you into thinking you actually live someplace worth being, can't it?" Cassie asks now, looking out at the lake. Obviously, she's not as scarred by our near-drowning incident as I am. She took swimming in Phys Ed our freshman year no problem. I had my mom write a note claiming "psychological trauma" to get out of it. That was a vile year. Tori Thompson saw the note and it got around school. Everyone called me "Psycho Skinny Sylvie Sydell." Then, of course, came the bits where I went cataplexic and my muscles melted while I accidentally left my body in class.

Let's just say the "Psycho" nickname has stuck.

"Racine sucks any time of year, Cass. And so does St. Anthony's," I mumble. "I'd better not have any classes with Tori Thompson."

"Ugh. Or Ashley Green."

"Tori's worse," I say. "But maybe I'll have a class with Kevin this year."

We make our way onto school grounds, then Cassie stops short. "Speak of the devil."

Snaking between cars in the parking lot are Kevin, Bryce Hensley, Ashley Green, and Kevin's appendage, Samantha Bauer. Kevin and Bryce are together, while the girls follow behind.

"Oh, no." Both Ashley and Samantha are wearing miniskirts and push-up bras. I look down at my covered legs and navy tank-top with the built-in padding. Luckily, I notice just in time that the foam insert where my left boob should be is pushed in, creating some sort of crater instead of cleavage. I shove my hand inside my top and poke it out, trying to look as casual as I can under the circumstances.

They're two feet in front of us now and that same giddy, nauseous feeling I get every time I see Kevin pulses through me. He's gorgeous. His hair has turned coppery-gold from the summer sun and his calf muscles flex as he walks.

Because Kevin went to grade school with me and Cassie, he never ignores us. But he never really says much more than, "Hey," either. Yet this time he says, "Hey," then does a double take and stops.

The rest of his group kind of stumbles and says, "What the—?" Then they spot us. Ashley and Samantha roll their eyes and mutter but Bryce and Kevin stand still, looking only at Cassie.

"Cassie Sanders?" Kevin pushes his sunglasses up into his hair. His eyes are darker than my dad's espresso. "Wow. Hi. You look…you've changed."

Cassie stops, arms crossed, hip out, posed like a model. She narrows her green eyes at him and pushes out her glossed lips. When she speaks, her voice is clipped and angry. "Really? Changed enough for you to speak to me now?" She tromps up St. Anthony's front steps and doesn't look back. Kevin and his clan look as shocked as I feel.

"Uh…well, 'bye," I say. They grunt some response and I hurry to catch up to Cassie.

"What was that about?" I grab Cassie's arm once we're inside the building.

"He's an ass, Sylvie. Did you see that? 'Cassie Sanders, you've changed.' What was I, a toad before?" She's practically yelling.

"Shhh. Of course not, you know that. But if you think he's such a jerk, why are you always pushing me to ask him out?"

"Because you like him."

"But why are you so mad?" I know the answer. I know it. I feel my voice go all squeaky. "You like him, too, don't you?"

"No!" Cassie shakes her head. "Maybe I overreacted, okay?"

I decide to let it drop for the moment. My stomach is wrenched into a knot. Kevin's noticed Cassie. And if she likes him, I'll never have a chance. Never.

Sam comes up and pokes me in the shoulder just as Cassie and I reach our locker. "Hey, uh, about lunch—" he begins but all of a sudden from behind me a voice, thick and gooey as taffy, drawls out, "Oh, look! It's Psycho Sydell! With a boyfriend? A little young for you, don't you think, Psycho? With glasses that thick you'd think he could see who he's hooking up with."

Tori Thompson and two of her friends stand a few feet away, teeth bared and claws sharpened.

Clueless, Sam shakes his head and says, "I'm her brother."

"Hmmm…I should have seen the resemblance," Tori coos. "Ugly runs in the family."

Thing about Tori is she's toxic. She actually hung around me and Cassie for, oh, about three days freshman year. But I guess she didn't like how well Cassie and I clicked. How we finished each other's sentences, how we shared everything. Cassie wasn't gorgeous back then, but she was still the more confident, the more with it, of the two of us. And of course she didn't have strange collapsing spells. So Tori cornered her one day and forced her to choose: Tori or me. Cassie chose me. The next day Tori decided to make my life miserable. She hasn't let up on me ever since.

Now Tori grins her venomous grin. "Should have known he wasn't your boyfriend. Because, Psycho, with a boyfriend? Not likely."

I don't need this. Not on the first day. So I ignore her and shove my books into the locker. I know from experience that she'll go away if I don't take the bait. I don't need the whole school seeing her make fun of me.

But Cassie, apparently, doesn't care about the whole school. "Just shut up, Tori. Leave Sylvie alone."

"Make me."

Heat rushes to my cheeks. "Leave it, Cass. She's not worth it."

"Oh, I'll make it worth your time, Psycho." Tori moves closer to us, swinging her hips.

Kevin comes up to us then and there. For a second, my stomach flutters and I remember the fifth grade. He's still a hero. He's here to save me. All that's missing are the braces.

"What's going on?" he demands.

*Bite her*, I think.

But the only thing that bites is the situation. Because Cassie glares at Tori, then Kevin. "Absolutely nothing's going on," she says and pushes me and Sam down the hall. "Come on."

My face is on fire. Once we're far enough away from Tori, I whisper, "Don't do that again."

Cassie looks surprised. "What?"

"Treat me like I'm a kid. Talk for me."

"Sorry. I was only trying to help."

"Don't." Now that Cassie has curves, she's acting like my mother. I'm sure she sees me differently than she used to. Now I'm Psycho Skinny Sylvie Sydell, her little friend who has to wear two pairs of jeans, one on top of the other, so as not to seem so disgustingly frail. Her little friend who can't be trusted to drive a car or ride a bike because her sinews might soften all of a sudden and cause an accident.

"Just don't," I say again, angrier than I know I should be.

The morning drags on forever. I check my cell between classes and Cassie's texted me an apology. By lunchtime we're friends again.

Sam catches up to us as we're walking into the cafeteria. "Can I sit with you?"

I stop and let the wave of people pass in front of us through the double doors. "God, Sam. Don't you have *anyone* to sit with?"

My brother looks down at his shoes—some sneakers Mom got at Target for $11.99. He's small and skinny like me—a little too fragile looking. It's only day one at high school, but I can already tell the next four years aren't going to be good to him. I mean, he barely got through orientation without crying.

So, while I really don't want him to sit with me (I see enough of him at home, okay?), I still want to keep an eye on him. Make sure he's doing okay. Plus, today is extra tough: I know Dad's leaving is killing him because it's killing me. "Fine, you can sit with us," I say. "Just for a few days."

Behind his glasses, his eyes close in relief. Then he nods and smiles and follows Cassie and me through the lunch line.

"I can't believe Mr. Crawford is doing it again." Cassie takes a cup and pours herself a Suicide Mix, every couple seconds moving the cup down the line on the soda fountain to put in a new flavor until it's full. The end result smells something like cat pee. "It was great and all the last couple of years, him giving out Twix bars for geezer rock trivia questions. But don't you think at some point the guy should teach Geography instead of the Rolling Stones?"

Moving my tray down the line, I wrinkle my nose. What *is* that—refried beans or vomit? "Really, Cass, you don't think knowing the length of Mick Jagger's tongue is as important as knowing where the Rocky Mountains are?"

Sam leans over, his eyebrows knotted. "What's a McJagger?"

I ignore him and keep talking to Cassie. "Yeah, well, you haven't had Trig yet. Mrs. Zimmer already gave us homework. Lots of it."

When we finally find enough stuff that resembles food, we head to the cash register. Kevin and his friends are right ahead of us.

"It's great that he's got *A* lunch," I whisper to Cassie, feeling my stomach roll at the sight of his back. "I thought for sure he'd change his lunch to *B*, to be with Samantha his beloved."

Cassie shrugs.

"Unless they broke up since this morning and we just didn't hear about it yet." I slide my tray onto the counter. "But why would they do that? They're inseparable."

Cassie shakes her head and pulls her wallet out of her purse.

I look over at Kevin, heading to the table with his friends. He glances back, eyes on Cassie.

*Oh, God.* He doesn't want to be with Samantha. He wants to be with Cassie.

I must be standing there with my mouth open, because the lady with the hairnet behind the cash register snaps her fingers in front of my face. "Three dollars!"

I pay. But it doesn't matter. I no longer have an appetite.

# five

## August: An In-School Out-of-Body Experience

Last hour of the day, I have my elective. Art. The familiar smell of turpentine pricks my nose as I take a spot behind one of the beat-up tables. Both Mrs. Stilke and my fellow art-freak, Nelson Strange (yes, that's his name, poor kid) smile at me.

Nelson gives me a thumbs up as I slide onto the stool next to his. His thumbnail is painted black. As are the rest of his nails, though somehow the overall effect is actually masculine. There's a hole in his nose where a ring should be. School policy doesn't allow obvious body piercing. However, there's apparently no policy against Nelson's electric blue hair. Go figure.

"Hey," I whisper, and nudge him with my elbow. "Looks like she's still got a thing for you." I'm talking about Melissa Scott, the center on the girls' basketball team, who's sitting on his other side. She sits next to him every year and flashes her long legs in his direction. She likes to play up her assets.

Nelson blushes and hooks a combat boot onto the rung of his stool. He narrows his eyes at me. "You okay, Sylvie?" Leave it to Nelson. Haven't seen the guy in almost three months and right away he knows something's up with me. Like every time I'm upset I have a tattoo on my forehead announcing it. Today it could read: *Shadows Sucked Me Pale* or *Dad Moved Out*. I don't talk about the shadows, but eventually I'll end up telling Nelson about my dad. After Cassie, he's really the only friend I've got. We sat next to each other in Mrs. Stilke's Art class freshmen year and hit it off from day one. He's got blue hair; I've got a blue outlook on life. Makes us buddies, I guess. Plus he's never called me *Psycho*, despite witnessing a couple of my "incidents."

Nelson's about to say something else when Mrs. Stilke stands up and demands our attention.

"Welcome back, ladies and gentlemen. I hope your summer was nice." She pushes a strand of jet-black hair from her face. "We'll be starting off simply today. Just a charcoal sketch." We all go to the back of the room and gather our materials together. When we're at our places again, Mrs. Stilke continues. "I'm going to need a model." Several hands shoot up like rockets—it's a chance to get out of actually doing the assignment and to just sit still for the next couple of classes.

I stare down at the table, my hands tucked between my legs. No way do I want my classmates to study my features, draw them on paper. I'd rather die first.

"Sylvie? I'd like you to do it," Mrs. Stilke says in a firm voice.

I whip my head up and let out a little squeak. All the blood drains out of my face, maybe my body, too. I'm sure if I get up, there'll be a puddle of it on the floor. "No...I... uh...can't, Mrs. Stilke."

"Yes, you can and you will. You're the one in this class who needs the least amount of practice sketching faces." She waves for me to come forward out of my seat. "Come on."

"But—"

"No buts. Come on. You've got an interesting face. Great for sketching."

*Interesting.* A nice way of saying aesthetically challenged. I swallow. Mrs. Stilke motions again for me to come to the middle of the room. Unless I commit suicide right here and now with the sharp point of my charcoal pencil, there's no way out of it.

The second I get up, all the blood I thought I'd lost comes rushing into my face. I walk stiffly around the semi-circle of tables towards the center of the room and the tall stool Mrs. Stilke has put there. I don't look around, just keep my eyes locked onto a point on the back wall. Big mistake. Because somebody put their foot out. On purpose or I just didn't see it. Either way, my foot hooks theirs and all of a sudden I'm kissing the floor. There's a loud thud as my forehead smacks the concrete.

*Ooof.* The pain. It's piercing and it squeezes, squeezes, squeezes my head. My body tingles and shivers. *Oh, no. No, no. Here it comes. Again.* There's a shifting at the base of my skull. And then smooth as butter, I slide out of my body and hover in the air right over a paint-splattered table. Mrs. Stilke is helping my skin and bones off the floor. Already there's a large, red lump on my body's forehead.

*Real attractive there, Sylvie.*

I float upward, through the ceiling and into Mrs. Zimmer's Trig class. I stop just above her desk. Her book, the teacher's edition, is open. And smack in line with my vision is page 3, number 13. I see the answer in red, $x = 30°$ *and x* *= 150°*. I'm about to commit the rest of the page to memory, when suddenly I feel a tug. I zip back down through the floor and with jolt I'm me again. The physical me.

"Are you okay, Sylvie?" Mrs. Stilke's eyes are concerned behind her purple glasses. "We should get you to the nurse."

I feel woozy for a second and kind of weave around as I stand up, almost toppling over. Mrs. Stilke grabs me before I fall. There are a few giggles and some gasps. This is where I know someone will sing-song, "Psy-cho!", but Mrs. Stilke whips around and the room is quiet. "Nelson, take Sylvie to the nurse. Now."

My head hurts like a son-of-a-bitch, so I'm actually glad to go to the nurse's office. Nelson gently helps me out of the room and we walk together upstairs. He's holding my arm, like I'm some old lady.

"Looks…uh…painful," he says.

"Yeah." I put my hand to my forehead. It's already swollen to the size of a Big Mac. "Geesh, the size of this thing. There goes my modeling career."

Nelson's blue eyes go wide. They're a shade lighter than his hair. "You never told me you're a model."

"Yeah. The Before pictures for plastic surgery."

His brow wrinkles up like an accordion.

"It's a joke, Nelson."

"Oh. Not very funny," he says and smiles at me. He has dimples when he smiles. "But you could be. You're pretty enough. Or you will be when the swelling goes down." He nudges me gently with his elbow.

"Yeah, right." I give a sharp laugh.

"Hey." He slows down. His combat boots make dull thuds in the hallway. His voice is unsure, questioning. "Are you okay? I mean, really?"

"What, now you're gonna start calling me Psycho like everyone else?"

He blanches. "No! No, hell, no. Besides, nobody calls you Psycho. "

"Everybody calls me Psycho, Nelson."

"Tori Thompson's not everybody. She doesn't even count as—"

We reach the nurse's office. "Here's my stop," I say, cutting him off.

"Want me to come in with you?"

I shake my head—a painful mistake. "No. But thanks."

He nods his blue head at me but doesn't let go of my arm.

"Uh, Nelson?" I say, looking down at his hand, and he finally loosens his grip. He blushes then turns back down the hall.

"That's quite a knot," Nurse Carey says as I come in. She asks me questions about the fall. I tell her everything. Well, everything that is except the leaving my body part.

I've got a good rap sheet here in the nurse's office. For all the times my soul's gone AWOL. Since freshman year, it's happened a lot. Any pain or strong emotion can send my spirit flying. Luckily, most of the time I go out and back in before anyone notices. But sometimes...sometimes the cataplexy kicks in and my body collapses. That gets noticed.

Not exactly the kind of thing that wins a popularity contest.

Nurse Carey pokes and prods and says, "Hmmm" a lot, but in the end she decides to believe me that it's just a plain old bump from a plain old fall and takes care of it.

She lets me stay in the office until the hour is over. When the final bell rings, she summons Sam to come and accompany me, then shoos us out. "Go home and get some rest in a stress-free environment," she says.

Sam and I almost burst out laughing. Stress-free? Our house?

As if.

# six

## August: Monday, Funday

Despite Nurse Carey's order to go home and rest, I don't. Sam and I head to our usual Monday extracurricular activities at the community center. Sam is part of Science for Scouts, a program that basically teaches five-year-olds about nature, like bugs and stuff. He has terrariums in his room with stick bugs, a praying mantis and other creepy things. They're illegal in most places, but since Sam teaches with them he's been alllowed to keep them as pets.

Luckily, no one at St. Anthony's knows. Because, can you say *loser*?

My thing is art class. For the after school program designed to keep little kids off the street. Last year I got paid. Just minimum wage and materials, but I made some cash. Then the program lost part of their funding and my job was cut. I was furious. Not because of the pay thing. But, because in my experience, adults don't want to help kids, not really. They just want to shut them up. Especially if it involves paying for a program to benefit kids who aren't even their own.

So now I volunteer.

Today there are about thirty kids in the center, ranging in age from six to twelve. Most of them are gathered around the table where the afternoon snack of the three C's is set out: cheese and crackers and carrots.

Angie, the director, smiles and waves me over. "Hey, Sylvie Sweetheart! Did you have a good summer? What d'ya got for today?"

I hold up a huge shopping bag, full of materials. It's a little crunched from spending the day in my locker, but nothing's ruined. "Paper bag kites. We can decorate them and fly 'em. Not much wind, but…"

"That's a big bump." Obviously, she's talking about my forehead.

"Yeah." I shrug. "I'm such a klutz."

We discuss her vacation in Door County and my summer stuck at home. The kids that are new, the ones who've come back. *American Idol.* I don't bring up bad stuff like my dad leaving. I talk as if life were normal. As if I were normal.

About half the kids do the kite project with me. We spend a good hour preparing the kites with paint, glitter, ribbons, and crepe paper. Most of the kids progress on their own, not caring if lines are straight or if the paint runs—what they want is to take the thing out to fly it. They hop up and down and push and shove to bring me their bags so I can punch holes and thread the string through.

Their excitement buoys me. Mondays are actually my fun days. Nobody here calls me Psycho, or treats me like I'm contagious, or forces me to eat bean sprouts. These kids have siblings who've died violent deaths, or parents who need to work three jobs. They've seen so much. Yet they still believe in the magic a grocery bag, glitter glue and a bit of wind can create.

And they allow me to believe it, too, if for just a thin slice of time.

When Sam and I get home, Mom is dressed in stiff brown pants and standing at the kitchen table with her hands on the back of a chair. *Oh, crap.* I feel a family meeting coming on.

I squeak past Mom and slide into the pantry. "Just getting a granola bar," I lie. Among the packages of prunes, rice cakes and Mom's huge jars of flaxseed, hidden behind the dusty ice cream maker is where Dad always stashes the chocolate. He hides it there for us so we can get proper junk without Mom on our case. I run my hand behind the ice cream maker and my stomach sinks. There's only one bar left. A cheerful red, white, and blue Nestle Crunch bar. Only I don't feel so cheerful. Now that Dad's gone, who's going to stock the pantry with contraband? And not only that. Now that he's gone, all of us have lost our sense of humor. Three months ago, Sam and I were still playing practical jokes on each other. In June, I poured Wasabi on his All-Bran and he froze my underwear. But now…who's going to *laugh* every once in a while?

"Sylvie. Come here, please. We have some things we need to discuss as a family." Mom sounds like someone's strangling her.

Sam is already sitting at the kitchen table. Mom motions for me to sit across from him.

I can't keep the sarcasm from my voice. "I don't see how we can discuss anything as a family: the whole family isn't here."

There's a heavy pause.

I sit down. "Sorry," I say.

Mom finally looks at me properly. "Oh, dear Lord. What happened to your head?" She moves towards me, inspecting the damage even though I hold up my hand to keep her away.

"I fell," I say. "By tripping. Like normal people do. Nothing strange, so don't even ask. The school nurse took care of it. I'm fine, really. It's just a big bump."

Mom rips off the checklist. The same list of questions as to what the nurse did or didn't test every time anything ever happens—dizziness, eyesight, hearing, memory…She'd make Dr. Hong proud.

When she's finally somewhat satisfied, she moves back to the head of the table and launches into her talk. "Your father and I discussed the…details of our separating this morning."

That was only this morning that Dad came? It seems like so long ago.

"We've decided that you'll both stay with me, at home, during the week. You'll spend Friday and Saturday nights with him." She holds up her hand, silencing Sam. "Nothing will change except for that. Your dad won't be living with us, but everything else will stay the same. You can still go to St. Anthony's. You'll still get an allowance. Life won't change that much."

Sam and I look at each other. *Yeah. Right.*

"Now." Mom sits down. "Did you want to talk about how you're feeling?"

We're silent. Then I open my mouth. I need to know. To make sure. "Why?"

"Well, because talking about how you feel just might—"

"No. I mean why did Dad leave?"

Mom's eyes fill with tears. "Because …I'm not…he's not… we're…" She sighs. "It's complicated, Sylvie. I don't know what to say."

So no one says anything.

Dinner that night is quiet. Mom asks us about school, but there isn't much to tell. It's the same torture as last year, all over again. All we say is "fine." We sit in silence eating our cremated kale casserole until we can escape to our rooms.

I'm at my desk dragging ink across vellum when Dad calls. Sam talks to him first, then knocks on the door and hands the phone to me. I consider hanging up right away, but instead I say, "What do you want?"

"Hiya. Just to see how you are. See if you have any questions about the arrangements." Dad's voice is soft and low.

"Yeah. I've got a question: why did you go?" My stomach twists. I know the answer.

He kind of moans and I can picture him on the other end rubbing his hand over his face. "We've talked about this, Sylvie. I told you that when you've been with someone for a long time you have to keep working at it."

"So work at it."

He moans again and exhales loudly. "Yeah, well, sometimes it's too late."

I get up and walk to my bedroom window. It overlooks our front drive. There's an oil spot where Dad's car should be. Sadness smacks me so hard in the chest, I can't breathe for a moment. When I do, it hurts. "Just try it with Mom again, Dad. I'll pick up your shoes. She won't have to. I'll even eat your All-Bran for you while her back is turned." Then I lie to him like I did to Dr. Hong, my voice breaking. "There haven't been any more incidents, Dad. I'm okay. Really. You and mom can try again."

He's quiet and then says, "Sylvie, it's not about you. Honestly. And I don't want to try anymore."

All the sadness I've been feeling, all the guilt, bunches into an angry ball. "Well maybe I don't want to try, either! Maybe I don't want to see you on the weekend and pretend everything is all right."

"Sylvie—"

"And it's your fault there aren't any more chocolate bars in the pantry. I'm too skinny to be eating rice cakes!"

"Sylv—"

But I hang up. I press the END button as hard as I can and then I throw the stupid phone against the wall, hoping it'll break.

A jolt of pain shocks me as I lean my sore forehead against the window pane.

It's dusk. A pink sky hugs silhouettes of treetops and telephone wires. Down below, next door, Cassie's dad is putting out garbage cans on the curb. Just as he is about to turn around, Cassie's mom comes up behind him, an empty bottle in her hand. She throws the bottle into the trash, then puts her arms around him. They stand there, hugging on the curb, for a long time.

My throat gets tight.

Cassie's parents really, really love each other. I mean, to the point where Cassie thinks they forget she even exists. My parents used to smile at each other over breakfast. They even used to hold hands. Until I ruined everything.

Cassie's parents saunter back into the house arm in arm.

Why can't my parents be like that? *How can they be, with you here, Sylvie?*

I think of Cassie instead.

Why can't *I* be like *her*?

## October 28th

*The ambulance turns the corner, and its sirens fade as it races further away.*

*I collapse on the sidewalk in front of my house. My chest is ready to burst and my head feels like it's going to explode. "This isn't happening this isn't happening" runs on a loop in my brain. Oh, God. I'm going to be sick. I crawl to the curb on all fours and vomit into the street. I start bawling. The noise of it is low and rough.*

*Behind my sobs, I hear Cassie come out her front door and run down the porch stairs. She's screaming something over and over. It's my name. No, it's his. No, I don't know. I don't know anything anymore. Oh, no, oh, hell.*

*I sit up on my haunches and Cassie squats down next to me. Her face is pale and her eyes wild. Tears streak her face. Her nose is running. She swipes at it with the sleeve of her sweater. She's bawling, too. And babbling. "Something happened to Sylvie. I don't know what happened. I don't understand. She just…The emergency people kept asking about drugs. She doesn't do drugs. We were just trying…"*

*Drugs. Could that be it? Maybe I'm tripping on something and I don't even know what. Maybe for once I'm really hallucinating.*

*Please, let me be hallucinating.*

*But I know I'm not. I feel the hard concrete sidewalk under my feet and taste the salt of the tears that are running down my face. This face.*

*The tears taste just like my own.*

*I'm stiff. Numb. But I need to hold on to something. Someone. So I reach for Cassie and she lets me. We wrap our arms around each other. Cassie puts her head on my shoulder; her tears soak my sweatshirt. Her soft hair is like silk against my cheek. Her shampoo smells like coconut.*

*I'm supposed to have silky hair, a tropical smell. Not, not... this!*

*Cassie's body is solid against my own. She's here. She's real. Where is he?*

*I don't know. But I'm here. And I'm in him. And it's real.*

*"Help," I whisper.*

# seven

## August: TGIF…or Not

The first week of junior year isn't any better than the first day.

I was barely out for a minute in Art class when I fell, but it's made for a good four days of entertainment. For everyone except me, of course.

*Psych Ward: 687-2222*

Someone's taped the note to my locker. Hilarious.

To add insult to injury, every time Kevin passes Cassie in the hall or the lunch line or the parking lot, his eyes lock on her like he's hypnotized. And she seems to be enjoying the attention. But he's not the only one to notice the new Cassie. Practically every guy in school walks past her panting.

Normally, I'm a decent student. All A's. But I suddenly can't concentrate. For the first time in my life, my classes are a nightmare. In Trig I do my homework every night only to find out the next morning that I did it all wrong. Mimi Wilder raises her hand in excitement when Mrs. Zimmer asks a question, but Mrs. Zimmer likes calling on everyone. So, in the first week I've managed to give the wrong answer nine times (who's counting?). In fact, the only right answer I give is to problem number 13, page 3. The one perk to my in-school out-of-body experience.

Mr. Crawford's class, where we answer music trivia and listen to classic rock instead of Geography lectures, should be fun but isn't. I never get the trivia questions right to win a Twix bar. And then suddenly he gives us a pop quiz to see if we've been reading in our Geography book everything he hasn't been teaching us—everything I haven't been learning.

Nelson's the new model in Art, so I don't even have him to talk to during class. He has to sit still on the stool, while we capture him from every angle. I draw the strong line of his jaw, the soft edge of his lips. As I shade in his eyes, something inside me stirs. He's got thick lashes. Like Kevin's. My mind wanders as I sketch and at the end of the period I realize I've drawn Kevin on the paper instead of Nelson. I smear the charcoal with the side of my fist before anyone can notice.

The goose egg on my forehead seems to get worse each day. All shades of purple and yellow and red. Just when I'm thinking I'm going to live through to the end of its transformation, Tori Thompson catches me at my locker.

"I think the bruise on your forehead is an improvement, Psycho. Takes people's attention away from the rest of your hideous face."

I stare at the vents in my locker (why do lockers need vents, anyways? so the freshmen who get stuffed in them by seniors can breathe?) and say low and even, "Leave me alone, Tori."

She raises her eyebrows. "You're telling me what to do?" Then she cackles down the hallway.

Even the news from Dr. Hong sucks. My test results are inconclusive. "I was sure it was narcolepsy, Sylvie. All the signs pointed to it," he says when I go to his office Thursday afternoon. "I think we have to re-explore the fact that this might be psychological." At the look I give him, he shakes his head. "The brain is very complex… Look, I want to get you back into the psychiatrist and the neurologist. For some more tests."

Luckily, there's no room with either of them until Halloween.

By the time Friday afternoon rolls around, I'm ready for the weekend.

"Free at last! Free at last!" Cassie's looking at her reflection in our locker mirror. She dabs a bit of lip gloss on her bottom lip and smears it around.

I stick with Vaseline; with all my allergies, anything else makes my lips peel. I end up looking like my mouth is molting. Ugh.

"I'm going out with Victor Moreno tonight. He said he'd take me to Milwaukee and we could sneak into the casino." Cassie pulls a package of Sugar Babies out of her bag, pours a bunch into her mouth and slams the locker shut. "Why don't you ask Kevin out and we could make it a double date?" she asks, mouth full.

Hasn't she noticed that Kevin has been undressing *her* with his eyes all week? "Uh…Hello? He's not interested, Cass."

She smacks her shiny lips together. "To be desirable you need to believe you *are* desirable."

"What've you been doing? Watching *Oprah* reruns?"

From the way her face turns scarlet, that's exactly what she's been doing.

I sigh. "Anyways, I've got to go to my dad's."

"Oh, yeah." She holds up the yellow bag of candy. "Sugar Baby?"

I take some. "You really think your parents will let you go to Milwaukee?"

She lifts an eyebrow at me. "They won't even ask where I'm going."

Outside the building, we meet up with Sam. He's chewing the skin around his fingernail again. His right thumb is bleeding.

"Come on, Sam. That's gross. If you're hungry eat a sandwich." I pull a wadded up bunch of Kleenex from my backpack and hand it to him. "Stop the bleeding."

Sam wraps his thumb, but doesn't say anything most of the way home. When we're on our street, he finally opens his mouth. "It's gonna be weird. Going to Dad's."

"Yeah."

I think about it. Dad living somewhere else. It doesn't seem possible. He was part of home. You could always find him at his desk working on the computer. Or at the kitchen table, a newspaper in his hand. Once in a while he left his post and took us places. He took me to the hospital for blood tests. To the DMV for my driver's license (which was useless since no one ever lets me take the car—"too risky" with the cataplexy). And he went shopping with me a few months back, but that was a disaster: being so small I still shop in the girls' department, and he kept picking out things with pink bows or princesses for me to wear. But mostly, Dad was around the house. Our house. And now, he's gone.

Then I think about how Dad has said he doesn't want to try with Mom, and yet here we have to give up our whole weekend to sit and listen to him tell us he loves us even though he left us. "Why should we have to spend time with Dad on the weekend, anyways? That's the only free-time we've got!"

Cassie waves her hands in the air the way my mom does when she's wafting incense around the room. "Come on, Sylvie. Cut your dad a little slack. It's not like you're ever that busy on the weekend."

Okay. That pisses me off. She used to stay home on weekends, too, before becoming Miss-I'm-All-That-America. I whirl on her. "Who *are* you? I thought you were supposed to be my friend."

"I am. I didn't—"

"Go on your date, Miss Good Times."

"You're not the only one with problems."

We're in front of my house now. Sam kind of slinks around me and walks towards the back door. (The front is for visitors.) I stand and look Cassie in the eyes. "Yeah, well, when your problems equal mine, let me know."

"You always think the world is out to get you, Sylvie."

"Haven't you noticed my life lately? The world *is* out to get me."

We stare at each other for a long time, then for some stupid reason she starts laughing. Despite the hot anger still boiling in the pit of my stomach, I feel the edges of my mouth turning up, and a giggle escapes me. She laughs some more and I finally can't hold back. We both laugh so hard our eyes leak.

"God, I'm such an idiot. I'm sorry, Cass," I say, wiping my eyes. "Give me a call after your date." I wave and head into the house.

A couple of hours later, my anger is still there, slippery and unsure of who to lash out at. But soon enough, I find a victim. From my bedroom window, I see Dad pull up. *That's it. I'm not going anywhere with him.* If he isn't going to try, neither am I.

"Sylvie! Your father is here! Come on down!" My mom's voice has changed pitch since Dad's left. Like by talking higher, she'll sound happier.

I pop my iPod into the holder, turn the volume on LOUD and stretch out on my bed. Thirty seconds later Mom is at my feet.

She's wearing a turquoise sweat suit. Mom is a massage therapist and regular energy freak. This weekend is some sort of Yoga convention at Festival Hall. Hundreds of women in their forties discussing chakras and sitting in the lotus position. She turns off my stereo. "Your father is here."

"I'm not going."

"Yes, you are. We agreed on this."

Now I sit up. "We didn't *agree* on anything, Mom."

She glares at me, her eyes wet. Again. "Don't do this, Sylvie. I'm having a hard enough time right now as it is."

"Oh, and I'm not?"

You'd think I slapped her for how shocked she looks. Her eyes peel back real wide and she claps her hands to her mouth. And then, all of a sudden, she sits down on the bed and wraps her arms around me. They're thin, but solid. She smells like lavender soap. "Oh, my baby girl. Oh, I'm so sorry, Sylvie."

It feels like I'm six again and waking from nightmares. She's hugging me with that same intensity, like if she squeezes me close enough everything bad will disappear. I give in for a few seconds and lean into her, wanting to stay like that forever. She's always been there for me. Put me first. From the moment I told Dr. Hong the truth about what was happening to me.

I still remember how the doctor's lips puckered with determination. "You're not having out-of-body experiences, Sylvie. You're hallucinating."

I still remember the look my parents shared when he said that.

I've looked it up. Online. Starting with the cataplexy and its link to sleep disorders. Then the out-of-body stuff. The first article I read said, "Neuroscientists have proven electric currents to the brain can create the illusion of an out-of-body experience…" Which didn't scare me. But when I kept skimming and saw the word *schizophrenic,* I was too terrified to read on.

I've gotten treated for everything, you name it. With no results. Just a spectrum of allergic reactions to all the medicines.

Even so, Mom sees me like her cooking: I'm a strange concoction she believes she can turn into something palatable if she tries hard enough. And like her cooking, she never gives up. No matter how obvious it is it won't get better.

Right now, in her arms, I crack. I know if I don't push Mom away, I'll start bawling. So I pull back and push hard. Despite the fact that I don't feel it, my voice comes out determined. "I'm not going with Dad, Mom. That's it."

She gently pulls my hand but when I refuse to move, her face turns stony and she nods. She leaves the room. I turn my stereo on again and fall back on my mattress. I wiggle my foot to the music and then Poof! The music's gone.

"Hey!" I sit up to see Dad standing next to my bed.

"You're coming with me, young lady."

"No. I'm. Not."

But suddenly he's grabbing me, scooping me off of my bed and over his shoulder.

"Let me down! I won't go! You can't make me!" I kick and scream as he descends the stairs, but it does no good. He's stronger than me. We pass Mom at the front door and I give her a dirty look. She hands my dad a bag with my stuff.

In the car, Sam is huddled under his seat belt in the front. I slide in the back, trying to make my anger as palpable as possible when Dad puts the car into drive. "You'll see, Sylvie. It'll be fun."

*Really?* What planet do my parents come from anyways?

Dad's apartment is small and beige and smells like vinegar. There's a bar in the kitchen but no table. He has folding chairs instead of real furniture. Dad shrugs. "I just moved in."

He orders us all pizza. We eat it on the living room floor. "Pepperoni and double cheese! Your favorite," Dad says as he slides about five slices onto my plate.

I cross my arms and refuse to look at him. "I'm not hungry."

My stomach growls like an angry bear.

Sam reaches into the pizza box. "Well, I am!"

I watch Sam suck down strings of cheese and cram two pieces of pizza into his mouth at one time. *Ugh.* I think I prefer him eating his thumbnails. I stand up. "I'm going to bed."

Dad, too, has his mouth full. Tomato sauce is smeared on his upper lip and he wipes it off with a napkin. "But I rented a Disney movie."

My eyes actually hurt I roll them so hard. "Then I'm definitely going to bed." Mom threw my pajamas and a toothbrush into the bag she gave to dad. I take it with me to the bathroom, which is the size of a Tic Tac, and change into my pj's. Then I go into Dad's study, where a blanket and a pillow have been laid out on the floor for me.

"I promise I'll get something more comfortable for you to sleep on for next weekend." Dad stands at the door. He has a plate piled high with pizza in one hand and a Coke in the other. "I know you're not hungry, but I'll leave this in here for the rats. I like to stay on friendly terms with them."

He still thinks I'm ten. If I weren't so angry, I might love him for it. Maybe.

He puts the plate on his desk and takes his laptop out of the room. My entire childhood is filled with memories of him writing. The newspaper constantly has deadlines; I know he won't be able to stay away from work the entire evening.

Despite wanting to make a statement by not eating, I snarf down the pizza right away because my stomach is killing me. I guzzle down the Coke and throw the empty can in the cardboard box doubling as a garbage can when Cassie calls me on my cell.

"How's it going with your dad?" she asks.

"Hmmm. Well, the apartment's practically empty and it smells bad. He forced me to come, Cass. Literally. He picked me up, put me over his shoulder and carried me to the car."

"Oh. My. God."

"The only good thing about being here is that I got pizza instead of Mom's lentil lasagna." I switch the cell phone to the other ear. "How was your date?"

"Victor didn't have any plans to take me to the casino," she says. "He drove way up to Grant Park just to make out. He was all over me, Sylvie! And when I told him to get off, he was blown away. He actually said, 'But I don't get it. I've got a condom.' Ugh!"

Even after all the dating she's done over the summer, Cassie's still shocked that guys are basically jerks. Too many years of no experience. We laugh about tonight, but she's lucky. Things could have turned out differently.

"Stick to nice guys from now on, why don't you?" I say before hanging up, meaning it.

*Just not Kevin nice.*

After the phone call, I can't sleep and I have nothing to do. I haven't charged my phone since Dad moved out. The thing's dying and Mom didn't pack my charger, so I have no internet access. There's no TV. No computer. Mom didn't even pack a book in with my stuff. And my backpack is out in the living room where either Dad or Sam must be sleeping on the floor. So, I have a lot of time for introspection. Mom would be thrilled: *introspection* is her word. Goes along with the yoga.

Dad doesn't have any curtains. The street light shines right into the room, right onto me like a spotlight in an interrogation: *Who do you think you are, anyways?* I lie on the floor, my thoughts keeping me awake, slamming constantly into each other in my brain, ripping away my resolve to stay stoic.

I think about the time we all camped out up north at Luna White Deer. I must have been six, maybe seven. Sam and I took turns jumping from a huge moss covered rock in the forest. On my third jump off, I twisted my ankle. That was before things got bad with me. Before I had lots of "incidents." There was no checklist yet as to what to test when I got hurt. No constant questions or calls to the doctor. There were just my Dad's strong arms around me and his kisses on my forehead. Just my mom's gentle grip on my ankle, doing magic with a bandage and her fingers. No one freaked. Instead, the four of us made popcorn by shaking a metal box full of kernels over the fire. Sam threw the burnt pieces towards the targets I drew in the dirt with a stick. And Mom and Dad fought over who got the last cold beer.

Not over the cost of my medical insurance.

Or whether all the tests are helping or hurting.

Or about their lack of time together as a regular couple.

Or because all my mom's energy is spent worrying. About me.

I break down. For the first time since Mom and Dad have separated, my tears get the best of me, and I cry until nothing more comes. My head is pounding and my insides feel like they've gone through a cheese grater.

*It'll be okay*, I tell myself. *Everything will be okay. All will be okay.* I concentrate so hard on making myself believe it, that I don't notice right away when my limbs go numb. I take a breath to brace myself, knowing I can't control what comes next. And with a pop I'm out of my body.

I wait, fear keeping me still and silent. But I don't hear the hissing. I slowly gaze around me. No shadows. No menacing fingers.

*Thank God. They ruin everything.*

Navigation outside my body isn't easy. I've been slipping out of my flesh for eleven years and I still move like I'm drunk. Plus, I never know how long I have before I'm sucked back into my skin. That's the worst part. The not knowing when it will happen and when it will stop.

I move towards the window and race through the wall instead, right through the layers of plaster and wood. It feels like going through a puff of steam.

Outside it's humid, and I feel the stickiness instinctively rather than physically. I bask in the night air, taking in the way reality is amplified when I'm not in my body. The whole experience is like it used to be, when I was happy and didn't encounter the shadows: it's soothing and lovely. The moon is honey gold, and paints the roofs with its glow. Fireflies create a light show in the darkness while crickets provide the background music. All the pain I felt earlier melts like chocolate in the palm of my hand.

I'm free and light and calm.

Sometimes this out-of-body stuff is a major affliction.

But sometimes, it's a gift.

# eight

A Memory: The Truth, Nothing but the Truth

Age thirteen was the year of sleepovers for me and Cass. I'm not sure why, except maybe because right after catching us in the backyard my mom was vigilant. The only way for us to have midnight conversations was to invite each other over to sleep, since no way in hell would Mom authorize a cell phone for me until high school.

It was also the year of "Truth or Dare." We did everything, from stealing gulps of Cassie's parents' gin to switching Mom's *Magic Masseur* almond massage oil with motor oil (to this day, Mom steers her clients away from that brand). And, of course, we delved into each other's deepest secrets. From Cassie's theft of a mounted butterfly from the Milwaukee museum, her first in a collection of many (butterflies, that is, not thefts), to my horrid fascination with HR Giger's art (Dad wrote an article on him. Scary stuff, but the guy can draw), to Cassie's birthmark on her left butt cheek, to how my allergies made my skin itch—everywhere. And of course we discussed how much I loved Kevin and how much she loved her boy-of-the-month (who never noticed her back then, just like Kevin never noticed me).

We knew everything about each other. Almost.

"Truth or dare?" I asked one April night, flashlight under my chin. We were at Cassie's so technically, we didn't need the flashlight: her parents didn't care what time we went to sleep or if we left the light on. But it was more fun this way.

"Truth." Cassie was huddled inside her princess sleeping bag. Good thing she didn't get asked to any other girls' sleepovers because they would have laughed her out of the house with that sleeping bag. I never got invited anywhere else, either, but I was equipped, just in case. My bag was plain old navy blue.

I turned the flashlight onto her, since she was in the spotlight. But mostly it was because I didn't want her to see the nervousness in my face. "Have you ever…left your body?"

She stuck her head out of her cocoon and lifted an eyebrow. "What kind of question is that?"

"Just a question. Have you ever felt like, well, like maybe you weren't actually in your body? Even for a second or so?"

She blinked at me, her pupils tiny dots in the brightness of the flashlight. "Does getting drunk count?"

"Yeah, if you leave your body," I said. "But you don't ever get drunk." When we drank her parents' booze, it was never to get loaded, at least not for Cassie. She did it to get even.

"Whatever. The answer is no." She raised herself up onto her elbows. "Why did you ask that?"

I moved the flashlight and my eyes followed the yellow circle of light around the room. "Truth?"

She just waited.

"I think that's what happens...when I 'faint.'" I'd accidentally left my body a few times in front of her. And like everyone else, she'd thought I fainted. This was still before high school. Before puberty or panic or peers made the whole situation worse. Before I turned from strange to psycho.

I switched off the flashlight while I waited for her to say something. Darkness swallowed the room. There was a long silence. Tears filled my eyes. I was glad I'd turned off the flashlight.

"That's really weird, Sylvie." When she finally did talk, her voice sounded hollow and a little freaked out. "But a little cool, too."

"No," I said. "Not cool. But weird, yes."

"I think it might be good sometimes to faint or leave your body or whatever. To just...forget everything for a minute." She paused. "I'd like that."

"You don't forget anything."

"But when you...faint...you always look so...relaxed."

"Relaxed? No. Not after." My words were a hoarse whisper. "Everyone thinks I'm schizoid. Maybe I am. Be glad your life is normal."

"Normal." Cassie let out a strangled laugh. It sounded sad and broken. And a few moments later I heard her start to cry.

I didn't ask her what was wrong. I didn't need to. Instead, I reached towards her in the darkness. My fingers found her sleeping bag and her skin. She slipped her hand into mine.

"I love you," I whispered.

Cassie gave my hand a squeeze. "And I think you're better than normal."

I want to believe we both told the truth.

# nine

## September: A Beer in the Hand is Worth Two in the Fridge

The second week of school, Kevin officially breaks up with Samantha Bauer. All week, he 'accidentally' bumps into Cassie between classes and 'mysteriously' ends up behind her in the lunch line. He tries talking to her, but instead, she'll pull me near and say things like, "Hmmm. Don't know... what do you think, Sylvie?" or "I've gotta run, but talk to Sylvie." Unfortunately, I get a bad case of conversation constipation near Kevin. I push and strain and only a tiny turd of a word comes out. Obviously, he doesn't stick around long with me there.

But I can see he's working up to something, because when he looks at Cassie it's no longer just gazing. His eyes are sparked with intention. I don't say anything to Cass. I just wait for him to strike.

He does it on Friday.

Cassie's new looks have brought her new popularity. And as her popularity has been growing, so has our lunch table. Instead of just me, Cassie and Sam, Sarah Chu and Michelle

Winston sit with us, too. Sarah has dark, smooth hair and wears silver eyeliner and T-shirts with Sesame Street characters on them. I'm not sure who she sat with last year. Michelle is what my mom would call 'pleasantly plump.' Her curly, blonde hair is cut to her chin and she's creamy white. Like a girl from a different era. She's new to St. Anthony's this year. Moved to Racine from Neenah. (That's somewhere north of here. If Mr. Crawford actually taught us geography, I'd know where.)

When Kevin gets up from his table and makes a beeline for ours, we've already gotten our lunches. I pick up a french fry from the pile on my plate. It's limp and lukewarm. School cafeteria food can even make Mom's tofu turnovers look good.

"Here comes Kevin." Cassie nudges me, but her cheeks are pink.

*She* does *like him*. I feel panic pushing at my insides. *Get a grip, Sylvie. It's just a boy.*

*No, it's Kevin. He's not* just *anything.*

"Hey," Kevin starts, his eyes on Cassie. *Oh, no. He's gonna ask her out. Oh, God, oh, no.* I think I'm going to faint. For real.

But Kevin's smart. He doesn't take risks. Instead he pulls a folded piece of loose leaf out of his pants pocket and smoothes it out on the table, barely missing a glob of ketchup in front of Sam's plate. "Bryce Hensley's parents are in Mexico and he's having a party tonight. Here's the directions." He makes a point of looking at everyone at the table. "You're invited," he says. "All of you." He stops when his eyes are back on Cassie. "It'd be great if you came." He ignores the collective gasp and walks away. He doesn't look back.

A group invitation. No chance of rejection there.

"Cool! An invitation to Bryce Hensley's! Doesn't he live on Lake Drive? I think his dad is some big-shot at Johnson's Wax or In-Sinkerator, or maybe he's a doctor. He's loaded anyways. And they shot that movie at his house...the one with the baseball players! How cool is that?" Sarah studies the sheet of paper with a rough map drawn in blue ink like she's going to be tested on it. She and Michelle are like me and Cass...inbetweeners, I guess: not geeks, not jocks, not Goths, not trash, not...well, just not anything, really. All of us at the table know that it only takes a few more invitations and some greetings in the hallways by the cool people to be bumped up to semi-popular. We will never actually say it matters to us to be popular. Not out loud. But it does. Just more to some than to others; Cassie, for example, doesn't seem to care.

"I don't know if I'll go." Cassie takes the map from Sarah and tugs at a long strand of hair that has come loose from the mass twisted into a barrette at her temple.

"You have to go. He was, like, talking directly to you." Michelle's blonde curls bounce as she bobs her head.

Cassie blushes again, and I feel my heart rate kick up.

"Whatever," Cassie says. "I bet Ashley and Rhea and Tori and all those biaches will be there."

"Think they'd let us breathe the same air they do?" Michelle giggles, only half-joking.

"But Bryce Hensley," Sarah argues. "He lives in one of the biggest houses in Racine. The movie, remember? Don't you even want to see it? I do."

"Me, too," says Michelle.

Cassie shrugs.

My palms start to sweat. I want to go. Not to see Bryce's house, not to be with the popular crowd, but to spend an evening close to Kevin—to maybe, maybe get a chance to really talk to him and not just say, "Hi." I know it's stupid. I know there's no way he even cares. And I know it's crazy how much I do care.

But I do.

Sam's quiet. He's looking down at the table. By now he should have made friends, should have been sitting with them at lunch, but he hasn't. The idea of a party terrifies him.

"Can you get your parents' car tonight?" I ask Cass. When she nods, I say, "Then we're going. No question about it."

Sam whips his head up. "But we're supposed to stay at Dad's tonight."

"We'll get out of it."

"We can't get out of it." Sam's right. I don't feel like reliving Dad carrying me out of the house again.

"Oh, please," Michelle says, dipping a chicken finger into the pool of mayonnaise on her plate. "My parents divorced when I was nine and all you need to do to get anything from either of them is lay on the guilt. Stuck in on a Friday night? It's ruining your life. And whose fault is it? Your parents'."

Sam looks uncomfortable, but I say I'll try.

The bell rings. Michelle hastily copies the directions to Bryce's into her History notebook. We all decide to meet in front of Bryce's house at 8:30.

"Bryce Hensley's?" Nelson asks during Art class, his voice cracking. "Why would you want to go there?"

"Well, they shot a movie at his house. That's pretty cool, don't you think?"

"That's why you're going?"

"Yeah, sure." I don't look him in the eye.

I can feel his gaze on me for a moment. Then he takes his X-Acto knife and digs furiously into his linoleum square.

Amazingly, Dad says yes. I go for the guilt, as Michelle suggested, and it works.

"This is our time together," he argues. "I don't get to see the two of you during the week."

"But that's not our fault, is it?"

It gets to him. Right away.

"Sylvie, you know I can't let you go just like that. Something could happen." Dad shakes his head.

"I don't have the right to a life?!" Tears threaten, so I inhale and lower my voice. "Dad, everything's been good lately. I promise."

He keeps eyeing me.

I smack Sam. He spits out, "I'll be with her the whole time. Both our cell phones are juiced to the max. And I know what to do if anything happens."

"Which it won't," I add.

Dad gives in. He makes me write down for him the who, what, when, where and why of the evening ahead. He gives us an 11:00 curfew. He checks the oil, the gas gauge and the air level in the tires of Cassie's car.

But he lets us go.

When we get to Bryce's house, his drive and most of the street in front of his house are parked full. Tori Thompson's convertible squats near the garage, and when I see it I have a split-second doubt about wanting to be here. With her here, it all could end up a disaster. But then I think of Kevin. And I have to take the risk.

Sarah and Michelle are standing on the lawn. Cassie, Sam, and I catch up to them and we all walk to the front door together.

The place is ginormous. I count twelve windows on the front of the house alone. A constant *boom, boom, boom* pulses out of them. On the porch we look at each other. We're basically a bunch of party virgins. "Do we ring the bell? Can they even hear it? " Sarah asks. "Or maybe we just go in?"

We don't know, so we ring the bell. The door opens three seconds later, frizzy-headed Tori Thompson on the other side.

My heart drops into my socks.

"Oh hoo!" She yells over the music. "Psycho Sydell and her lame-ass friends! Wrong neighborhood, people. You're looking for Loserville." She starts pushing the door closed.

Cassie sticks her hand out to stop the door. "Kevin invited us," she says loudly.

Tori crosses her arms in front of her chest and looks Cassie up and down. "You mean he invited *you*."

"No, *all* of us."

Tori considers this, then opens the door wider. "Fine. Whatever. If he wants to slum it, let him."

We move in, but she stands in front of me before I can walk further into the house. "Don't think this changes anything, Psycho."

I glare at her and wait for her to move, my heart pounding. Then I follow Cassie and the others into the frenzy.

It's like those parties you see in movies where there are too many people, too much beer, and absolutely no supervision. It seems like the whole freakin' school is here drinking, smoking, or giggling themselves high. The place smells like smoke and beer and perfume and vomit.

"We're gonna check out the place," Michelle grabs Sarah's arm and they go off to sneak around in closets and dresser drawers.

"Help me find Kevin," I say to Cassie and Sam.

A group of guys in the kitchen are pouring beer into a funnel placed in Richard Melmick's mouth and shouting, "Chug, chug, chug!" What a bunch of idiots. As we squeeze past them Cassie yells in my ear, "Maybe tonight you should tell Kevin exactly how you feel about him, Sylvie."

I can't look at her, instead I watch Richard's adam apple bob up and down as he drinks. But I say what I haven't dared say the past two weeks. "Come on. You have to have noticed Kevin drooling over you, Cass. I think there's more of a chance that he'll tell *you* how he feels."

Cassie stops walking and puts a hand on my shoulder. "Why would I go out with him? I know how much you like him."

"Well, yeah," I say. "But I think it would be great if you could be friends."

"Like that'd work." Sam shakes his head.

I hurry down a set of stairs to the basement and they follow.

There's a huge television screen on the back wall. Someone has put on porn, and a group of senior guys are cheering and hooting as a woman with boobs the size of watermelons begins wriggling out of her underwear on screen.

"Ugh. Let's go back up," I say. But then, out of the corner of my eye, I spot Kevin in a room off of the main one. "Wait! There he is."

We hurry past the TV (well, Cassie and I do—seems like Sam takes his time) and arrive in what must be Bryce Hensley's bedroom. There are less people here. Kevin's sitting in a corduroy bean bag chair throwing a baseball into the air and catching it. Bryce is on the bed, leaning over and rolling a joint on the nightstand. Ashley Green is next to him, drinking beer with a straw. A few other people are there: Ryan Witteck, Latisha Harper, Rhea Silverman and Tyrone Dickson (making out in the corner) and, of course, Tori Thompson. She must have made a beeline for Kevin after answering the door.

Bryce and Kevin are in the middle of a conversation, but they stop talking when they see us. Kevin smiles at Cassie. "Glad you came," he says. Then he takes in me and Sam. "Uh…all of you."

Ashley and Tori exchange looks. Bryce arches his eyebrows and leaves the room. Two seconds later he's back with beers for us. "A beer in the hand is worth two in the fridge," he says.

Cassie's gone to a couple parties. This summer, with the barrage of boys she's suddenly been dating. But me and Sam, never. I feel ridiculous with this crowd, totally out of place, and Tori's staring at me doesn't help. Yet Kevin's here. And being so close to him outside of school fills me with a sweet ache that drowns out any other feelings. He stands and clangs beer cans together with us.

"Cheers!" His gaze lingers on Cassie, but when his eyes finally meet mine over the foam oozing out of his can of Schlitz, he winks.

*Oh, God. Somebody get a defibrillator. I think my heart just stopped.*

Bryce lights the joint he's rolled. He takes a drag, then motions for us to sit on the floor. Kevin drops down next to Cassie.

"So we were talking about Kevin's step-mom," Bryce says, smoke escaping his mouth with every word. He passes the joint to Ashley. "That woman's messed up. An effing head case."

"Just wait. There's more." Kevin says to Bryce, then glances at Cassie. "It started with her having the baby."

This is what I know about Kevin's family: His parents are divorced, but he lives with his dad. I have no clue where his mom lives. Two years ago, he got one of the country-club ladies as a new mom. She wanted her own kid, and now, at sixteen, Kevin is big brother to a ten-week-old screamer.

The suffocating, sweet smell of marijuana creeps around the room. Next to me, Sam's making little gurgling noises, trying not to cough.

Ashley offers the joint to Kevin, but he waves it away and keeps on about his step-mom. "So get this, this is all she's been talking about the past few weeks: she's convinced she, like, left her body while she was squeezing David out. Says she saw herself yelling while she floated around the ceiling in the hospital."

My breath catches and my head starts spinning. I feel the can of beer slide out of my hand and drop to the carpet. Sam reaches over and sets it upright, giving me a dirty look as he does so. One phrase reverberates inside my head: *she left her body.*

"Okay, I don't even understand what you mean, dude," Bryce says while running a finger up along Ashley's leg. She giggles.

Kevin bunches his eyebrows together. "She says she thinks her soul…left her body."

"She was on drugs," Ashley sighs.

"Not even," Kevin says. "No drugs."

Ashley tries handing the joint to Cassie, but Cassie shakes her head and raises her beer, "Don't like to mix my medicines." So Ashley holds the joint up in the air and Tori takes it from her.

"If she wasn't on drugs, then what?" Cassie looks at Kevin.

"She says she thinks the pain drove her out of her body. She wasn't dead, but she could go through walls and everything, like a ghost. At least, that's what she's been saying."

"Whooooooo." Bryce lifts his hands in the air and pretends to be a ghost. Ashley, Latisha, and Tori all laugh like it's hysterical. (It's not even the beer—they always act that asinine.)

Kevin runs a hand through his copper hair. "Thing is, now she's convinced she can do it again. She got books from the library. Googled it. Thinks she's some guru. When she's not stuffing a bottle into David's mouth, she's meditating, trying to send her soul out again. I don't know why Dad married her—she's psycho."

I feel my face heat up at the word *psycho*, but butterfly wings bat like crazy inside my chest. *I'm not the only one. Oh, my God. I'm not the only one.*

*Maybe I'm not such a freak.*

*Maybe I'm just a normal girl with a paranormal problem, that's all.*

*Maybe—*

Tori comes over and waves the now miniscule joint in front of my face. "Not gonna ask *you* if you want a puff,

Psycho. You're too goody-goody. Besides, you'd probably pass out on us."

All eyes are on me. I consider taking the joint and smoking it, just to get Tori off my back. But it won't work. She'll never be off my back. And I just don't give a damn right now. Right now, I want to hear more about Kevin's step-mom, so I ignore Tori.

Bryce nudges Kevin with his foot. "So what's up now with your step-maniac?"

Kevin bites his bottom lip like he's not sure if he should really be saying anything. When he finally talks, his voice is low. "Last night she said she did it. That it worked."

Bryce holds up his hands and shakes his blond head. "Whoa, dude. What worked? You mean she, like, left her body?"

I shoot up like a rocket but keep my mouth sealed shut. *She left her body on purpose?*

Kevin picks at a seam on his jeans and answers Bryce. "Yeah. I know it's such bull, except…"

"Except what?"

Kevin looks at Cassie, like he's talking only to her. "Late last night I snuck out my bedroom window and met Bryce to T.P. Mrs. Zimmer's house."

Now Sam straightens up. "The math teacher? You toilet papered her house?"

"She gives too much homework."

Sam shakes his head. "She yelled at me today because when I came to class I had toilet paper stuck on my shoe!"

I close my eyes and wish we weren't related.

Bryce laughs out loud. Kevin grins, punching Sam in the shoulder. "Sorry, man." Then he turns around and looks at Bryce. "But my step-mom knows we did it."

"Derp. Why'd you tell her?"

"I didn't. She says she saw us when she was floating around out of her body."

Ashley giggles. "Come on!"

Bryce shakes his head. "Someone must have seen us and told her."

Kevin's face crumples like he's eaten something bad. "I don't know. She said she was right next to us and could even hear us talking about Coach. She got it right, too."

"This is messed up, dude," Bryce says. Everyone goes quiet.

"So she controlled it?" I break the silence. "She decided then and there that she was going to leave her body and go somewhere and she did it? She controlled when she went out and when she went back?"

Kevin bites his bottom lip again. "That's what she says."

"And you believe her? You believe she did it?" I feel Cassie's eyes on me, burning through me, but I don't look at her. *If I could control it, really control it…if I could go where I wanted, do what I wanted, when I wanted, maybe that would change everything. Everything.*

Kevin shrugs. "No, I don't believe her. It was just freaky, that's all."

"But," I say. "But…if it were true…if she could really control it…imagine the kind of power she'd have. She could follow you around whenever she wanted. Pretty powerful stuff." *Cool. Very, very cool.*

Everyone in the room stares at me.

Kevin studies me for a long time, then he turns to Bryce. "I'm hungry. Let's grab something to eat." They get up and all of us follow them to the kitchen, except for Rhea and Tyrone who wave and shut the door behind us. On the way up the stairs, I feel fuzzy and lightheaded and it has nothing to do with the beer.

Cassie pokes me in the shoulder and whispers in my ear. "Hey, you okay? Are you weirding out on me, Sylvie?"

"Did you hear Kevin?" I whisper. "His step-mom leaves her body! Like me!"

"You *are* weirding out." Cassie bangs her knuckles on my temple. "Earth to Sylvie."

We haven't ever talked about my out-of-body experiences since that one night of truth and dare. And especially not after the whole hallucination debacle with the doctors. But I've always assumed she believed me. I mean, she knows to shake me when I melt on her. And when she does, she always smiles at me and says, "Welcome back."

But maybe she never knew whether to really believe me or not.

*Well, can you blame her, Sylvie? You didn't know whether to believe you.*

In the kitchen, things go on around me, but I stand still, thinking and leaning against the wall. For once, I don't care what anyone else thinks. Bryce pulls out a pack of marshmallows from the cupboard. Sam says something to him and suddenly the whole group is cheering around the microwave, watching the marshmallow blow up to ten times its normal size. Bryce pulls it out and offers it to Ashley, who laughs as it deflates before her eyes.

*Kevin's step-mom left her body.* All this time I wasn't sure what was actually happening to me when I slipped out of myself. Whether it was real. Whether I was crazy. After seeing the schizophrenic reference that one time, I was afraid to research it more. Afraid to talk to anyone. Afraid of what I'd find out. I've been living with this…thing all by myself. But now…someone else did it. And then wanted to do it again. Figured she'd learn to control it. Saw the power in it.

"So." Ashley comes up to me, licking marshmallow off her fingers, breaking my concentration. "Having fun?"

"What's that supposed to mean?" My voice is sharp. We've been in the same English class since freshman year, but this is the first time she's ever talked to me to say something other than, "Faint much?"

"Uh…duh…it's supposed to mean 'are you having fun?'"

I look at her for a minute, taking in her smug expression and the casual way she flips back her chestnut hair. I'm not sure if she's really trying to be nice or making fun of me. But before I can decide, she sucks in a breath then exhales loudly, "Bitch!" She goes back to Bryce, wrapping her arms around his waist and leaning over to whisper something to Latisha.

Heat rushes to my cheeks. I should have given her the benefit of the doubt.

Sam pokes my arm with a sticky marshmallow finger and smiles. "This is great, but we gotta go. It's almost 11:00."

Ten minutes later when we get into Cassie's parents' car, Sam bursts out, "They were nice to me!"

Cassie grins. I turn around to look at Sam. "Did I miss something?"

"The marshmallows…can you believe they'd never microwaved them before? I thought everyone had done that."

"Didn't you notice Bryce and Kevin and all them were slapping Sam on the back?" Cassie turns off of Bryce's street and heads towards my dad's place.

They like *Sam*? I shake my head. No. I didn't notice.

"Next time it's Mentos in Coke." Sam is practically beaming. I've never seen him like this before.

"You were pretty quiet at the end, there, Sylvie. If it's about Kevin sitting next to me, it's not my fault. I was kind of worried, what with the beer and everything that you might get upset. " Cassie glances at me with pleading eyes, then focuses once more on the road when the car swerves.

"No, everything's fine. I was just…thinking, that's all."

"Find something good, will you?" Cassie points to the radio with her chin. I fiddle with the control, stopping on a station that's playing *Satisfaction* by the Rolling Stones.

"'Cuz I try and I try…" Cassie and I sing. We've heard it trillions of times in Mr. Crawford's Geography class. But Sam hums along and asks, "Who sings this?"

"Hey," I say. "We've got to get rid of the beer smell on our breath." I pull gum out of my purse and hand it to Cassie and Sam.

Sam raises his T-shirt to his nose. "What about the smoke?"

"What did you do, when you went to those parties this past summer?" I ask Cassie.

"*I* didn't do a thing. My parents don't care what I do."

"I wish that were the case for us right now." I yank the pine tree air freshener from off the rearview mirror and rub the thing all over my clothes. "This is gonna have to do."

She lifts one eyebrow. "Pine scent? That's…creative. Too bad I don't keep Febreze in the car like Evan. He had a whole slew of stuff he did after a party. Called it his 'Smelling Sober' ritual. I told you that."

Evan. One of the guys she'd dated over the summer. "No you didn't."

She just shrugs. "Maybe I don't tell you everything."

I look at her French manicured fingernails on the steering wheel, then down at my own unpainted ones, cut short. I think of tonight's conversation at the party and of all the times I've left my own body. *Yeah. Well, maybe I won't tell you everything, either.*

When we pull up to Dad's apartment building, Mom's car is parked outside.

"Oh, no. We're dead." Sam slides further into the back seat, deflating like the marshmallow Bryce offered Ashley earlier.

"Come on." Both of us get out and wait for Cassie to speed off before walking the twenty steps to the apartment building. It's a decent complex: sandy brick squares with large picture windows and wrought iron rails on the balconies. Despite Dad's move seeming sudden to me, I know he was actually looking for a place for a while. To get away from her. From me. From us. Maybe from everything.

When we walk into his apartment, they're arguing. Of course.

"—in your care. How could you let them go?" This from my mother who looks on the verge of tears. She always looks on the verge of tears lately.

"I'm still their father and I—" Dad sees us and put a cheesy smile on his face like we're three years old and can't understand what's happening. "Hello! I see you two are on time, just like we said." Here he gives an 'I told you so' look to my mother. But her eyes are probably too full of tears to see it.

Mom turns to us and throws up her arms. "I was worried sick about you! Going out so late! You two never go out. Where were you?"

*That's it. We're toast.*

But for once I'm glad for the tension between the two of them. My dad stands up straighter and says in a steely voice, "Nicole, they're my responsibility on the weekend."

Mom looks from him to us. She drops it for now.

"Why're you here?" I ask.

She pulls an army green backpack off of a folding chair Dad has in the living room. "Sam, you forgot this. I figured you'd need it to do your homework."

Sam shrugs. "I finished it all; Mrs. Leonard wasn't there fifth hour and then I had study hall."

Mom looks almost crushed. "Well, then." She puts the backpack on the chair again, but doesn't make a move to go.

When we'd walked in, the anger in the room was palpable. Now, though, it's dissipated into something else. Dad shuffles his feet and sighs. "Did you want to stay for a drink? Not long. Just until the kids are ready for bed."

Mom pretends to hesitate, but she's not fooling anyone. Least of all Dad. "I suppose I could."

Dad still doesn't have a table, just the bar with stools. Mom gets on a stool, her legs dangling. "I'll have tea, please Michael."

"No tea here."

"All right, then. Fizzy water?"

Dad's lips get tight and a muscle in his neck pulses. "There's coffee, beer, Coke, and milk."

Mom is lactose intolerant. She doesn't do coffee. Or Coke. I wait for her to ask for tap water but she surprises me and shrugs. "Fine. Give me a beer."

While Dad's taking the cap off the bottle, Sam and I get Cokes out of the fridge.

"What are you doing?" Mom looks from me to Sam. "It's almost midnight. You are *not* drinking Coke this late."

Sam puts his back, but I open mine and take a long swig. I don't know why. I just can't help myself. I want to piss them both off. I want them to scream at me.

"Sylvie, caffeine will aggravate your condition!" Mom yells it.

"Sylvie!" My dad says it through his teeth.

"No prob. I'm done anyways." I set the can on the sink, burp and go to put on my pajamas.

In my room, or Dad's office, really, I listen at the door. I hear the door to Dad's bedroom close. That'd be Sam. Sent there since Mom and Dad are discussing or fighting or whatever. Sam is supposed to sleep on the new sofa bed in the living room.

I can hear Mom crying. Every once in a while her voice gets high. I hear Dad say, "You don't know me anymore, Nicole. You haven't even noticed me for years." And then I crawl onto the new inflatable mattress and pull the blankets over my head. An emptiness eats its way through my insides.

If it were just Sam, they'd still be together.

From my jeans pocket comes the beep-beeping I get when someone texts me a message. I grab my jeans from the floor and pull my cell phone out: Cassie.

*"Got mssg frm Kevin 2 go 2 mvie 2morrow. I said NO."*

I blink at the screen and at the same time I blink back tears. *Why the hell is she telling me this? To ruin my night? Just in case it's not bad enough the way it is?*

I turn off my phone.

I hear my mother's tinny voice and then the front door shutting. Then the sound of the clang of a bottle as my dad grabs another beer from the fridge. Pretty soon, I'll smell cigarette smoke seeping through the crack under the door.

I lie down on the mattress again, but can't get comfortable. I roll onto my stomach and then onto my back. But nothing helps.

I'm not even comfortable in my own skin.

# *October 28th*

"Help," I whisper to Cassie, again.

This time she pulls away from me and searches my face. "What? What did you say?"

"I need your help. I'm not who you think, Cass. I'm not. I..." I swallow, hoping I can spit it out. I'm not sure I can voice what's really happened. But I don't know what else to do. "I'm...I'm Sylvie...stuck...in this body. I got stuck and I tried but I can't get out. I know it doesn't make sense, but it's true. And I'm freaking out, Cass. You've gotta help me." The words sound far away, almost distant. Like someone else is saying them.

Someone else *is* saying them. In a way. Ha. If it weren't tragic it'd be hilarious. I start laughing and can't stop. Big hiccoughing laughs that hurt my stomach. My head. My heart.

"Why are you saying this? Why are you doing this? Stop laughing!" Cassie's voice is trembling.

But I can't stop. I can't do anything.

"Shut up." Cassie narrows her eyes at me.

Finally, my laughter dies and I take a few calming breaths. The only way to convince her is to list our secrets, so I do: "We're blood sisters. Since age ten... You collect butterflies... Your parents—"

*But Cassie cuts me off. "Stop talking!" She screams it, loud and clear for everyone on our street to hear. "I don't know why you would do this, but if you say one more word, I swear I'll scratch your eyes out!"*

*I open my mouth, then close it right away. She's got killer fingernails. She could easily do it.*

*Behind her, her dad's voice calls out hoarsely, "All right, I'm ready. Let's go." He steps out onto the porch, his hair mussed, a bleary, worried look on his face. "Your mom…can't make it right now."*

*Hearing this, Cassie's eyes flash like they do when she's angry, but it lasts only a second. She turns to me. "I'm going to the hospital."*

*"Take me," I whisper. I have to get to my body. And maybe… maybe he's in there. In me.*

*"Take yourself."*

*"I can't. Please. I've gotta go there. Now."*

*But she ignores me and walks to the car, sliding into the passenger seat. Her dad backs out the driveway. I hesitate, but only for a moment. Then I leap towards the moving car and yank open the back door. I dive in and slam the door behind me.*

*"What do you think you're doing?!" Both Cassie and her dad turn around to yell at me.*

*"I need to get to the hospital," I say, my voice low and even.*

*Cassie glares at me. Her dad shakes his head.*

*But no one kicks me out.*

# ten

## September: Puttering with the Paranormal

I wake up Saturday morning with a start and look at my watch. 5 a.m.

Bryce's party seems like it took place years ago and I wonder if I dreamt it up. Especially the bit about Kevin's step-mom. I sit in the semi-darkness, thinking. I want to know more about what she did. About what *I* do. Now that I know I'm not the only one, I'm not so afraid anymore. My eyes drift to the desk and I can't believe my luck. With all the Mom confusion, Dad left his laptop in here last night.

I can go on the net and research the whole thing.

I get online and take a deep breath, typing in *leaving your body*. The results aren't what I was looking for:

*Leaving Your Body to Science*
*Full Body Treatment: Leaving your Body Beautiful*
*Leaving on a Jet Plane*

Then I try *outside your body*. The first link gets me:

*Astral Projection and Out of Body Experiences: Traveling
Outside Your Body*

I click on it and tug at my hair, anxious and excited. The
site itself has some weird mystical music playing. Right away
I pound the mute button. I don't know if Dad would be cool
with me using his laptop without asking. There are pictures
of a naked man lying down while what looks like his double
hovers above him. They're connected by a silver rope. I scroll
down to the text and start reading:

*Astral projection, sometimes called etheric projection or out-
of-body experience (OBE): when one's soul or etheric self leaves
the physical body to enter the astral realms.*

Okay. I read it twice without understanding but keep on.
I finally get to:

*In astral projection one consciously leaves one's body—to bob
about the room, to travel the earth, the universe, or different
planes of existence.*

*That's it. Holy crap. That's it.*
I keep scrolling down, then click on another link full of
testimonials, my heart ramming against my chest. There are
hundreds of accounts of people doing it, by chance or on
purpose: a prisoner-of-war who left his body when he was
tortured, a woman who 'visited' her sick brother in another
country, victims of car accidents, high fevers and, like Kevin's
step-mom, women who had extremely painful deliveries.

It's happened to other people. Lots of them. And this whole time I didn't know…I can barely breathe.

They're not hallucinations. I'm not crazy. And I'm only one of many. My eyes sting with tears of relief. I tip my head back and blink at the ceiling until I know I won't cry.

I click again.

*Learn Astral Projection in Fifteen Minutes Flat! Double-click here to order your trip to freedom! Only $69.99!*

I try a different link. And another one. And another one. They all say I can learn astral projection. Several give general directions, saying to lie down in a darkened room and relax, but I can't find anything detailed.

Most of the sites refer to books or DVDs to buy. It doesn't seem like I'm doing more than scratching the surface on the net. They want to sell their books, not give the info away for free.

Click.

*At Your Own Risk! Danger! The Dark Side of Astral Projection*

Getting lost. Evil entities. Demonic possession. Death. All are listed. I think of the shadows. But nothing like that is mentioned here. Here they talk about astral enemies and demons with blood red eyes. No shadows that drain your energy and leave a bitter taste in your mouth.

Click. All the other sites refute the dangers. *There is no risk. Anything that scares you comes from your own imagination.*

I'm not sure that makes me feel better.

But, hell, I've done it. I know it's not dangerous. Not really. I mean at times it's scary and strange, but other times it's magical. Most of the time.

The next sites make voluntary astral projection sound easy. I just need specifics.

Someone turns on the shower in the bathroom. I look at my watch. Wow! 7:30. I've been on the computer for over two hours! The sun's come up, but it's barely visible. Dark, black clouds smother it. The first raindrops splatter against the windows, a sporadic drumming.

I stare at the screen in front of me, a rainbow-colored drawing of people flying in space. I exit the site and erase the history. Yet the image is still in my head.

When I've left my body, it's been uncontrolled. Erratic.

But this. Astral projection. Knowing how to do it consciously would be like knowing the formula to give myself a superpower.

I can't ignore it.

Sunday, I lie to Dad about having to do some research at the library for school. So he leaves me off while he and Sam go to play video games.

I love the library: the hushed voices, the smell of books, even the way the wrinkled old ladies behind the desk look at you like you're up to no good. And the Racine library is great. Its ceiling to floor windows look over the football field and, beyond that, Lake Michigan. Today the lake is choppy and grey. The sky is like what's called Ivory Black on my watercolor palette at home.

I set my books on a table near the windows and go to find the place in the stacks for the books on astral projection.

And plow right into Kevin Phillips.

"Oh…uhh…sorry," I say, my voice a squeak. He's got a bunch of books in his arms, but I look at his coffee eyes and breathe in the musky scent of him. I think of my dream and feel my face burn. I have an urge to run my tongue across his bottom lip.

"Hi." He hugs his books to his chest. "What are you doing here? Studying for the Chem test?"

"No…yes…no…I…" I want to tell him that I think what his step-mom did is something I do, that I'm here to read about it. But I can't choke it out.

"Or is this how you spend all your Sundays?" He gives me a wide grin.

"Just…just today."

He nods and glances over my head (like everyone else, he's a whole head taller than me). "You here with Cassie?"

"Nope," I say. His shoulders droop a bit.

"I gotta go. Swim team tryouts today. Gotta go through the drill every year. I don't wanna be late and piss off Coach." He rolls his eyes. "He's such an ape."

*Ape.* That's what he called Randy Lang when he stood up for me in grade school—a stupid ape. I feel my body sway at the memory.

I want to ask him to study with me sometime. Tell him I've got a system down pat for memorizing. I'd be a great partner. But I don't get further than, "Uh…"

"See ya," Kevin says and walks off.

"Bye!" I call out after him and get shushed right away by a librarian.

I walk down three aisles, which is where the books on astral projection are. Half the titles listed on the library's computer must be checked out since they're not there. But there's enough left to keep me busy. I don't even go back to my table; I just sit on the floor next to the shelf and page through books.

I scan a story about a sleep-deprived woman who let her body sleep while her astral self checked up on the baby at night, skim through an outline of an experiment done to see if astral projection is real, and read through a detailed description of techniques to leave your body.

I stay for a good long time.

It's only when I'm downstairs, by the main doors, that I wonder why Kevin was there. Didn't he say something about a test? *Crap.* That's right. I'd completely forgotten about Chemistry. The whole junior class gets a grilling this week.

Dad pulls up and I get into the car.

I hug my bags of books close. This is it. I now have more than enough information on voluntary astral projection to look through…and to try it.


Dad gets us back home by dinnertime.

Sam gets out of the car, but Dad puts his hand on my arm to make me wait. "Here," he says and hands me a plain paper bag.

"What's this?" But when I look inside, I understand. There are several Nestle Crunch bars, a couple of Snickers, and some Reese's Pieces. I've been sneaking home candy I bought from the gas station, but getting this from him is almost like before. *Almost.* My throat feels blocked up, so instead of saying thanks I just nod and follow Sam inside.

Mom is at the kitchen stove heating up her Leftover Surprise for dinner—the surprise being that we actually eat it.

The second we get in, she wipes her hands so she can set them on her hips. I think she's going to heave warnings at us about going out on weekends, but she doesn't. She narrows her eyes at us and asks, "Did you eat *anything* that didn't come from a fast-food place this weekend?"

Fruit Loops don't seem to count.

We eat our overcooked and excruciatingly healthy leftovers to the hum of the refrigerator. Even after two weeks, it's hard to get used to a meal with just the three of us.

Next door, in the glowing light of the kitchen window I can just make out Cassie through the lace curtains. She waves to me and holds up her phone and two seconds later my cell rings.

"You're having Leftover Surprise, aren't you?" Cassie sounds amused.

"How'd you know?"

"I can tell by the weird smell coming from your place. Come over after. You'll still be hungry. My mom was in a great mood today and cooked. I'll save you some of her sausage lasagna."

My mouth waters thinking about it. "You're a goddess."

"I know," she says, dead serious.

Mom gives me the okay to go next door once my supper is done. I go and knock on Cassie's front screen door. I can hear her parents laughing somewhere in the house. I shuffle my feet on the porch. When was the last time my parents laughed together? Then a memory hits. Last year. We all rented an old Cameron Diaz film. Mom and Dad were practically limp they were laughing so hard. So was I. And then I lost the hold I had on my body. And my bones collapsed without me holding them up.

Everybody stopped laughing.

Now Cassie answers the door, a smile on her face, beautiful. "I got my car!"

"No way!"

She pulls me to the driveway, where a shiny yellow Toyota stands at attention. "It's used, but it looks great, doesn't it?"

We sit inside. It's weird, the car is used but it smells like new. I wonder if they bottle that smell at all car dealerships. "You're so lucky, Cass. My parents won't even let me take the stupid station wagon, let alone buy me my own car."

Cassie eyes sparkle. "Wanna go for a spin?"

The weather is clearing up, and the air is humid but warm. We drive up and down streets, the windows open wide, the radio blasting, singing at the top of our lungs. We drive past the lake and honk at the seagulls and the people jogging. And we bust up laughing as Cassie squeals her tires around a corner.

"I've got something else to show you, too," Cassie says when she pulls into her driveway. "My Morpho Godarti from Peru arrived yesterday." A new butterfly.

In her room, she points to a bluish-silvery butterfly in a frame on the wall, squeezed next to all the other butterflies in frames on the wall. "Isn't it great?"

"It's pretty," I admit, admiring how shiny it is. I sit down on her bed, grab a fuzzy purple stuffed heart and pet it. Her room is girly. Pink and purple and turquoise fuzz everywhere. And then there are the butterflies. From white to orange to yellow to black, she has them all; well, all that are legal, anyways. "So what's it now? 115?"

"This is 117."

"You know, you can use that wall," I say, pointing to the only place where not one frame is hung. "I don't mind."

Almost three years ago I painted a mural on the wall opposite her windows. Butterflies, of course. I did it after our eighth-grade graduation ceremony.

The day of the ceremony and dance, her parents went off to some friends' house for a lunchtime barbecue that Cassie didn't want to go to. So we spent all day at my house getting ready. Painting our nails. Playing with each other's hair. Even cold-waxing our legs (big, big mistake—though not as bad as armpits). But when it was time to go, her parents weren't back and her dad wasn't answering his cell. So Cass came with us to the ceremony. It was supposed to be a big deal, the best time of our lives. But Cassie didn't enjoy one minute. She was angry they weren't there. Scared they weren't, too. I don't know how many times my mom tried calling that cell. Then, around 7 pm, just when the ceremony was ending, they showed up in a flurry, completely mortified.

They'd forgotten. Simple as that.

That's when Mom stopped the long chats with Mrs. Sanders on the front lawn, when she started in on Dad if he had a beer with Mr. Sanders. And that's when I painted the mural. Because I wanted to put a smile back on Cassie's face. (So did her parents. They paid for the paint.)

When I'd started painting, I thought butterflies all looked the same, that just the color of the wings changed. But I used Cassie's mounted ones as models and saw that each was unique. The body larger here, skinnier there. Some wings longer, some fatter. Some shiny, some matte. Part insect, part angel. Both ugly and beautiful at the same time. And then I thought how caterpillars leave this strange little straightjacket of a cocoon to become these more complex creatures, free as air.

Since then, I can appreciate that Cassie finds butterflies lovely. They are, in a strange way.

Even so, I would never share my bedroom with over a hundred little corpses.

Now, Cassie sits down next to me. "No way am I covering up that wall to hang frames," she says. "I love it too much. Besides, it took you two months to do. I can take down my bookshelves—that'll give me lots more room. I'll just put my books in the den."

"Cass, if you add more butterflies, you're going to have to start charging admission. If it weren't for your bed, I'd swear I was in a museum already."

"It does kind of look like a museum, doesn't it? God, I'm a complete loser. Good thing you're the only one who knows."

"Takes one to know one." I smile at her and she grins back. But it wouldn't matter if she had a thousand butterflies. She might not realize it yet, but she's no longer a loser. Beauty changes everything.

Even friendships.

"So Kevin asked you out, huh?" I pick at the heart shaped cushion and don't look her in the eye.

"I told him no, don't worry." Her voice is kind of harsh.

I look up and meet her gaze. "I'm not worried."

She blushes and turns away quickly. Suddenly, it feels like I'm wearing one of those lead aprons they put on you at the dentist's for x-rays.

I'd planned on telling her about astral projection. About me and how I've had what the websites called OBE's—out-of-body experiences. But our little exchange about Kevin puts me into a mood where I don't really feel like sharing.

That's when Mrs. Sanders' honey voice calls from the kitchen, "Sylvie? I saved you some lasagna. Do you still want some?"

Cassie whispers, "My mom didn't start with the martinis until six today, so the lasagna turned out perfect." We giggle and follow the smell of garlic and herbs to the kitchen.

"Hi, Sylvie, baby," Mrs. Sanders says. "Like Cassie's car?"

"Awesome."

Mr. Sanders is leaning against the counter next to Mrs. Sanders. He turns a martini glass around in his hands and starts telling me about horse power and four-wheel-drive and the like. Mrs. Sanders puts my lasagna on a plate while Cassie opens and closes cupboards.

"Mom," Cassie says. "Where are my Sugar Babies? I thought you went shopping."

"I did go shopping. But I couldn't remember what candy you liked. I got Milk Duds." Cassie's mom puts the lasagna on the table and motions for me to sit.

"Sugar Babies. Not Milk Duds."

"Oh, Cassie, they're both small and round."

"I've been eating them every day for like two years. How can you not know what I like?"

"Honey, there are so many products at the supermarket it makes my head spin." Mrs. Sanders picks up her glass from the counter and takes a sip.

Almost under her breath, but loud enough for us all to hear, Cassie says, "It's not the products that make your head spin, Mom. It's the gin."

The room is suddenly still. I stop chewing and feel my heart bump up a notch. Cassie's mom looks at me, then Cassie, and lets out a loud laugh. "Oh, my, you are a riot, Cassie. Isn't she a riot, Phil?"

"Hilarious," Mr. Sanders says, eyebrows puckered together. Then he smiles at his wife over his glass.

Cassie looks ticked.

"Sylvie, let me ask you," There's a bit of bitter in Mrs. Sanders' sweet voice. "Would you rather your parents bought you a car or a bag of candy?"

"Uh…" I glance at Cassie. I don't want to let her down.

"It's not a trick question, Sylvie." Cassie's mom won't give up.

"A car," I answer, and mouth, "Sorry, Cass!"

I mean, really, no matter how upset Cassie is about the Sugar Babies she has to admit the car's a damn good deal.

Cassie rolls her eyes at me.

"You've got to learn to let the little things go, Cassie, honey." Mrs. Sanders strokes Cassie's head. Cassie still looks a little pissed, but she doesn't pull away.

"Okay, then." Her mom moves over to me. She comes real close and squeezes my shoulder. "And how are you holding up?"

"All right," I say, taking in the scent of her: cooking herbs, Chanel, and vermouth.

Mr. Sanders fills his glass and turns to me. "You might need an ear to bend. We're here if you need us."

I nod, but don't say anything because I feel a lump growing in my throat. I can barely remember a time when I didn't know the Sanders. And even though I can understand Cassie's getting annoyed with them because of their drinking, they've always been really nice to me. Yes, they've had some bad parenting moments. But look at them. They're together. They're trying. For themselves. For Cassie. That's something *my* parents sure aren't doing.

Mr. and Mrs. Sanders smile at me warmly. If you forget the fighting, if you forget they drink a little too much gin and you look at them like that…see their faces together with Cassie's, lovely under the yellowy glow of the light, they look like something from one of the Norman Rockwell prints my mom has hanging in the kitchen. They look like a family.

And just like that, something ugly yawns and stretches inside me.

Jealousy.

I try swallowing it along with the sausage lasagna. In the end, though, I have a hard time digesting it.

# eleven

## September: Howling at the Moon

Things change Monday at school. Bryce and Kevin high-five Sam and punch him in the arm when they see him in the hallway.

"It's Sam the marshmallow man!"

"Sam-I-Am!"

Even I seem to shed some of my Psycho persona. So maybe Ashley and Tori don't treat me differently, but now Kevin winks at me when I pass him. Like I'm normal. Like I'm beautiful. It makes me feel drunk.

But seeing him and Cassie together sobers me up fast.

They don't *do* anything. Just share a smile in the hall. But I can feel that smile down to my bone marrow.

I catch Cassie's eye and she breaks the connection fast. "What?!" she says. "It's nothing."

But it's something.

Mrs. Stilke wants to use the prints of our linoleum cuttings for silk screening. We've already dug out a picture with a St. Anthony's theme. "Now's the time to perfect it," she says.

Nelson shakes his foot and taps his thumb on the table while he's trying to think of what else to do. I give him a couple subtle looks, but he doesn't get it.

"Hey, Nelson," I say eyeing his foot and hand. "Do you mind?"

He looks down at his moving body parts and his eyes get wide. "Whoa, sorry!" He stops fidgeting immediately.

"It's all right," I say. "But I can't concentrate when the table's shaking."

"I can't concentrate at all." He leans a bit closer to me. He smells good. Like vanilla and Elmer's glue. I'm surprised at how all of a sudden I want to breathe in the scent of him. "How was Bryce Hensley's house?" he asks. "As swag as you expected?"

"Yeah, it –" I stop and think. To be honest, I can't remember a thing about Bryce's house. I was too concentrated on Kevin and his stories. "—it was pretty big."

"Uh huh." Nelson taps his pencil on his lips. "Hey, hold still a second."

I do and suddenly his hand is flying across his paper. After a few quick strokes he holds the sketch up. "What d'ya think?"

I frown and say, "Doesn't look like me." He's drawn a girl. Pretty. With upturned lips, deep-set eyes and a strong jut of the chin. She's got straight hair like mine, but…

Nelson looks at the paper and then back at me. "Looks just like you."

"Whatever." I go back to my linoleum square, adding detail. After a couple minutes, I feel Nelson leaning towards me again.

"You suck," he says.

"Excuse me!?" My voice gets high, but I stifle a laugh.

Now he turns into a Rocket Pop: his hair blue, his face red, his neck white. "No," he pleads, shaking his head. "I didn't mean you suck as in you suck and can't draw but as in you suck because you've already got something near perfection and I'm still struggling with how to make mine work."

I stare at him.

He looks down at his black fingernails. "I mean, you really don't suck, ever. Far from it."

"Okay, Nelson." He glances up from his hands and I punch his arm. But before I can pull my hand back, he grabs it and squeezes it with his own. He only touches me for a second; the weight of his fingers is warm on my knuckles, then gone. But my heart rate kicks up and every little bit of me tingles.

*What the hell?*

I whip my hand back and focus on deepening the lines of my design. I don't look back at Nelson the rest of the hour.

I just listen to my pulse pounding in my ears.


We make 'stained glass' in the after school program out of colored tissue paper and black cardboard. All the kids cut their own design and glue tissue paper to it. Then Angie and I tape them up to the large window in the snack room.

The window faces west, and the sun is shining in just as we hang the mosaic of designs. The room is bathed in purple, blue, yellow and red.

"Wow." Seven-year-old Selena sucks in her breath as the colors dance on her skin. "Look. I'm pretty."

I tug on one of her braids. "You already were, kiddo."

But she's right, the colors make everything appealing. It feels other-worldly. Like the far side of the rainbow.

I stand with her in the middle of the room, laughing at the collage of colors on our arms.

We pretend we are caterpillars, turned into butterflies.

At night I read the how-to sections in the books on astral projection. It's all about deep relaxation. About keeping control while letting go. I figure it shouldn't be too hard for me since I've done it before—accidentally, but still. So I try it. And try it. And try it.

No matter what the websites say, this isn't something that can be learned in fifteen minutes.

At 2:00 a.m., I'm wiped. Relaxing is hard work. Frustration crawls under my skin, but I'm just too tired to keep trying. I close my eyes and let my body melt into the mattress, all the tension from trying to project leaving me. And just when sleep is about to take me, I know I can do it. I think the words from the formula in one of the books: "Leave now. Sit up and leave your body behind."

Inch by inch I imagine pulling a rope, hand over hand, the ethereal part of me creeping upward while my body stays flat on the bed. It's slow, but with every little movement I feel myself getting closer to success. Finally, when I feel I'm sitting straight up, my body tingles like I've just stepped into an overly hot bath.

It sounds like a melon splitting when it happens. And it's like I'm free of a heavy shell.

*Yes!*

This time the shadows stay back. I can sense them. But I don't hear or see them.

*Screw you*, I think. *I'm doing this.*

I bob near the ceiling, looking over the sleeping body of a girl. Me. My hair makes long, dark lines on the pillow. The faint bruise on my forehead shines in the moonlight. Everything around me looks brighter—the blue of my bedspread, the white of the walls. A hushed glow emanates from it all.

I look down at my astral self. My arms and legs and fingers kind of glow from within, like a low-wattage light bulb, a bit fuzzy around the edges. There's a faint sort of silvery cord connecting me to my body, like a tether.

I move outside and watch the moonlight lick the grass. It's beautiful. Everything seems clearer, more alive than it normally does. The bushes are laced with white, the edges of each tiny leaf visible and shining. The little patch of geraniums in the window box is a bright spot of red in the dim light. I stay outside, waiting to get yanked back into my body. When it doesn't happen, I realize that for once, I'm in charge. I can go where I want.

*Kevin's house.* I want to go there. I've always wanted to go there.

I zip through town, unable to control my speed or my exact trajectory. I whip through telephone poles, tree branches, and chimneys. If anyone saw me they'd die laughing.

*Slow down, Sylvie. Keep your cool.* I'm able to stop moving and then I concentrate on making my astral body go where I want it to.

I make it to Kevin's bedroom.

Kevin's room! I can't believe it—I'm actually inside of Kevin's room! Posters of women in bikinis, Brewers' baseball pennants and postcards from around the world cover three walls. On the far wall, instead of posters, several shelves bend with the weight of all the medals and trophies stacked on them. And in front of those shelves is Kevin, on the bed. Sleeping.

*Oh. My. God.* I move towards him. He's in his clothes, a notebook face down on his chest. His bedside light is burning. I move closer to him, close as I dare, and take in the velvety curve of his lashes, the firm line of his chin.

I float around his room, swearing when my hand goes right through everything I want to touch. If only I could rummage through his drawers, check his e-mail...But all I can do is look. His laptop is off and closed, a grey rectangle at the foot of his bed. Pairs of shoes surf on the waves of clothing strewn about his floor. There's a box of baseball cards on his desk, next to a banana peel and a half empty can of Coke.

On the other side of the door, a baby wails. It spooks me and before I know it SNAP, like a rubber band, I'm back in my body. My limbs burn. I blink and stay on the bed. The burning feeling passes and my mind clicks in.

I did it. I went to Kevin's house. I totally did it. I controlled it.

"YEEEEEEEEES!" I pound and kick my mattress with joy until I'm slick with sweat. Outside the window, the moon shines bright and round. I howl at it like some wild dog. It seems closer than usual, bigger.

Like reaching it is so very possible.

# twelve

## September: On Top of Spaghetti

I'm hoping to get through Tuesday quickly and uneventfully, so that I can just run home and go astral. But the day doesn't cooperate. It starts off ordinarily enough: in Trig I watch Mimi Wilder pop her zits between problems. In English, I'm forced to listen to a debate between Ashley Green and Kayla Conroy on real nails versus nail tips. By the look on Mrs. Huggan's face when they start talking, I'm sure they didn't get the subject approved by her ahead of time. But it's lunch that makes the day unbearable. Enter Tori Thompson and life will always go downhill.

I'm swirling orange strings of spaghetti around on my plate, wondering how the school could even manage to ruin pasta, when it happens. Dwayne Fischer, linebacker on the football team, stops in front of our table. Michelle makes a little squeak (she does that near anyone with a Y chromosome), but Dwayne stands right in front of me blinking his blue eyes and running sausage fingers over his shaved head. I have time to exchange a quick, questioning glance with Cass when all of a sudden, Dwayne gets down on one knee. He grabs my right hand, making my fork skid across the table and onto the floor. My heart starts slamming around and for a split second I can't believe someone like Dwayne is actually holding my hand. But when he looks back over his shoulder to his lunch table full of guys the size of water buffalo, fear burns through my insides: something bad is going to happen.

"Sylvie," he says loudly. He looks down to his free hand, where he's written something in pen on his palm. His voice is the monotone of someone who's a bad reader. "I know it seems unbelievable, but I have a thing for you. Will you hook up with me?"

I stare down in confusion at his hand holding mine and can barely breathe. "Uh…"

"Just kidding. 'Cuz with the way you pass out all the time, you've got to be so dead in bed. And I'm not into"—here he squints at his palm—"necro…necrophilia," he says and drops my hand. Laughter erupts behind him at the water buffalo table. I can hear them hooting. Everyone at my table is dumbstruck. Then *snap, crackle*…I pop out of my body. I hover over Dwayne's left shoulder. I can see the wax in his ear.

Tori Thompson comes from behind Dwayne, holding her phone up, taking a video. "What an actor! Looks like we know who to cast in the lead of this year's *A Christmas Carol*." She pulls five dollars out of her pocket and gives it to Dwayne. Then she looks at me. "What? You didn't really think he was serious, Psycho? Did you?"

But, of course, my limbs have loosened without me in them. My body slides down my chair, my head hanging.

Tori points to me, her eyes glittering, a hyper laugh bubbling up. "Whoa! Psycho's at it again!"

There's a moment of silence when everyone near us seems to hold their breath. Then there's some giggling and some gasping. I see Mimi Wilder run toward the cafeteria doors where Mr. Paige is engrossed on his iPhone. Cassie swears at Tori, who's still laughing, and Sam gets to work at shaking me. Hard.

Sam holds me up for a second until I'm back inside myself. My limbs tingle. Nausea rolls over me. My body jerks back to attention .

Cassie lets out a long breath and turns to me. "Welcome back."

*I don't want to be here. I don't want to be me.*

Holding back tears, I say to Tori, "I'll get you when you least expect it. I will."

"Yeah. Keep dreaming, Psycho." She spots Mr. Paige with Mimi and scurries back to her table of the week.

No one at my table says a word. They're too shocked. They all pat my shoulder or reach for me, but I shake them off so I don't start blubbering. I swallow back a raw feeling in my throat and stare at the cold pasta on my plate until the urge to cry passes.

Mr. Paige comes up with Mimi, looking annoyed. "Sylvie? Are you okay? Mimi told me you fainted." Mr. Paige is anti-social and doesn't like 'teen energy'. He avoids unnecessary interaction with students at all costs. He's the chemistry teacher but he'd much rather be working in a professional lab than at St. Anthony's. We know this because he tells us. Actually, he tells us he'd rather work *anywhere* than St. Anthony's.

"No, no fainting," I say, trying to keep from panicking. "I'm good. See?" I lift my arms as if to show him I'm not being propped up or something. I look at Mimi with pleading eyes. *Come on. Back me up.*

Mimi shrugs her shoulders. "Ooops?"

Mr. Paige glares at both of us and takes off, mumbling, "Damn kids" under his breath. Mimi apologizes, "Sorry. I got scared."

"It's okay." I try to smile at her. I'm surprised anyone did anything.

The bell signaling the end of lunch rings. Mimi leaves and all of us start gathering our stuff. Sarah and Michelle take off like they're being chased.

Kevin comes up to our table. He has something in his hand. "Hey," he says, glancing at me. "What was so funny that whole football team cracked up? We couldn't hear a thing back there."

"Nothing," I say before Sam or Cassie can answer.

"'Didn't Dwayne do something?"

"Dwayne's a—" Sam starts, at the same time Cassie says, "Pfft. He—"

But I put my hand out to stop them both from finishing. "Nothing worthwhile," I murmur.

Kevin's confused, but doesn't push the issue. Sam takes off for class, and Cassie and I stand to go. But Kevin puts a package of Sugar Babies in front of Cassie. "For some reason, when I was at the store last night I saw these and thought of you."

*Sugar Babies?*

Cassie's cheeks turn pink. "Thanks. But why would they make you think of me?"

"Oh. You don't like them? Sorry. I didn't know, I just thought—" He puts his hand on the package, ready to take them back.

Cassie smacks her hand quickly over his. "No! I like them. A lot, actually."

Kevin doesn't move his hand away and neither does Cassie. They stay like that forever, like they're paralyzed. So do I, watching them. It feels like someone has emptied all the air out of the room. Finally, Kevin smiles, takes his hand out from under Cassie's and says, "In that case, keep 'em."

He goes off to his next class. Cassie catches my eye and shrugs. Then she seems to remember the whole Dwayne incident and gives me a pitying smile. "Tori and Dwayne are such a-holes. They're perfect for each other. But I still can't believe they did that." I know she means it to be supportive, but it just makes me feel worse. She holds out the bag of candy. "Sugar Baby?"

"I don't really feel much like eating now, thanks." I hike my bag onto my shoulder and walk to class alone.

There's giggling around me when Tori's near. But amazingly, there's not as much laughter as I expect.

Keri Nielsen leans towards me in Morality to whisper (quite loudly) that both Dwayne and Tori are pissheads. "Plus, Dwayne stuffs his pants with socks," Keri says. "He's really the size of a Lil' Smokie." Keri's been around. She'd know.

In Art, Nelson comes out with, "Dwayne Fischer is a Neanderthal."

I nod quickly and feel my throat closing up. Word's around the whole school, then. Nelson doesn't even have the same lunch hour as I do.

He hands me a sheet of paper. He's drawn Dwayne as a cave-man. A really derpy, ugly caveman, with a sloping forehead, a drooling mouth and Dwayne's buzz cut. It's good. If I weren't feeling so awful, I'd probably laugh.

"I thought we could decorate his locker in his likeness after school." Nelson holds up a thick, black permanent marker and grins at me.

"What for?"

"Because he's a complete dickwad, for starters."

I stare at him. "You mean deface school property?"

Nelson grins even wider.

It almost makes me cry, knowing Nelson's still okay with being my friend even after what the whole school thinks of me. I grab the table and look down at my legs. My skinny, skinny legs. Out the corner of my eye, I see Melissa Scott rub a shapely calf, accidentally on purpose bumping into Nelson as she does so. She apologizes with a flip of her hair and a tongue across her lips.

It's stupid, but she looks sexy doing it. I think of Kevin. By now he knows. And for sure when he thinks of me he doesn't think *sexy*. He thinks *spaghetti*.

"No. No locker art," I say to Nelson. "I just want to forget the whole thing."

I don't wait for Cassie or Sam after school. I try to get out as fast as possible, without anyone seeing me. As I'm going out the back door, I hear Nelson's voice behind me: "Sylvie! Wait!"

But I don't wait. I sprint down the steps and across the street. Back at school, there's shouting, a horn honking. Without breaking my stride, I look back and see Nelson pounding on the hood of Dwayne Fischer's truck. Dwayne guns the engine and squeals out of the parking lot, leaving Nelson looking ticked off. As Dwayne's truck comes down the road I cross through someone's yard, and take a different route than usual so I won't bump into anyone.

When I'm finally home, I lie on my bed and let myself cry. I cry big, sloppy tears. I hate Dwayne. But more than anyone, I hate Tori. She's made my life hell from day one.

My cell beeps. I pull it out of my pocket. The message is from Cassie: "*u ok? Can I cme ovr?*"

But I'm not in the mood to talk to her or anyone. "*No thanx*" I write back.

My cell beeps again. This time it's Nelson: "*Wanna talk?*"

I write "*No thanx*" again. Then I turn off the phone and wipe my tears.

Sam bangs on my door, "Sylvie? Can I talk to you?"

"NO!"

"I just…come on, Sylvie."

"I said no. Leave me alone."

Then my mom knocks, quietly. "Sylvie?"

But I can't face anyone.

It happened again today. Psycho me. That bit that I do at the worst times—what the library books call a 'spontaneous projection'. I let a bitter laugh escape. And here, just yesterday I was thinking it was like a superpower. Yeah, right. What good does it do to slip out of your body every time you hurt?

*Come off it, Sylvie. Yesterday you controlled it. It* is *a super power.*

I close my eyes. That's it. I need to *do* something with it. Something real.

# thirteen

## September: Just Like Heaven

The shadows are there when I slide out of my body. I can hear them, their strange language a harsh hissing in my ears. Their long fingers wrap around me like tentacles. I struggle and start to scream, but then something strange happens. Their cold breath tickles my neck. And soothes me. It feels…good…so good. *Why have I been fighting them all this time?*

I stop struggling and the hatred and hurt in me swell to something strong, something majestic.

My fear falls away and I let the shadows in.

We ascend through the attic, out the roof and past the trees. Below me, Racine is a pattern of lights against the darkness, getting smaller with every moment. We speed up higher, up farther until I'm surrounded by stars. Earth is just a marble in the distance.

Quiet as steam, the shadows meld with me. I can feel their power in my core. Thick as tar, cool as metal. Their language suddenly makes sense. They tell me I can be whoever I want to be. I can inhale the galaxy and exhale the universe.

I've never felt so strong, so smart, so sure.

It's divine.

I am beautiful out here. I know I am. The knowledge courses through my veins like an elixir. It sweetens every move I make. Its power tastes like heaven.

Then I tumble back down to Earth, back through the trees, the roof, the attic, and back to my room. I collide with my body and watch as the shadows disappear, along with my confidence.

So I slip out again and call back the shadows to spend the night in their embrace.

## *October 28th*

*We drive to All Saints Medical in silence. The only noise is my heart, this heart, pounding loudly in my ears. Sweat trickles down my spine, though it's freezing in the car and I'm not even wearing a coat. I do all I can to not go completely crazy. I pull at the hairs on my forearm. I chew my tongue. I shake my legs. I count backwards from a hundred but have to start over three times because I can't concentrate enough to even get down to eighty. What I really want to do is scream and rip up the upholstery. Instead I tell myself, "Everything will be okay, Sylvie. Breathe in. Breathe out." Maybe he's in my body by now. Maybe we can get together and figure out how to go back to being ourselves.*

*I spread my fingers out on the back of Cassie's seat, amazed at how they stretch across almost the whole thing. I pull them back and form a fist.*

*I run my hand across the slight roughness of his cheek, still able to feel the smoothness of the skin underneath the spare whiskers. As I move, I smell the tang of sweat and I know it's coming from my armpits.*

Mr. Sanders creeps along the road. He's careful. Utterly and annoyingly careful. He slows at every traffic light, even if it's green. He doesn't exceed the speed limit.

Cassie says something, but it's soft. Mr. Sanders doesn't hear her. She shifts in her seat and looks out the window at the ugly store signs as we pass. McDonald's. Walgreen's. Family Dollar.

She says it again, only louder this time because she's still facing the window: "What if she's not okay, Dad?"

"She'll be okay, Cassie."

"But what if she's not?"

Mr. Sanders doesn't answer. He just shakes his head.

Suddenly, I can't get enough air. I push on the little button that makes the window go down, and I stick my head out. Like a dog.

That's when we pass the cemetery. The tombstones glow eerily in the light from the hospital sign just next door. Neighbors in sickness and death.

I silently will Mr. Sanders to go faster.

# fourteen

## September: My Jawa Audition

The confidence I get from projecting isn't there when I wake up Wednesday morning and remember the whole spaghetti incident from the day before. I so do not want to go to school, but there's a Trig exam that's worth a third of our grade. Plus, instead of handing us the box of All-Bran for breakfast, Mom serves us tofu on burnt toast like it's something special. "I thought I'd make the two of you a meal this morning," she sobs between sniffles. "Because you both are everything to me." Sam and I exchange terrified glances and get out as fast as we can.

All morning, I scrape my tongue against my teeth. It tastes like something moldy is in my mouth, thanks to the shadows. My eyes look bruised, the circles under them are so dark.

I wear my brown hoodie to school to avoid the stares of the other kids. I shrink down inside of it every time I walk the halls.

At lunch, Cassie hisses, "We can figure a way to get revenge on Tori, Sylvie. But take the hood off. You look like those little Jawas in *Star Wars*."

"It helps, Cass." The hood works like blinders. I don't have to see Tori gloat in the hallways, at lunch, or in Morality class. And no one has to see me.

"But you look like a freak."

Sam and Michelle and Sarah nod their heads. Actually, today Sarah and Michelle have moved a seat over at our table so they're across from Sam and Cassie but no one is across from me.

"Deal with it," I say and poke at my stale nachos. I let them carry on as if I'm not there.

My hoodie becomes a part of me. A shelter. I figure I'll wear the thing until I die, and then I'll probably even be buried in it. But Art class gets me to take it off. I walk through the door and shove the hood off my head, but right away, I put it back on. Our silk-screened tees are ready, and mine is draped over the table at my spot. Most of the class is gathered around it. They lift their eyes from the shirt to stare at me. *Oh, God. Now what?*

"You've got fans, Sylvie. Your design turned out beautifully." Mrs. Stilke smiles at me. I blink at her, and then at the group by my place. My stomach twists in fear—I've had enough being the center of attention—but it's true: nobody is looking at me in disgust or pity or indifference. They're looking at me with…respect. I swallow hard.

"Put it on!" Nelson's practically ecstatic. He grabs the T-shirt and holds it out towards me. I walk the length of the room and take it from him.

Melissa Scott says, "Looks really cool. You should wear it."

I hold it up to my shoulders like you would a shirt you don't really want to try on in the store.

But Mrs. Stilke sighs. "Take the sweatshirt off, Sylvie, and put your T-shirt on over your clothes. I want to see how it looks." She gestures to the rest of the class. "All right. Everyone to your place." She crosses her arms and waits for me to put the stupid shirt on.

So while the class is moving around, I quickly slip off my hoodie and pull the T-shirt on over the one I'm wearing.

At first glance, my design looks like a giant lace circle. But when you look again and see the details, you can make out the teachers at St. Anthony's, St. Anthony himself, parts of the building and icons to represent different subjects weaved into the design. I smooth my hands over the shirt and look up at Mrs. Stilke. She nods and winks.

Nelson nudges me in the side and gives me a quick hug. As he pulls away, he brushes a stray hair from off my forehead. "Lookin' good, Sylvie," he says softly.

Other kids have their T-shirts on, too, showing cartoon characters in front of the school, or the St. Anthony's seal, or books and rulers in a pile. Nelson's shirt has St. Anthony himself on it, ears pierced and wearing combat boots under his robe. I can't believe Mrs. Stilke let that be printed. The principal would have a cow.

"There's a contest to design the yearbook cover. The winning design obviously gets on the yearbook, but also on the T-shirts to sell for the fundraiser," Mrs. Stilke announces when everyone is sitting. "I've already submitted everyone's work." Here she rolls her eyes and looks at Nelson. "Well, almost everyone's. Let's hope someone from this class wins." Then she goes on about our new assignment.

Once we all get started, she comes up to me and whispers, "Would you be okay with helping a student from another class? He's really struggling and I think he might respond better to a peer's help."

"You really think I could help him?"

"That's why I'm asking you, Sylvie." Mrs. Stilke squeezes my shoulder.

"Sure," I say, suddenly feeling better.

As the hour progresses, confidence builds inside me and I know I want to do something other than hide away in a hoodie for the rest of my life. I want to take back some control.

"Psst." I poke Nelson. "Your offer to personalize Dwayne's locker still stand?"

"Hell, yeah." He grins. "I'm gonna make him a masterpiece."

Nelson's work *is* a masterpiece. And for once my projecting serves us well.

"Look," I say when the halls are free of students. "You draw. I keep watch. But I'll do it from around the corner over there."

Nelson frowns. "How can you see from there?"

"Trust me," I say. Then I hide and go astral. I watch from above as Nelson recreates the cave man drawing on Dwayne's locker. He bites his lip in concentration and drags the marker over the metal. It squeaks under the steady grip of his fingers. The veins on his hand pop out in relief, and the muscles on his arms create a solid surface under his long sleeved T. He's lovely, in a way, and I almost forget to watch for the custodian because I want to keep watching him. But then I float around the school and see Mr. James making his way up the stairs. Had I stayed solid, we'd probably be caught. But instead I'm back in my body and tugging on Nelson just as Mr. James comes into view.

We run down the hallways, our shoes slapping on the marble floor. Nelson grabs my hand and we practically fly down the stairs and out the back door of the school. We bend over to catch our breath, but we're laughing hysterically. It's been too long since I've laughed this hard.

"I can't believe we did that," I pant.

Nelson shakes his head. "That was epic! What have you got, some sixth sense in order to know Mr. James was on his way?"

"Something like that."

Our breathing slows to normal and we stand up. Nelson's eyes look turquoise in the sunlight. The second I notice them, my insides tilt, like I'm going high and fast on a swing.

"Want a ride home?" Nelson asks, keeping his eyes on me.

But right then the pool building door opens and a bunch of guys come out, Kevin Phillips among them. His hair is still damp, and he sees me.

That's when I realize Nelson and I are still holding hands. I let go.

Kevin saunters over to us.

"Hey," he says. "I gotta get this thing for Art in by tomorrow—I gotta draw a bowl of fruit. Mrs. Stilke just texted me to say maybe you could help?"

In the back of my mind, a little voice is saying: *The struggling student is Kevin? I freakin' love you, Mrs. Stilke!* "Yeah," I say out loud. "Yeah...uh...yeah!"

"Cool," he nods. "Can we go to the art room? Now, maybe?"

"Yeah...uh...yeah." My eloquence is staggering.

"Later," he says to Nelson.

But when I look at Nelson to say good-bye, I hesitate. I notice the spark has gone out of his eyes. The effect is like a kick to the chest. I mean, we just had a great time together, defacing school property and all. Maybe it would be…nice… to spend a little more time with him. "Or else maybe tomorrow—" I start.

But Nelson cuts me off. "Gotta go. Guitar lesson."

"I didn't know you played guitar," I say.

"There's a lot you don't know about me." His voice is angry and for some stupid reason I feel tears prick the back of my eyeballs. "You guys better get to the art room before Mrs. Stilke leaves." And he takes off, without looking back at us.

I watch him walk to his car, sudden annoyance taking over. *What the hell?*

"Okay?" Kevin nudges me.

I nod and follow Kevin back inside the building. We go down to the basement. Mrs. Stilke is in the storeroom. When she sees us, she comes out.

"Hi, Sylvie, Kevin." She smiles at me. "I appreciate your helping out, Sylvie. I've got to get some of this inventory done, since I didn't do it the second school started. So your being here giving pointers frees me up."

I nod. "Sure."

"Plus, I think it's good experience for you to teach a bit." Mrs. Stilke gets out a wooden bowl a banana, an apple, some grapes, a pear, and a pineapple. She sets it on the table closest to the storeroom and says, "Go for it…oh, and Kevin, don't bother asking Sylvie to draw it for you. I'll know." Then she goes back to taking inventory.

Kevin and I look at each other. Six years of Kevin-worship erase any worries about Nelson's strange behavior. Because Kevin is here to spend time with me. *Me.*

My breath is stuck somewhere between my lungs and my mouth. I have to remind myself to exhale.

"So Mrs. Stilke didn't like my take on the still-life." Kevin pulls a heavy piece of peach colored paper out of his backpack. The charcoal is smudged quite a bit, but I can see he's drawn the fruit bowl. The bowl is lopsided and the fruit is basically floating in the air. It's messy and obviously quickly done.

I raise my eyebrows and say, "Oh."

"I'm not an artist."

"Uh. Yeah."

At first I have Kevin try drawing the still life on scrap paper, giving him pointers, trying my hardest to explain what seems natural to me. "We need to work on your perspective. Right now everything looks flat. I know the front lip of the bowl isn't really lower than the back, but you've got to draw it that way for it to look round…see how you can shade this in? See how it gives it depth?"

I have him start again on the bowl, but already it's too shallow. I reach over to stop him, my fingers touching his. Lava surges through my veins.

He doesn't pull away. I don't dare breathe but feign nonchalance as I wrap my fingers around the charcoal pencil with his and guide his hand. His fingers are thick and strong but so, so soft. If only I could lace mine in with his, if only –

"How's it going?" Mrs. Stilke breezes into the room with a bunch of paintbrushes in her hand.

I yip like a little dog and jump up. Both Kevin and Mrs. Stilke widen their eyes at me. "Uh...you scared me." I sit back down, only stiffer now.

"Nice start," Mrs. Stilke looks over our shoulders, then disappears into the storeroom again.

We get back to work, and Kevin manages to get the bowl looking somewhat like a bowl and the grapes and apples are more than just circles. When we start on the pineapple, he puts down the pencil and stops. "You're okay, Sylvie."

"Huh?"

"You're okay." He smiles at me, his eyes warming up as he does so. "I mean, some people give you a hard time 'cuz you...well, you know...but you're okay. Most girls will sit around and bitch about other girls. But you don't. And you're wicked with charcoal," he says holding up the still-life.

I can't do anything but snort out a little laugh.

"I heard about what Dwayne did yesterday." His eyes are on me.

Now I really can't do anything. I'm too mortified to move.

"Sometimes we hang around the same crowd. So I know him. A little. They should really get him in for scientific study; he's the only human alive who is functioning without a brain," Kevin says, shaking his head. "Plus, have you noticed the size of him? He's probably a mutant, too."

"Like Randy Lang?" My voice is so quiet, I'm not sure he even hears me.

But he bunches up his eyebrows, remembering. "Holy shit. Yeah. Like Randy Lang. I'd almost forgotten about him. Man, what was he? Part gorilla?"

And amazingly, unbelievably, we both burst out laughing.

I have to remind myself this is real. That Kevin is not even six inches from me. He smells like Polo cologne and chlorine. His lips are Rose Petal Pink and his eyes dark as Hershey chocolate bars. I've been dreaming of this moment for six years. The moment where he tells me he doesn't think I'm a freak. The moment where he tells me I'm lovely and smart and everything he's ever wanted.

When we've finally stopped giggling, he tilts his head and I know he's about to ask me something. I feel my hands shake.

"Can I ask you something, Sylvie?"

*Oh, yes, oh, God, yes.* "Mmm hmm."

"You don't think you could draw the pineapple for me, could you?"

"I HEARD THAT!" Mrs. Stilke yells from the storeroom.

"Was worth a try." Kevin shrugs, grinning. "My dad says, 'Try until you succeed.'"

I hand him the charcoal. "Okay, then. Try this."

# fifteen

## September: A Bitch in Time Saves Nine

Dwayne goes insane when he sees his locker. He charges through the hall like a rhino and when he comes up to me I can tell he's barely holding it together. "I'll get you, Psycho," he whispers in my ear. Fear trickles through me like ice water.

I don't tell anyone about Dwayne's threat. Not even Nelson. Besides, he's forgotten all about Dwayne and is focused on Kevin instead.

"So how did the art lesson go?" He keeps his eyes on his work as he asks.

I'm about to apologize for the whole thing yesterday, but then I realize that I have nothing to apologize for. He's the one who took off in a fit. So instead, I remind myself of Kevin's soft fingers and how he said I was okay. "Good."

"You gonna do it again?"

I stop working and blink at him. Again? I hadn't thought of that. But I could help Kevin out regularly. Then maybe... maybe it could turn into more. Definitely more. What did Kevin say?

*Try until you succeed.*
"I think I will." I nod.
Nelson doesn't reply.

I avoid Dwayne for a few days. I also have another tutoring session with Kevin. We are two inches apart, breathing
each other's air. But he doesn't seem to notice more than his
pencil on the page. I shouldn't be surprised, after all. And I'm
not. But it doesn't stop me from being disappointed.

What is surprising, though, is that Dwayne's not as dumb
as I thought. He doesn't talk to anyone about wanting to
pound me. He keeps a low profile and the days go by with
people believing he might actually have a sense of humor
about the whole thing.

After another art session, Kevin goes to the pool for an
extra practice and I start on my way home. Everyone else left
an hour ago and all's been quiet on the Dwayne front. So I'm
not expecting Dwayne to pull up in his truck the second I
step off school grounds.

I run. Panic sends me the wrong way. I should run back
to school, where if he touches me he's out on his ass, but I go
towards home. And take the park as a short cut.

On the other side of the park is the grade school and its
high, gated fence. Today's a school day. I'm not worried about
it being locked.

But it is.

*Crap!* I reach up, but the edge is too high for me to grasp,
even on tip-toes. And the boards are smooth and slippery. No
place for a toe hold. My heart pounds. I have to go around.

I can hear Dwayne's footsteps whacking the pavement. He
catches up to me before I can go anywhere and pounds me

against the wooden boards. The noise is deafening, but no one comes out to see what's going on.

*Don't project. Don't go astral. Stay inside. If you don't, you're dead.*

"You little bitch!" Dwayne's hands are on my shoulders now. He slams me against the fence. Once, twice, three times. Tears spill onto my cheeks as he grinds my spine against the wood. Visions of Randy Lang and fifth grade swim in my head. I picture Kevin biting Randy, picture his heroics.

Only now, Kevin isn't here to save me.

So I save myself. Kevin style.

I turn my head and bite Dwayne on his large hairy hand with all my force. He tastes like sweat and rotten salami, but I keep digging my teeth in until I realize he's actually screaming.

Dwayne backs away. His eyes are wide and wild. He looks at me like I'm the one who's the monster. "Fucking psycho bitch! I'm gonna need rabies shots now!"

I spit the taste of him out at his feet and sprint towards home.

Once I realize he's not following me, I collapse onto some stranger's front lawn and gulp down deep breaths. When I stop shaking and realize the terror has seeped away, I start laughing.

I laugh and laugh until I cry.

# sixteen

## September : The Gateway Drug

Every day after school I astral project.

I project to Kevin's and watch him lounge in front of the TV. I project to Mrs. Zimmer's and get the answers for the Trig test. I project to Tori's to figure out how to get even. I project everywhere I want, but then I come home and come back to being me. It's like the longer I'm out, the more I want to stay out. The more I want to forget who I am. It's a strange high, and the crash back to reality is always brutal: Someone rips the ANIMAL CONTROL page out of the Yellow Pages and tapes it to my locker. Tori puts the video she took of me in the cafeteria on YouTube—on it, I wilt like week old lettuce, sliding under the lunch table while Tori's laughing makes the soundtrack. My mom erases my dad's name from our answering machine. Cassie and Kevin seem to have whole conversations with just a look. My little brother is already a hell of a lot more popular than I'll ever be.

I stay strong. And I'm no longer afraid of Dwayne. Now that he believes I'm certifiable, I have no reason to be scared. He's more scared of me.

But it's lonely. And it hurts. All of it.

So I go astral as often as I can. Every day the shadows are waiting to cradle me, their touch cold as winter frost. But I've learned to like the chill. To crave it.

The whole experience leaves a permanent bad taste in my mouth. I go through packs of mint gum to get rid of it.

But I never think of stopping. I can't. I'm addicted.

# seventeen

## September: The Inside Counts for Crap

Kevin comes up to our table at lunch and invites us to a party that same night, this time at his own house. "You gotta come," he says to us. "Wear your swim suits, 'cuz I've got a pool." His eyes hesitate over Cassie, then move to me. "Hey," he says. "Got a C+ on that Art project."

Anything below a B is bad news for me. But Kevin smiles. "She was failing me. Getting a C+ is major." He slaps the table in a little drum roll, then winks at Cassie.

After he walks away, Cassie lifts her eyebrows at me. "Wow. You've made him happy."

I enjoy a little swooping in my stomach at the thought.

Then she whispers, "Looks like you'll finally get to see the inside of his place." We've gone past Kevin's house probably 300,000 times since the fifth-grade, with me wanting to see him and yet ducking behind a bush anytime he's been around.

"Yeah." She doesn't know I've done better than see his place, I've seen his room. Well, in a way.

Michelle suddenly slams her Diet Coke onto the table. "Wait! My dad's using the car tonight."

Cassie smugly sucks up the last of her Suicide Mix with a loud gargle. "I've got a new car, people. My *own*. I can pick everyone up."

The bell rings and we all head to our next classes. Cassie and I have religion class—Morality. It's the junior class's curse. Not only is the subject unbearable, the teacher reeks like B.O. If you get him last hour, your eyes actually water from the stink.

The tardy bell rings just as Cassie and I slide into empty desks.

"All right, Ladies and Gentlemen. Today you are going to split into two groups: male and female." Mr. Walker begins waving all the boys over to one side of the room, while we girls form a circle with our desks. I try to get mine as far from Tori as possible. Ever since the whole thing with Dwayne's locker, she hasn't let up.

Mr. Walker sets a large piece of paper before me and explains the assignment to the group. The smell of his armpits almost knocks me out. "You will define the perfect male. You have twenty minutes to do so."

The others start to give ideas so quickly I can barely write them down fast enough.

"Blonde."

"No way, I like 'em dark."

"Tall. Six feet. Or taller, even."

"Not too tall."

"Athletic."

"But smart. Like making lots of money smart."

"What about gallant?" This is Cassie's input, surely because we're reading Jane Austen in English. I start writing it down, but the other girls laugh like she's made a joke. "I'm serious," she says.

Across the room, the boys are debating on the merits of the perfect female. I hear things like, "Big tits" and "Long hair" and I swear I even heard someone say, "Cassie." I glance at Cassie, but she seems to not have heard it.

"Keep writing, Psycho," Tori drawls. "*The Perfect Male.* You do know the difference between a man and a woman, don't you? Or do you need me to draw you a picture?" Then her eyes flit over to Keri Nielsen. "Or Keri could draw it for you. She knows, for sure."

Keri sticks out a pierced tongue (that somehow got past the authorities) and gives Tori the finger.

Tori gets up. "Gotta use the little girls' room." Everyone except Mr. Walker knows she really goes out to smoke.

I write down our final list for the perfect male, but I'm really thinking about the party tonight. How I can get Kevin to look at me and forget to look at Cassie. Mr. Walker takes our paper and gives us another blank sheet. This time we have to list out the perfect female. Tori slides back into her desk reeking like cigarettes. She rolls her eyes at the new heading on my paper, but she doesn't give me a hard time. The suggestions come quickly.

"Pretty."

"Friendly."

"Can keep a secret."

"Is loyal." This time everyone agrees with Cassie.

When we're done. Mr. Walker collects the second list and then tapes all four to the board. "Do you think God's list for a perfect male and perfect female read like this?" He points a chubby finger to one of the lists. "Size 38DD bra. Long legs." He grimaces toward the group of boys, who double up in laughter. Then Mr. Walker points to one of our lists. "Or this? Tall. Rich. Muscular."

He faces us and stares at us, one by one, with those hard eyes shoved into folds of flesh. "Ladies and Gentlemen, you'd better think a little more about this. Those lists? Perfect Male and Perfect Female? They should be the same. The perfect human. There shouldn't be different criteria for men than for women. Because it's not the outside that counts. It's the inside. Don't let the wicked world convince you into thinking otherwise."

There are some groans from the boys' side of the room and some simulated barfing from the girls'.

The bell rings and everyone leaves the room in a herd. Tori Thompson bangs into me. "Oh, sorry, Psycho. Too bad for you that inside counts stuff is a load of shit."

Cassie gets her face right into Tori's. "You're such a bitch."

Tori just laughs.

"Shut up, Tori," I spit out and pull Cassie with me down the hall.

The day drags on a lot longer than usual, which is saying something. Just the thought that in only a few hours I'll be at Kevin's house makes those hours seem like days.

Finally, my last class. Before the bell rings, Nelson turns to me. "Hey, there's a bunch of people gonna have a bonfire on the beach tonight."

"Yeah?"

"Yeah. It'll be fun. I can pick you up if you wanna go." He fingers a hole in his jeans as he says it.

It would be the first time we'd do something together outside of school, which could be cool. But not tonight. Not when I get to go to Kevin's. "Thanks, Nelson. But I've got plans." *Big plans.*

"Oh, yeah. Of course." He nods and turns to the front of the room.

Mrs. Stilke gives us a heads-up on the next project. "If you can start with this today, great. But if not, I want you to think about it over the weekend, because it's a big project. We'll be working on it for a while." She sits on the paint-splattered table at the front of the room which serves as her desk, tucking her long skirt underneath her.

"Home. What do you think of when I say that? Now, I'm not just talking about the place where you live, although that might be what you call home. But some of us have other places we like to call home, or places we feel really at home. I, for example, feel the best when I'm fishing in the Root River." Here the class stifles giggles—no one can imagine Mrs. Stilke with her funky dresses and thousand necklaces wearing rubber boots and a fisherman's hat. But she ignores us and continues. "I want you to think about where you feel best. We'll start painting that place, in acrylics, on Monday, but if any of you want to get a head start, you can."

I think of my house and the emptiness that has taken over the place since Dad has gone. I won't paint that as home. It doesn't feel like it anymore. But Dad's place definitely isn't home either. Neither is school. Thing is, I'm not at home anywhere—not even in my own body.

How sick is that?

I rub my thumb over a dried blob of red paint on the table. I think of how things look when I leave my physical body: the way my astral body glows, the way even normal everyday objects seem more colorful, sharper and bright, of how the dark is no longer scary, but intriguing, inviting. Amazing. Lately I really only feel at home when I do astral projection. I take a deep breath and get a smock and some brushes. I prepare my paints and canvas and sit down.

Then I pick up my brush and start.


After school, I run out to the parking lot. Cassie and Sam are already there. Sam's leaning on Cassie's car, telling a couple other freshmen guys he's invited to Kevin's party.

"Come on," I tease him. "You'd better get into Cassie's car before your head grows so big it won't fit."

As Cassie pulls out of the parking lot, I pound the passenger side floor with my feet and sing out, "YES! We're going to Kevin's! We're going to Kevin's!"

Cassie laughs then looks at me, her eyes narrowed. "Why don't we make you up tonight, Sylvie? Get Kevin's attention."

"Are you kidding? Don't you remember the last time I used make-up?" I'm allergic to all sorts of things. Well, not many foods, luckily, just watermelon. But medicines are a nightmare, and I break out in hives if I get stung by a bee; I sneeze like crazy around cats. I turn red and scaly if I use powder or base, and the last time I tried eyeliner, my eyes swelled up. My only friends are Vaseline, ph neutral soap, and hydro-cortisone cream.

"Yeah, but I don't think you've ever used expensive make-up. The really good stuff. They have make-up for people with allergies. And even if it's not a hundred percent, it might be worth a bit of itching if you look good at the party tonight."

"Look good? Puh-leeeze. Not possible." This from Sam.

I glare at him. "You watch it, derp."

I look back at Cassie, at the way her lips glisten, the way her eyes seem all the more seductive darkly lined. I'd love to be able to wear make-up. I've watched all the soupy films about the girl being turned into a goddess with a bit of lipstick and a good haircut. I'd give anything for that to happen to me. Maybe Kevin would finally give me a second look. But I know from experience to be cautious. "I don't know."

"My mom just bought some hypoallergenic stuff because her skin was getting weird with her regular brand. I can swipe some and bring it to your Dad's."

"Well…"

"Come on, Sylvie. Lately, you look like someone's sucked the life out of you. Or like you got punched in the eyes. Make-up can cover that."

Side effects of my shadow addiction. "Okay. Maybe if it's decent make-up."

She claps. "Yippee! This will be fun."

I hope so.


Cassie comes to Dad's apartment with us for dinner. We all eat KFC and ice cream together and then she holds up a large, floral make-up bag. "Mr. Sydell, we've got to get ready."

We shut ourselves into Dad's tiny bathroom. I sit on the toilet seat while she bends over me with her brushes and Q-tips. I love the satiny feel of the blush over my cheeks, the slight pulling of the mascara wand on my eyelashes.

Cassie drags lipstick over my lips. Then she stands back as far as she can and grins. "Stellar!"

I look in the mirror.

Whoa.

The girl who looks back isn't my usual horrid self. She's normal. Almost cute. I can't believe it. I blink at my reflection. I pucker my lips a couple times. "Wow, Cass. Thank you."

She runs a brush and some serum through my hair until it's smooth and shiny. Then she nods. "Great. Now for the rest. Hey, do you have a skirt you could wear?"

"Umm, legs like toothpicks? No skirts."

"Okay. Fine, whatever." She shrugs and pushes me to the door. "Let's show you off."

When we come out of the bathroom, Dad looks at me funny and makes a big deal about my face. " I can't believe how fast you're growing up."

Ugh.

We leave as the evening melts into darkness.

Sarah and Michelle both live on the other side of town. On the way to pick them up, Cassie juggles steering and popping Sugar Babies into her mouth. "Hey," she says, mouth full. "Wasn't that thing we did in Morality class interesting?"

I look at her like she's just spoken Chinese.

She shrugs. "What? I thought Mr. Walker had a point. In a perfect world, we wouldn't judge people by their looks, but by who they are. And why do we have different criteria for men than we do for women?"

I have to stop her watching those touchy-feely talk shows. She's starting to sound like a pop-culture scholar. "So, you don't think looks are important?" I ask. "That it's only the inside that counts?"

From the back seat, Sam gives one sharp laugh. Cassie ignores him and answers, "Yeah, I guess so."

"That's because you're pretty."

"No. No one ever told me I was pretty before this summer and I lived my life just fine."

"Get off it, Cass. People have always gone on about your hair. God, it's the first memory I have of you. Your hair shining. Even as a kid I would have gladly traded with you."

"Really?" She whips her head towards me. Her hair bounces mockingly.

"Yeah…Anyways, if looks don't count, then you would have no problem being me?" I ask slowly. Every nerve in my body prickles, like her answer means everything.

She laughs. "Of course not."

"Oh, come on. "

"You act like you're covered in scales or something, Sylvie. I wouldn't have a problem being you. You're cute. Scout's honor," Cassie holds up the first three fingers of her right hand.

"You've never been a scout, Cass."

She shrugs.

"You couldn't pay *me* to be you," Sam says to me from the back.

"I didn't ask you," I bark at him then look back to Cassie. "I think I'd like being you," I say to her.

"Ha! You'd have to deal with my parents."

"I like your parents. At least they're trying to do things right."

Now Cassie shakes her head. "Sylvie, even apart, your mom and dad are better parents than mine ever are. I mean it."

But my parents wouldn't be apart if it weren't for me. They'd still have time for each other. Time for Sam. Time to stay a family.

We pull into Michelle's driveway and Cassie beeps. Michelle's out the door in a flash, a streak of white clothing in the dark night.

A few blocks from Michelle's we pick up Sarah, and then we head back across town to Kevin's. He only lives a couple miles from me and Cassie in one of those split-level houses scattered about the north side. I know what the outside is like: an apple tree in the front, an in-ground swimming pool in the back. And from projecting, I've now seen the inside. Well, his room, anyways. But now I'll get to go inside because I was invited. Because Kevin wants us there. All of us. Me included. My stomach see-saws at the thought.

My eyes start itching about ten minutes before we arrive. I ignore it, and think of Kevin's reaction to the new made-up me. He did say I was okay. Maybe now he'll see me as more than okay.

But when we park outside his place, Cassie says to Sarah and Michelle, "Check out the new Sylvie!" and turns on the dome light.

All of them scream in unison.

With shaky hands, I put down the sun visor on the passenger side and open the mirror. *No! No, no, no! Not tonight!* I might as well be covered in scales. I'm already bright red and my left eye is so puffed up, I can't believe I can actually see out of it. I can't see for long, though, because the tears are already starting to make everything blurry.

"Oh, hell. Oh, no. I'm so sorry, Sylvie. It's my fault; I shouldn't have made you up. But I thought...Oh, God."

Cassie puts her hands over her face and peeks at me from between her fingers. "You can't go in there."

Sarah and Michelle agree. "No way."

"Yeah," Sam says. "You look like a DNA experiment gone wrong."

I glance at Kevin's house and put a hand over my mouth to stifle a sob. This is so, so not fair. "Fine," I say, when I'm able to talk. "Let's go then. We can rent a movie at my dad's place."

But they all just look at each other.

"What?"

Sarah puts a hand through her jet-black hair and lifts her eyebrows. "We're going to the party, Sylvie. Just because you can't go shouldn't ruin the night for the rest of us."

"I've got to show them the Mentos trick." This from Sam. Michelle just opens the car door and gets out.

I look at Cassie.

"I'll drive you home and come back." She waits until the others are all out of the car and then starts it up again.

We're almost to my dad's when I say, "You can't leave me, Cass."

"But—"

"It's your fault I'm like this! You said the makeup was all right!"

"But I've got to bring the others home! I can't stay with you."

"They've got their cells. They'll text when they need a ride." Truth is, I'm afraid to leave her alone with Kevin. What'll happen if they're together without me? Plus, I'm so disappointed and confused and angry. The one night I get to go to Kevin's, the one night things are going my way, Cassie wants to make me up. The thing is, she of all people knows how allergic I am to everything.

She wouldn't have done it on purpose, would she have?

I hope not.

I decide to go for the guilt and hold up my index finger, showing her the little scar there. "I thought we were blood sisters."

Cassie looks at me for a long time, and I know she wants to be back at that party. But she sighs, holds up her finger and wraps it around mine. "Fine. Blood sisters forever."

Dad, however, takes one look at me and sends Cassie away. "I'm taking Sylvie to the walk-in clinic. You need to stay with Sam." Cassie looks relieved and hops into her car before he can change his mind.

For a Friday night, the walk-in clinic is dead. I'm in and out within an hour. I must look devastated, because when we get back to the apartment Dad actually offers to play Parcheesi instead of work. It's such a bad suggestion, though, I figure he's hoping I'll say no so he can write anyways. It doesn't matter. I want to be alone. I blow him off and shut the door to my so-called room.

I scream into my pillow, kick the blow-up mattress and cry myself weak.

Kevin's having a party and I'm not there.

*Screw it.* I'll leave my body and go to that damn party anyhow.

# eighteen

## September: Is That a Knife in My Back?

I split from my body and see myself lying there on the blow up mattress, face swollen, arms stick-thin and pinned to my sides. It's like I have no connection to that frail-looking creature. It could be anyone, not me.

I wonder if Kevin's party is still going strong. I barely complete the thought when the shadows surround me. Their cool breath lifts me up and pulls me there.

I'm in Kevin's kitchen. It's huge and sleek, all metal and granite. I reach out to touch the wall, and my hand sweeps right through it.

Around the kitchen island, Sam, Bryce, Kevin, Cassie, Sarah, Michelle, Ashley and a few others are all laughing and wiping themselves off with paper towel. On the island stand two almost empty bottles of Diet Coke and an empty pack of Mentos. Diet Coke is splattered everywhere.

"Cool, dude." Bryce says this to Sam. "A geyser."

"Yeah. That was the shit!" Kevin nods at Sam, then turns to Cassie. "I've gotta say you look fantastic doused in Diet Coke."

"Shut up." Cassie grins.

Kevin goes to the fridge, opens it, pulls out a can of 7Up and shakes it. "But I wonder? Would you look so good doused in 7Up?" Now he cracks the can open in Cassie's direction, letting the spray fizz out over her and several others in the kitchen.

The place goes wild with screams and laughter and even more so when Cassie opens the fridge and gets a can to spray at Kevin. Soon everyone's spraying cans of soda. The floor is wet and slick. Kevin grabs Cassie and slides a couple feet on the floor with her, like they're ice-skating partners, only then they fall down hard together.

Cassie stays on the floor, giggling. *Get up, Cass*, I think. *Get away from him*. Kevin stays next to her. He reaches out and tucks a wet strand of hair behind her ear.

"Ugh. I'm all sticky," Cassie says, patting her hands to her cheeks.

"Come on." Kevin gets and up grabs her hand, pulling her after him. They slide around the kitchen once more then slip out the doors to the patio. The swimming pool is a turquoise rectangle in the darkness. It's a warm evening, but breezy. I can hear the wind shaking the leaves on the trees.

Kevin yanks off his Abercrombie sweatshirt and the T-shirt he's wearing underneath. He stands there in his tan Bermudas. His chest is lean but muscular. His skin looks almost iridescent in the light from the pool. It's beautiful. I reach out to touch him, but that's when he dives a perfect arc into the deep end. When he comes up, he shakes his head and grins at Cassie. "You got your suit on, right?"

"Yeah…but…"

"It'll get the 7Up off." Then he dives under the water again.

Cassie hesitates for a second but undoes her jeans and whips off her top. She's wearing her jade green bikini. I was there when she bought it this summer. Both of us stood in front of the mirror, gaping. Wondering who the hell the gorgeous babe in the green swimsuit was.

Of course she bought the damn thing.

Kevin comes up out of the water just as she's descending the pool stairs. He wipes water from his face and stares. I see him swallow and know the bikini has worked its magic.

If only she'd burp or fart or vomit. Then maybe she wouldn't be so freakin' gorgeous. But she doesn't. She glides gracefully under the water and ends up about two feet in front of Kevin, near the ladder. She climbs it and sits on the edge, shivering. "Got a towel?"

Kevin hoists himself up out of the water and goes to a little shed at the back of the yard. He comes back with two beach towels. One he wraps around her, the other he drapes over his shoulders.

"Warm enough?" He sits down, leaving barely an inch between them.

"Sure," Cassie says. *Move away from him, Cass. Get up and move away.*

"Man, I'm glad my parents and brother are gone. I get to breathe."

Cassie just raises an eyebrow.

"Do you ever get the feeling you're living your life for other people?" Kevin's voice is bitter and he keeps his eyes on the water.

Cassie looks at Kevin curiously, her eyes searching his face. "Sometimes."

Kevin moves his jaw back and forth, like he's trying to decide something. Then he turns to Cassie and says softly, "Or like nobody even cares if you're there?"

Now it's Cassie who looks down at the water. She blinks a few times, then closes her eyes. When she opens them, they're glistening.

*What the hell?* I can't believe it. They have two minutes of conversation and already Kevin has Cassie down pat! He knows exactly what to say to her.

"Do you feel like that?" Cassie hugs her towel tighter to her chest.

"My dad wants me to be the best swimmer. The best baseball player. He'd probably keel over dead if one day I came in last place. When I'm playing real good, he calls me 'Champ', otherwise it's 'young man'. I think he forgot what my actual name is."

A smile flits across Cassie's face. She looks at Kevin, then back at the pool. "My parents actually do forget my name sometimes." She takes a shaky breath and lets it out. "They like to get too plastered to remember they have a kid."

Cassie has never told anyone in the whole world about her parents drinking. No one. Ever. Except me. I'm the only person who knows how her parents really are. It's always been one of the greatest secrets in our friendship. And now she's telling Kevin. My weightless form suddenly feels heavy, like instead of golden light I'm made of lead.

Kevin leans toward Cassie and brushes his lips against hers. And she lets him. She totally lets him. She takes in a quick breath and he bites her bottom lip.

Then they're at it. Kevin's hands pulling at Cassie's hair, Cassie holding tight to his shoulders.

*NO!*

I didn't know you could feel pain outside your body, but a pain so intense slashes through me, the next thing I know I'm on the mattress in Dad's study, gasping like I've just been gutted.

*Oh, my God. Oh my God. Cassie and Kevin kissed.* I hug myself tight and do my best to hold back tears.

I knew it.

I could spy on Kevin every day. Learn all there is to know about him. Tutor him until he's freakin' Picasso. But it still wouldn't change the fact that *I'm not her. All he wants is her.*

I feel dizzy and nauseous and empty. Completely empty. I can't believe Cassie did this.

*Come on, Sylvie. It's not like you really have a chance with him. It's not that big of a deal. You love her. Let her be happy.*

But it is a big deal. And she's also supposed to love me.

With numb hands I reach for my cell, and dial her number. I mess up three times before I'm able to actually complete the call. I hold the phone to my ear as it rings. And rings. And rings.

Finally, she answers. "Hey."

"What are you doing?"

"Huh? I…we're at the party. You know that."

"Having fun?" I can't keep the sarcasm out of my voice.

She doesn't answer right away. I can hear the sound of splashing and yelling in the background. Other people have finally made their way to the pool. "Yeah. It's fun. What's going on?"

"Forget it," I say and hang up.

I sit and stare at the wall forever, letting time stretch out and out.

Then I hear the apartment door open and shut; Sam is back.

I go out into the living room. Dad's on the couch with his laptop. He looks up and says, "Oh! I thought you were sleeping." I just shrug and move past him to sit at the bar and wait while Sam makes himself a peanut butter and jelly sandwich.

He squishes his two pieces of bread together, takes a big bite and half-sits on the counter. It's odd; one thing about Sam is that he always looks…I don't know…like his clothes don't fit right, or maybe like he isn't comfortable in them. But standing there with his PB and J at this particular moment, he looks at ease.

"Whoa," he says when he notices me sitting there. "I forgot about your face. I hope it's better by Monday."

"The doctor said it will be. Mostly."

Sam nods and I mouth that I want to talk to him about the party, but not in front of Dad. So he comes into Dad's study with me.

He leans against the desk, but suddenly can't stay still. He paces the room as he talks. "It was so awesome, Sylvie. I think…I think they're my friends now."

I swallow a rawness in my throat. They're supposed to be *my* friends.

"They were nice. Not fake. And then I did the Mentos trick—they'd never tried it before."

"I thought everyone had done that," I say. But I'm stalling, what I really need to know is if Kevin and Cassie hooked up.

"But that's not the big news—"

I brace myself. *This is it.*

"—the neighbor called the cops! We had to book out the back and through that same neighbor's yard to get away!" He looks at me and shakes his head. "We were all ready to crap our pants!"

The news isn't as juicy as it normally would be. In fact, I'm barely listening. "And…uh…Kevin? At the party? Did he… or Cassie…did they, like…get together?"

Sam looks embarrassed. "Kevin and Cassie?"

"Yes, Sam. Kevin and Cassie."

"Look. I don't want to talk about other people and what they do, okay? If you want to know, ask Cassie. Don't ask me." He's got his thumbnail in his mouth and he's gnawing at it like he's starving. That's all I need to confirm how uncomfortable he is. All I need to confirm that the kiss I saw was real.

I nod and turn toward the window. He leaves and I sit staring out at the streetlight and the dark sky behind it. My stomach is churning.

I lie down on the mattress and wait for sleep to come. But before it does, I slip out of my body. I'm surrounded by the shadows and their incessant buzzing. They whip out words I can't quite grasp. But they repeat a phrase, over and over. I know they're trying to tell me something, but I can't seem to concentrate on the meaning.

They go with me to Chicago, where I hover above the John Hancock building and look at the lights of the city. I try to enjoy its beauty. Try to get the same high I usually get when I'm out of my body. But it's lost its edge.

When I'm back in my body, the air in the room is chilly. My mouth tastes like hell. I can still hear the shadows' buzzing, like an echo, inside my head. I can still feel their forked tongues tickling my ears. All of a sudden I get clarity and hear their words as one liquored voice:

*Become her.* It says. *Figure out how.*

In the morning, Cassie calls to tell me how the police took down people's names and how they threatened Kevin that if he had another party they would give him trouble. But, apparently, this time they just wanted to scare everyone. They didn't call Kevin's parents. But Cassie says Kevin almost wished they had so that he could let the cleaning lady scrub the place down. As it was, he, Bryce and Ashley were going to have to spend all day doing nothing but mopping up.

"So, how do you know all this?" I push the phone closer to my ear.

"Oh…Kevin called me. To let me know how things turned out. Since we left without knowing."

"He called you."

"It's not like that, Sylvie."

"What happened last night, Cass? Between you and Kevin?"

She hesitates and I think she's about to tell me. Instead she sighs. "Nothing. Nothing for you to worry about."

"I'm not so sure."

"Let it go, Sylvie."

But she should know I can't.

# nineteen

## A Memory: Stupid Girls

The summer we were ten years old, Cassie and I held our fingers over my mother's biggest, shiniest knife and looked into each other's eyes.

"Ready?" Cassie asked. Her eyes shone. She dragged her front teeth across the plump cushion of her bottom lip.

The knife was her idea, not mine. I would have gone with a needle.

But a few hours earlier Cassie had come over to my place with tears in her eyes, upset about her parents drinking. As usual.

There was never any violence. Never anything to get too freaked out about. But sometimes it wore her out. Like this time. This time she wilted against the back of the couch and whispered, "They barely notice I'm there."

I laced my fingers in hers. We sat a long time, dangling our flip-flops from our toes, the too-sweet smell of honeysuckle coming in from the open windows.

Suddenly, Cassie sat up straight. Her left flip-flop dropped to the floor. "You're my best friend, right?"

"Yeah."

"We've been through everything together."

We had. From what everyone called my 'fainting spells', to getting our pants pulled down by the neighborhood boys, to an attempt at running away, to living through Sam's practical jokes. And more.

"And we'll be friends forever? We'll always be able to count on each other, right?" Cassie spoke quickly now, her grip on my hand getting tighter.

Her intensity wasn't exactly scaring me, but it did make me squirm just a little. "Forever."

She narrowed her green eyes at me. "Prove it."

So it came down to this: An extremely sharp knife and an oath to always be best friends. Which is why we were standing there, in my kitchen, my mom's cutlery in our hands and why Cassie's face was flushed with satisfaction and mine with fear.

"The oath," Cassie prompted. We said it together, our two voices melding into one:

*Blood Sisters, blood sisters as long as we live. Always together. We always forgive.*

*Best friends forever, best friends for life. As proof we share our blood with this knife.*

"On the count of three," Cassie said.

"Uhhh…"

"You can't hesitate, Sylvie. If you hesitate that means you don't take it seriously." She fixed me a look that managed to be both demanding and pleading at the same time.

Where we gripped the handle, my palm was slick with sweat.

She started to count: "One…two…three…"

Both of us slid the pad of our index fingers down the blade at the same time.

The blood came first. Bright, bright blood. And then the sharp, stinging bolt of pain. The knife dropped to the tile floor with a loud clang. Cassie sucked in a huge breath. I stared at the red dripping onto my feet and cried out.

We'd been intending to rub our blood into each other's cut. But before we could, I felt a prickle of fear and then nothing. Nothing at all.

Dizziness seized me as I hovered near a cobweb ·in the corner, watching as my mom ran into the kitchen and took control, her voice strange and surreal from where I was.

"What are you girls thinking?" she shrieked. "Do you know what kind of infections and diseases you can get from doing this kind of thing? You're lucky you didn't cut your fingers off!" From above I saw my body go limp, my head pitching forward and my legs buckling. "Oh, my Lord, Sylvie! Don't faint!" When Mom thrust our hands under cold water, I came back to my body with a jerk. "Stay with me!" pleaded Mom as she shoved my raw and aching finger further under the rushing tap.

Mom cleaned our cuts and wrapped them in Barbie Band-Aids. It was only then that Cassie and I touched fingers. We hooked them around each other and squeezed, the pain from the fresh cut throbbing up to our elbows. But no fluids were shared, so officially we were just two kids with deep cuts. Not blood sisters.

Even so, we took that oath—Band-Aids or not we took it. "We're blood sisters," Cassie says even now, six years later. "No matter how mad we get, we have to forgive."

Or do we?

## October 28th

I think I'm going to lose it, but then we finally arrive at the hospital.

The smell of antiseptic bites at my nostrils the second we pass through the sliding doors, reminding me of all the time I've spent taking some sort of medical test. I wish now that those tests had shown something. Anything. So I wouldn't be here. Like this.

The hospital is busy for the middle of the night. There are people standing in clumps everywhere. We follow a nurse's directions. My parents and Sam are in one of those hallway sitting areas, holding paper cups and looking shocked. I'm not surprised to see Mom and Sam, but I can't believe my dad's already here, too. He's sitting next to Mom like they've never been apart.

The sight of them makes me stop in my tracks. The three of them look so much like a family.

"Any news?" Mr. Sanders asks.

"She's not waking up," my mom says. "They're…they're…I don't know what they're doing. They're trying to wake her up." Mom looks pale. And scared. "This is all my fault. Dr. Hong told me to keep an eye on her."

"It's not your fault." Mr. Sanders shakes his head. "Don't think that way." The rest of the group stays silent. My mom must have said the same thing at least twenty times already.

I stand stiff, watching my parents look lost and my brother chew his thumbnail into oblivion. Panic strangles me. Being in this body is like wearing a cheap Halloween mask: I can see and breathe just fine, but I still feel half-blind and near suffocation.

I want to ask where my body is but can't open my mouth. I kind of squeak without meaning to.

"What are you doing here?" Dad points his chin at me.

My family's eyes are on me. I look down at myself and see the men's tennis shoes. The dirty jeans.

The low pitch of my voice startles me. "Uh…I'm…Cassie's friend."

Dad looks at Cassie. "They'll be testing for narcotics…" He trails off, rubbing his hands over his face.

"I told them she doesn't do drugs," Cassie whines. "That's not it!"

"They've got to cover everything in order to help her. In order to find out what happened."

But I know they can't help me. They'll never find out what happened. Because they'll never believe it.

I can barely believe it myself.

# twenty

## September: Something's Rotten in the State of Wisconsin

Sunday my face is almost back to normal, apart from the dark circles the shadows left behind, so Dad thinks we should enjoy the fall weather and take a hike outdoors.

"A hike?" Sam isn't the physical type.

"Well, a walk. In the woods. It'll do you both some good." Dad drives out to Petrifying Springs Park in Kenosha, parking the car near the edge of the lot. The colors of the leaves on the hundreds of trees are already starting to change. In a week or two I'll need to come out here with my sketchbook and some paints.

The sky is clear and the air warm. I take off my itchy wool sweater and tie it around my waist. Sticks crackle under our feet as we walk away from the lot. Somewhere, someone is having a barbecue; we get whiffs of the smoke on the wind.

Dad is extra happy, downright cheerful, almost forced. Sam and I exchange glances: something has to be up. But once we're in the woods a while, Dad's cheerfulness doesn't seem so odd. He talks about the different trees and the origins of the park. He almost catches a chipmunk. He gathers chestnuts and gives them to us like we're five, but it's kind of fun. We sit at a picnic table among the squirrels and have summer sausage sandwiches and Coke. The texture of squishy white bread against firm slices of summer sausage is something I love. I chew with gusto and give Dad a smile. This is probably the best time I've had with him in years.

Of course, he has to go and ruin it.

"I wanted to tell you two, so you would be in the loop right away: I'm serving your mom with divorce papers." He tries to say it nonchalantly, like you would tell someone to pass the salt.

I let my sandwich drop to the ground. What's left in my mouth I swallow with difficulty.

"I wanted you to know, because your mom will probably be...upset about it."

"Oh? You think?" I say, my voice hard. "So, she doesn't know yet?"

"She knows it's what I want. She'll find out tomorrow I meant it."

"You didn't tell her the papers are coming?" Sam's voice quavers.

Dad looks embarrassed. "She wouldn't have let me get a word in edgewise. But this way..." He sighs and runs his long fingers down his face. "You kids can't understand."

"And what are we supposed to do? Keep this a secret? Break it to her?" I yell, the loudness of my voice out of place in the quiet of the park. Dad opens his mouth to answer, but I don't let him. Instead, I let my emotions take over: "You're so pathetic! I hate you! Both you and Mom are pathetic!"

Hatred boils inside me, bubbling over. But it's not really Dad I hate. Mom, either.

Dad stands up and stretches a long leg over the bench of the picnic table, smashing his lunch bag into a ball as he does so. I can hear him talk. I can see the anger in his face. But it's from a distance. Because I've slipped out of my body so fast, even I don't notice at first.

"I am your father, Sylvie. I do not need to answer to you, nor do I need to listen to you when you talk like that. You are to show me some respect." Dad's voice is hard and authoritative. And then my body falls from the bench and makes a dull thud on the ground.

"Sylvie!" Both Dad and Sam shake me until I come back into my body. When I stiffen up, Dad searches my eyes. "How do you feel?"

The back of my head aches where it hit the ground and Sam's grabbing my arm too tightly, but all I say is, "Don't tell Mom this happened. She's got enough to worry about right now."

No one says a word in the car, and I can tell Dad hasn't decided what to do yet. We're not angry with each other anymore, because the sense of despair fills the car so fully there's no room left for anything else.

Even though it's early, Dad pulls into our driveway. "I'll keep quiet just this once," he says. "But I might call Dr. Hong myself."

I nod silently and he hands me a paper bag full of candy bars.

When we're inside, Mom pokes her head out of her work room. "You two are home early! I've got another massage here today, okay?"

That's Mom Code for: "I'm working! Don't interrupt me." We don't need to answer. Thank God, because neither Sam nor I would know what to say.

I feel sick to my stomach and lock myself in my room, holding my trash can in my arms, just in case I puke.

I look at my Salvador Dali posters, at the paintings I've made over the years hanging on my walls. At my stereo, at the pile of blankets in a heap at the bottom of my bed. At my art supplies spread all over my desk. Nothing gives me any comfort whatsoever.

I want to get away. Just leave. Be somewhere else. And despite my bad experience visiting Kevin's party, I think of astral projection again. It's the only way I know how to escape.

*You're such an idiot, Sylvie.*

But I do it anyways.

I set the trash can on the floor and lie back. I take several deep breaths, and imagine my body loose as jelly.

Eventually, I'm able to leave it.

I go through the wall and outside the house. Where do I want to go?

I should go to China, or Iceland, or Morocco.

But the shadows are with me, and they whisper his name, so instead I go to Kevin. Again.

Okay, Sylvie. Can you say *stalker*??

I can't help it. I want to be wherever he is. And even though I don't know where to find him, in a matter of seconds I'm next to him.

He's in his Camaro, across from Lakeview Park. On his lap is a Cool Whip container with holes poked in the top. He stares out the window to the park. I get as close to him as I dare, amazed that he doesn't feel me there. He squints over his shoulder and runs a hand through his hair. It's getting darker now that he's no longer at the beach all the time, but it suits him. I wish so much that I could touch it.

I look at what he's staring at and feel a jolt of surprise: Cassie's on a swing, her shoes kicked off. She swings slowly, dragging her toes in the sand.

Kevin gets out of the car quietly, then leans through the open window and takes whatever is in the Cool Whip container out, cupping his hands around it. He crosses the street and stands behind Cassie. "Hi."

She nearly falls off the swing, then starts giggling. "Hi. You scared me," she says.

They look at each other. Then she turns away, her cheeks pink. "I wasn't gonna come."

Kevin nods and bites his bottom lip.

*They planned this meeting!?!* Rage fires through me.

Cassie's voice wavers. "The only reason I came was because you said you had something to show me. And I'm still not sure I should be here. It better not be lame."

"It's not." He kneels down before her in the sand and for a second I think he's going to propose. But instead, he moves his cupped hands right in front of her at chest level and opens them. A Monarch butterfly sits in the palm of his left hand, its orange and black wings spreading tentatively.

"Oh! Gorgeous!" Cassie breathes, her eyes bright. "It's almost October, though, it should have migrated already. Where did you find it?"

Apart from opening its wings, the butterfly hasn't moved. Kevin looks down at it, then up at Cassie. "My secret."

I can't believe it. *A freakin' butterfly! She told him? Him?* I'm the only one who knows about her butterfly fetish!

Cassie's voice is soft. "I hate for it to be all alone. And we definitely can't keep holding it. What if we sneak it into the butterfly exhibit at the zoo?"

The zoo entrance is across from the park, just steps from where Kevin's car is parked. Kevin makes a strangled noise between a cough and a laugh. "Great idea."

That's how he got the thing, I'm sure of it. He just snuck it *out* of the exhibit.

I follow them. Kevin, hands cupped, but looking like he's itching to drop the butterfly and put his arm around Cassie, and Cassie all quick steps and excitement. Kevin tells Cassie to take his wallet and pay, so she does, while he stands to the side, his back to the cashier. They hurry past the kangaroos, go around the pyramid covered with mountain goats and monkeys and make it to the building in the middle of the zoo where the butterfly exhibit was just inaugurated a few months ago.

First one set of sliding doors, then another, open before them as they step forward. Even without my body, I can sense the change in temperature. Not feel it so much, but know it. It's hot, mostly humid. Tropical flowers create a jungle around Kevin and Cassie, and a waterfall splashes in the background. All different colors of butterflies flit inside the greenhouse, stopping on a flower or a rock before moving on. Cassie has been here plenty of times, but I can see she's still enchanted.

"Should I let it go?" Kevin holds his hands out, and at Cassie's nod opens them. The Monarch stays put until Kevin wiggles his fingers. Then it flies up and out of sight.

Cassie smiles at him and touches his arm. "That was worth coming out for."

I shouldn't have trusted her.

They walk the exhibit and the rest of the zoo. When they stop in front of an orangutan that has gotten a hold of some gum and is blowing large, pink bubbles, Kevin leans over, lifts Cassie's mass of auburn hair and drags his lips across her neck.

My astral body suddenly goes numb.

Cassie closes her eyes as Kevin's lips move along her hairline. She gently pushes him away and starts to walk, smiling back at him as she does so.

I begin to follow them, but I hear someone calling my name. It's faint at first, a question, "Sylvie?" then louder and louder almost to the point of a scream, "Sylvie!"

My mom. *No.* I don't want to, but I have to go.

I speed back into my body. Mom is banging like crazy on my bedroom door. I take a moment to reorient myself, then unlock it.

Mom's eyes are wild and her hair messed up. "Good Lord, Sylvie! When I tell you to open that door, you open it! No locking it! You scared me!"

"I was asleep."

"I've been out here screaming for you. I was ready to go out to the garage and get a ladder so I could climb in through the window!"

"You're serious?"

The look on her face tells me she is. "Dinner," she says. I walk past her and go downstairs. The kitchen table is set. Sam's in his spot.

"Do we say something?" he whispers.

*Say something?* It takes me a second to realize he's talking about the divorce papers. That was today? Spending the afternoon following Kevin around has made everything else seem far away. But the whole deal with Dad comes back like a hammer to my chest.

"Are you kidding? Don't say a word," I whisper before Mom comes in the room.

All throughout dinner, Sam and I avoid talking about Dad or anything, really. We've never downed our food so fast or with so little complaint. I can't look Mom in the eyes, so I keep my gaze on the table. Every once in a while, though, I sneak a peek at Cassie's house to see if she's home yet.

"So Mrs. Cabrini told him, 'If that's what you want.'" Mom lifts her fork into the air and gives a light laugh. Then she eyes me and Sam. "You two aren't even listening to me."

Of course we aren't. "Sure we are, Mom," I say. "Mrs. Cabrini."

Mom puts her fork down and wipes her mouth with her napkin. "Did something happen at Dad's?"

Both Sam and I burst out, "No!" at the same time. Total confirmation that something did happen.

"Well?" Mom says, waiting.

I've been going back and forth between hating Mom and hating Dad. Hating myself. Hating the world. Right at this moment, though, Dad takes the cake. I thought Mom was the weak one because she cries all the time, but at least she has the courage to say things to Dad herself. And yet...and yet there's a reason Dad never says anything to her. You can't say anything to Mom. She's a know-it-all dictator in lots of ways. She's stiffer than a rod of uncooked spaghetti; she doesn't bend. She only snaps.

I wonder if she'll snap now. "Dad's serving you with divorce papers. Tomorrow."

Mom stares at me until goose bumps form on my arms and a chill shimmies down the back of my neck. Then she excuses herself from the table and takes the cordless from its cradle. She goes upstairs, leaving a mess in the kitchen, something she never, ever does. I sigh and look at Sam, who is practically eating his whole hand.

"Sam," I say.

Sam immediately takes his fingers out of his mouth. "You said not to say anything. Why'd you tell her?"

"She knew something was up. I couldn't pretend."

Sam nods and brings his hand back to his mouth. This time I say nothing. Let him have his comfort. He looks so worried and sad, like the time when he was four and he lost two of the polyester peas in his stuffed pea pod. He slept in Mom and Dad's bed for almost a month after that.

It feels like I've swallowed barbed wire. I stand up. "We should do the dishes."

I wash and he dries. Then I wipe down the table. Muffled yelling comes from upstairs. Sam pulls his iPod out of his pocket and sticks the phones into his ears.

That's when I see Cassie through the lace curtains of her kitchen window. She's home. Finally. I rinse out my dishrag, then move to the living room and draw the blinds.

# twenty-one

October: There Is No Santa Claus (It's your parents lying to you. Again)

Monday morning, Mom serves us our breakfast and gives us our lunch money like some sort of zombie. Apart from 'good morning' she says nothing. She moves like she's on rails.

Sam and I get out fast, and on the ride to school with Cassie I think about the butterfly and the zoo and I say, "So, what'd you do yesterday?" I know I can forgive her if she tells me the truth.

Cassie glances at me and shakes her head.

"Go ahead."

Her eyes flick up to the rearview mirror, to see if Sam's listening. But Sam makes a point to shove his earbuds further into his ears.

"I had a really fun weekend, Sylvie," she starts.

I swallow a raspy feeling in my throat. *I had a really fun weekend.* The unsaid is *without you.*

But it's even more than that. "Part of that fun was talking to Kevin." Cassie doesn't look at me, just keeps her eyes straight forward.

I feel like I did when Cassie told me at age seven there was no Santa ("It's your parents lying to you," she'd said then). Everything in my life felt like a farce. Including Cassie's friendship.

"So," I say now. "What happened this weekend? I need you to tell me the truth."

But she doesn't. She's quiet so long, I can't take it anymore. We pull into the school parking lot, and I get out before she's even fully stopped the car.

"Nothing happened!" Cassie yells to me before I slam the door.

"I'm not stupid," I shout back and sprint to my first class, hoping to outrun my tears.

At lunchtime, Sam announces the big news: Bryce told him he could sit at their table. Sam doesn't hesitate.

"Sorry to leave you all hanging." He makes a show of apologizing to us as we walk through the line in the cafeteria.

"Don't sweat it, Sam," I say, holding up a ladleful of mashed potatoes, wondering whether or not to whip it at him. "We were trying to figure out how to get rid of you, anyways." I shake the mashed potatoes onto my plate. This is nuts. I thought Sam would end up with the pale-faced weirdos who eat boogers and make up math equations for fun, not the guys I want to be with.

I get to the cash register at the same time as Cassie, wondering if she's got any intention of telling me the truth. We've been stiff around each other all morning. But something's got to give.

Sam sits down at Kevin's table between Bryce and Tori-the-table-hopper-Thompson.

Cassie, Michelle, Sarah, and I sit down at our usual table and begin to eat. We talk about Mr. Crawford's Geography test, but everything feels strange. Like we're in some parallel universe.

"Can you believe Sam's at that table?" Michelle is having a hard time keeping food in her mouth it's hanging open so wide. "What's the deal with that?"

"He's their mascot," Cassie says. "A little frosh to carry the flag for the group. They're having fun and they like him."

"He *is* more fun than he looks. But still. Why him and not us?" Michelle shrugs her shoulders and adds unconvincingly, "Not that I care."

"Me neither," Sarah agrees quickly, not fooling anyone. "What about you, Cassie? I would think after the weekend, they'd have asked you to sit at that table." Sarah's eyes narrow to straight lines.

"Well, they…" Now Cassie's glance flicks over to me.

"They what?" Sarah pushes.

"They don't want…well, Tori and Ashley said…"

"You're talking to Tori now?" My voice sounds like I've swallowed glass.

"Well, it was Ashley, really. Tori was just there and agreed."

"But I thought you hated her."

"I do. She was at Kevin's, though. Can't avoid—"

Sarah breaks in. "But what did she *say*, Cassie? About the lunch table."

"She said…" Cassie's gaze points to me, then she purses her lips and shakes her head. "Doesn't matter. I'd rather be here."

Sarah and Michelle look at me now like I have some rare disease. Which, I suppose in a way, I do. *Freakitis.* "It's you?" Michelle asks me.

"It's no big deal," Cassie says.

*No big deal?*

I hate her sometimes. Really hate her. "I have to use the bathroom." I push my chair back and leave the cafeteria. It's all I can do not to run.

I lock the stall door and push my fists into my eyes. *Don't cry. Don't cry.* Now Cassie's sticking by me at lunch out of pity? Because she feels sorry for me? Because no one else wants to be around me?

She's supposed to be my best friend.

My chest shudders as the first sob escapes me. I grab onto the toilet paper dispenser and rest my head on the wall of the stall, right where someone has scraped into the paint: *Keri Nielsen is a slut.* I can't stop the sobbing now. All I can do is hope no one will come in.

But that's too much to ask for.

"Sylvie?" It's Cassie. Alone. At least it's not Tori.

I stifle another sob.

"Look. I don't know why you're upset. I choose to sit with you at lunch, don't I? We share lockers and everything."

"I'm not forcing you to." The words come out a wail.

"I know. I want to…but you need to know that doing things on my own sometimes, not as the Cassie and Sylvie team, it's…interesting."

"*Interesting?* What the hell does that mean?!"

"People like me for me."

"*I* like you for you." Then it hits me: "What are you saying? That people don't like me?" Not that this is news. But Kevin...he said I was okay.

"Sylvie, you don't like *yourself*." Cassie's voice is hard. "So you don't let others see how great you can be—you act different around everyone else. You say things...Like at Bryce's party. You offended Ashley by ignoring her. You...you jump to conclusions."

Anger sparks a fire inside me. I throw open the stall door and glare at her. "Like I'm jumping to conclusions about you and Kevin?"

She flinches. "Don't even go there, Sylvie."

"No, you're the one who said you wouldn't go there."

Cassie's eyes flick away from mine and land somewhere over my left shoulder. "I'd just like a little credit for sticking by your side, that's all."

"I'm not a charity case."

"I didn't say you were."

"Why are you even friends with me? So you can tell everyone else how I hold you back? So everyone will feel sorry for you? The martyr Cassie stuck with Psycho Sylvie Sydell as a friend."

"Stop it. Now you're being stupid."

"No, you stop it. Admit that you want to get rid of me. You want to be with Kevin and Bryce and Ashley. You don't want to be friends with some loser who shucks off her body like she shucks off dirty clothes."

The bell signaling the end of lunch rings. We have three minutes to get to class.

Cassie slowly shakes her head. "You need help, Sylvie. You've got a real problem, you know that?"

"Yeah, Cass. You're my problem."

She doesn't say anything to that. She just walks out the door without looking back.

It's a difficult task to ignore your locker partner. But I manage pretty well all afternoon. I wait until she grabs her books from her shelf before even attempting to get mine. I sit far from her in Morality and let my insides boil every time I think of all she's said. I go from anger to self-pity to bitterness and back around again in the course of the next couple hours.

By the time I get to Art, I'm back to anger, laced with the desire to inflict pain. Preferably on Cassie, but unfortunately, she's not available.

Nelson sets up his canvas next to mine.

"Hey, Sylvie. Everything okay? You look like you could use some cheering up." He dips his brush into some red paint and dots it onto his nose. "How about a clown? I've got the hair for it."

Any other day I would laugh, maybe paint his cheeks, too. But not today. He waggles his eyebrows at me and it reminds me of Cassie and her one eyebrow-trick. That pisses me off. "Nelson," I say, my voice harsh. "Leave me alone. For once, just leave me alone."

His blue eyes get big and he wipes the red paint from his nose. He gathers his stuff together and moves to the other side of the room without a word.

I hate myself sometimes.

When I get to the community center, I'm so worked up I'm not sure I'll be able to teach the kids. My dad's deserting the family was hard enough. But Cassie deserting me? It puts me over the edge.

My eyes sting. And I keep breathing in those damn hiccupping sobs that come on after I've cried too hard. Angie drops what she's doing and comes over to me. "Sylvie Sweetheart, what's wrong?"

And that's when it hits me. I will never get Kevin. I'll never be pretty like Cassie. I'll never be normal. And my family will never be whole. And my knowing how to control astral projection can't change any of that.

Thick and tricky as quicksand, a sense of despair settles over me, pulling me under. It gets into my lungs, it blurs my vision and it paralyzes me. Numbness trickles through me and I feel a tug. Then I'm out, the shadows wrapping their long fingers around my astral self, like ice on a wound.

Angie screams as my body crumples before her, collapsing into her arms. The kids in the room run towards us, eyes and mouths wide open. Fear circles the room like a vortex, pulling everyone in.

I want to go back to my body, reassure Angie and the kids. But the shadows feel so…nice. They suck my depression away and replace it with something stronger. Anger. Hatred. Selfishness.

I stay in their arms only forcing myself back to my body when I see Angie pull out her cell phone, ready to dial 911.

Once I'm in, the taste lining my mouth is so rotten, I almost retch. "It's okay," I manage to say to Angie. "Don't call anyone! Please!"

"I have to."

"Please, Angie. Please," I sob. The last thing I need is more tests and more questions from Dr. Hong. More worry for Mom.

She hesitates, but puts down her phone. I see her eyes and the eyes of a dozen little kids looking at me. But not the way they usually do. Not with admiration, or joy, or pride. They look at me with unease. They look at me like I scare them.

A thread of pain winds its way around my heart. This is the one place I've always felt welcome.

I know I won't come back.

When I get home, I expect Mom to be giving massages late, as she does every Monday. I don't expect for her to be in the kitchen. And I really don't expect her to be surrounded by three gallons of Ben and Jerry's ice cream.

She holds up a spoonful of Cherry Garcia as I walk in. "Want to join me? Misery loves company."

"But, Mom! You're lactose intolerant!"

She holds up a business sized envelope. "Your dad sent it. The bastard." Taking a wad of Kleenex out of her pocket, she blows her nose.

"Oh, no." I slide into a chair, still feeling a bit wobbly from my OBE. I grab the carton of Chocolate Chip Cookie Dough.

Mom finishes the Cherry Garcia and reaches for the Mint Chocolate Chunk. "You know, your dad was crazy about me in college. Every time I turned a corner, he'd be there with his goofy grin. Even after we got married, we adored each other. We'd spend hours just cuddling each other. And when you and Sam were young, too. It's crazy. One day we were happy and the next we barely crossed paths. I can't even remember the last time we kissed. I don't know what happened."

But I know exactly what happened. I started leaving my body. And taking up all her time. My stomach hurts, a sharp crampy pain, yet I keep eating the ice cream. "You still love him?"

"Yes. But I guess not enough to have done things right." She sets the ice cream container on the table. "Some people say that you can't be in love with one person your entire life. That we're not made that way."

I'm not so sure. I wonder if I'll ever stop loving Kevin. It's been six years already.

We eat in silence for a while. I think about Cassie and our fight, my stomach aching even more. Cassie The Perfect. So perfect she pushes away the only friend she's had for more than ten years so she won't have to be seen with her and her imperfections.

Cassie wouldn't lose her shit in front of a bunch of grade school kids.

Cassie wouldn't come home to see her mom torturing herself with milk products.

Cassie wouldn't…just wouldn't.

"Mom?" It's almost a whisper. "Do you ever wish you were someone else?"

She gives a bitter laugh. "Sylvie, that's all I've been doing lately." Then she thinks for a moment and reaches across the table to grab my hand. "Not that I would ever, ever give up you and Sam."

I hear a faint humming then Sam opens the door. He's been smiling, holding himself in that self-assured way again.

But it all collapses when he sees Mom, the ice cream and the envelope. "Oh, no."

Mom wipes her eyes. "Oh, yes."

Sam falls into a chair and looks at the cartons of melting ice cream. He must be upset by the sight of Mom eating dairy, because he doesn't even grab a spoon. "I'm really popular at school, Mom," he says.

Mom pats him on the knee. "That's great, honey."

"It is great. It's awesome. But," his voice breaks. "I come home and with what's going on, I don't feel great. I feel... sad."

Leave it to Sam to get eloquent about it. If only I weren't here, maybe he'd still be happy.

I do my best to hold back tears.

Mom doesn't hold back at all. Sam's words gets her bawling all over again.

"You moron," I mouth at him while Mom's blowing her nose.

Then I see movement in Cassie's house. She's standing there, behind the lace curtains in her kitchen, watching us. When I catch her eye, she reaches up and pulls the shade down hard.

1:00 a.m. My mind is on overdrive. I can't sleep. I slip my hoodie over my pajamas and pad downstairs to the backyard. I lie on the grass. It's cool, but soft as velvet. The air smells like fall. The sky is clear, and I can make out the Big Dipper among the stars. I can never remember the other constellations.

I rip a handful of grass out of the ground and let it fall back down like confetti. I think about the fight with Cassie today. She thinks she's better than me now that she's so good looking. Now that Kevin's interested in her. Why stick with someone like me?

I roll over onto my stomach. The grass is still green enough to smell tangy. I breathe in its scent and feel like crying, but my eyes stay dry.

All of a sudden I hear the faint squeak of a screen door. *Crap!* It's Cassie. I plaster myself to the ground. *Don't see me, don't see me.* Her head bobs around above the hedge, then suddenly nothing. She must be settling down on the lawn.

Just seeing her perfect head for those few seconds gets me ticked off again. Anger comes off of me in waves. I yank at the grass and take deep breaths and wait for Cassie to go back inside.

But she doesn't go in. She must have seen me because she says, "I was supposed to go out with Kevin tonight." Her voice is just loud enough for me to hear her through the hedge.

The anger is practically strangling me now. I pull and pull at the grass. I've already pulled enough to feed a small cow. "Oh?" I say, trying to keep my voice even. "But you didn't?"

"Well…you don't want me to, do you?"

"And that's why you didn't go out with him tonight?"

She's quiet a minute, then she says, "No. I had to stay with my mom. Dad's working and she… couldn't leave her alone."

My anger melts. Her mom's been drunk and pulled this on her before. Several times. Passing out. Crying fits. Suicide threats. That kind of stuff. I move to get up. To reach across the hedge and give Cassie a hug. Because I always have. I always do. Because I'm her friend and I love her. Despite it all.

But a little voice in the back of my head stops me.

*Okay, let's get this straight. Cassie turns into a beauty queen and no longer spends Saturday nights with you. She embarrasses you to no end in front of your lunch table, then gets ticked when you get upset about it. She kisses and decides to date the one boy she knows you are completely in love with. And you want to be her friend?*

Well. When you put it that way.

I hear a bit of movement and then Cassie's standing behind the hedge, her arms crossed over her chest. "I want us to be friends, Sylvie. You're...like a sister."

A pain sharp as a razor blade pierces my chest. I love her. I hate her. I feel sorry for her. I envy her. "So you'll leave Kevin alone."

She crosses her arms tighter. "No."

I leap up and stand facing her across the hedge. "In that case, I already have a sibling, thank you very much."

"Face it, Sylvie. You were never gonna make a move on him!"

"I was! I just didn't have the chance."

"You've had since the fifth grade!" Cassie's voice gets loud enough to startle me.

"Shut up," I hiss. "You wanna wake my mom?"

"I just wanna do what I want for a change, Sylvie. I never, ever get to do what I want."

"You've gotta be kidding me!"

"I'm not. I always do what I think is best for everyone else. But I'm sick of it."

I blow air out of my mouth in disgust.

"Sylvie, it's like Kevin was made for me. Now that I know him. He understands me, I think. Usually boys are all about themselves. He's...different."

"I could have told you that." My voice is steel.

"Get off it. Why don't you go out with Nelson? He's perfect for you."

The nerve. "I can't believe you! What, you're hoping to pawn me off so you can steal Kevin without feeling guilty?"

"Come on, Sylvie. We've always been together, no matter what. Don't let a boy come between us." She holds up her finger. "Blood sisters forever."

I take a step towards the hedge, its scraggly branches poking me in the stomach and legs. "I don't know why you want to be my friend, Cassie. You're not acting like one. You're the one letting the boy get between us. Go out with Kevin, you backstabber. You can eat at his table and play with Tori. I don't care. I don't want to be your friend anymore, and I'm definitely not your blood sister." I march to my back door and step inside the house. I hear Cassie say my name, but I let the door shut behind me.

I lean against the closed door taking deep breaths. For a split-second, I go astral without meaning to. The shadows surround me the moment I'm out. And when I slip back in my body, like dark smoke, the shadows fill my mouth, nose and lungs. Something happens deep inside me. Like a black stain slipping about then grabbing hold of my soul. I can feel it eat away at me, leaving behind only the oily residue of hatred.

And at the back of my mind is that voice that says, *Become her. Figure out how.*

# twenty-two

## October: Speaking in Tongues

In the morning, I look like hell. My face is blotchy and I'm this putrid gray color, like I was up all night.

I did wake up. A lot. All night I had dreams, nightmares, and even once or twice I wasn't sure if I had an OBE or was just dreaming it. God, I've got to stop hanging around with the shadows. They may make me feel good, but they also make me look like crap.

I stare into the mirror and swear. I don't even need make-up. After last night, I'd fit right in with the Goths.

I sneak out, hoodie pulled up, before Mom can see me and call Dr. Hong.

Cassie and I manage to not meet up at our locker even once. I glimpse her in the hall, walking with Ashley and Tori, but we don't come near each other. At lunchtime, I stop just outside the open cafeteria doors. Cassie is sitting at Kevin's table. Sarah and Michelle are with her.

My whole table has deserted me. Just like that.

*Did you really expect anything different, Sylvie?*

"You want me to sit with you?" Sam comes up behind me. He doesn't want to sit by me. He's just being nice. Though I hate to admit it, he's what they call a good soul.

"Thanks, Sam. But I've got stuff to do." It's really better that both of us don't fall to loser status.

I say I want to work, so Mrs. Stilke lets me spend lunchtime in the Art room. I get on my smock and take out the painting I've been working on: 'Home.' Everyone else's work shows an actual place. Mine is the only one that could be considered abstract. But it isn't abstract. It's very concrete, just unrecognizable to all but me. It's the silver cord and the strange, golden, fuzzy-light way I see my hands and feet when I astral project. On a background of Prussian Blue to represent the nighttime sky, the whole effect is oddly eerie and comforting at the same time.

I'm pretty much finished already, but I'll keep at it and at it for the rest of the year if I have to. There's no way I'm going to sit at a lunch table alone.

I don't really talk to anyone all day. And no one tries to get me out of my funk. I can't even imagine how scary I look.

Nelson stays away from me in Art class. For some reason, this makes me feel hollow. I go to the sink when he's there and tell him I'm sorry for how nasty I was yesterday. "Yeah, sure," he says. But he still sits across the room.

I walk home alone.

Alone: it's something I need to get used to.

I eat in the Art room by myself all week. And the following week.

I sit at Mrs. Stilke's beat up table, a wilting watercress sandwich lying pathetically before me (bad idea to have asked Mom to pack me a lunch). The faucet in the back of the room drips, a metallic plonking sound alternating with the tick of the clock. Plonk. Tick. Plonk. Tick. If I strain my ears hard enough, I can make out the din from the lunchroom above. During Homecoming week, there are always food fights between the classes. The juniors in the lunch room will be sticking together regardless who usually sits where. *Yeah, whatever.*

I take a bite of my sandwich but don't feel like eating the rest. I shove it away from me and go to the supply room, hoping to take my mind off things. I'm in front of the pans of watercolors when the door to the supply room swings open.

It's Nelson. "Oh," he says, looking uncomfortable. "I thought you were Mrs. Stilke."

"Nope. Just me," I say.

"Hey, well, I'm skipping out on study hall. I should probably go back." He turns to leave.

"Don't go," I say before I realize it even comes out of my mouth.

Nelson stops. His voice is quiet. "What are you doing here? Don't you have lunch now?"

I keep my eyes on the watercolors. *Indian Yellow, Cadmium Orange, Faience Blue.* "I eat lunch here," I say.

I can feel him go still. "Since when?"

"Since the other day. Since I fought with Cassie. Since I fought with you. Since I have no more friends, basically." I can feel my eyes burning with tears but I force myself to look up and give him a smile and a shrug, like I don't really care.

"Who needs friends, right?" My voice catches and tears leak out onto my cheeks.

Ugh. Could I get any more pathetic?

Nelson must find me pretty pathetic, too, because he comes over and wraps his arms around me. I stiffen, then let go, leaning into the warmth of him.

My face fits perfectly into the crook of his neck. He's solid and smells like a vanilla milkshake. While I cry, he rests his jaw on the top of my head. I feel it move as he speaks. "I'm sorry, Sylvie. I was a dickwad for not talking to you. Won't happen again. "

I pull back from him and wipe my face. "I can't believe I'm crying."

"When you cry, it makes the grey of your eyes more intense. Makes them silver."

I laugh at that and smile up at him, so glad he's back to being my friend. He smiles down at me, the dimples in his cheeks deep lines on either side of his mouth. The dimples disappear along with his smile, and he suddenly looks serious. His hands slide onto my hips.

"Feeling better?" His voice is low and masculine and amazingly sexy. He leans down and I can feel his lips on my forehead. His breath is warm and sends shivers all down my body. The shivers stay and pulse somewhere between my legs.

*What the hell is going on?* I close my eyes in confusion and suddenly, his lips are touching mine. Suddenly, we're kissing.

*We're kissing.*

*What are we doing?* I open my mouth to say this. Nelson takes it wrong and his tongue touches mine.

Zap! An electric current couldn't have shocked me more. I back into the row of metal shelves and feel something sharp poke at my back. That's all I need to lose grip of myself.

In a split second I'm above the two of us, by the buzzing fluorescent lights. My body stands there for a moment then kind of sags against the shelves. Nelson's face is filled with horror. "Sylvie?"

The shelves are those flimsy stand-alones you can get at someplace like IKEA or Home Depot. The weight of my body topples them over. There's an enormous crash, and tubes of paint, brushes and single-edge razors go flying. Nelson yelps and it brings me back to myself.

"Oh, crap," I say surveying the damage and rubbing my sore back.

"What happened? Are you okay? " Nelson's eyes are open so wide I can see the white all around them.

"I'm fine. An X-Acto knife or something poked me in the back. That's all. Freaked me out a bit." I avoid looking at him. I'm still reeling from the fact we kissed.

Kevin was supposed to be my first kiss.

Nelson puts his hand out to help me up. "You…you fainted or something."

*Or something.*

"Maybe we should take you to the nurse," Nelson continues.

"No."

"You sure?"

"I said no, Nelson." I grab his hand a bit too tightly and he pulls me until I'm standing. I let go the second I'm up.

"Didn't know I was good enough to send girls swooning." He attempts a laugh but it comes out sounding forced.

I feel like I'm on the Tilt-A-Whirl. Like all my emotions are churning around inside me in two different directions. Like I can't find my footing anymore.

"I'm sorry if I —" he starts.

I cut him off and motion to the downed shelf. "Mrs. Stilke is gonna kill me."

Silence. Then: "She doesn't have to know." Nelson grapples to put the set of shelves upright. I grab the other side, jumping on the chance to do something. Something other than talk about what just went on.

We work without saying a word until the end of the period. When the bell rings, everything is back in its place. Very little ended up being wrecked or broken.

"There," Nelson says, as we shut the door to the supply room. "Like it never happened."

"Yeah," I say, thinking about my spontaneous projection, about my crying. About the kiss, that kiss that came out of nowhere. Now that I'm no longer bawling, Nelson's probably feeling just as strange about the whole thing as I am.

"Yeah," I say again and look directly into his eyes. "Let's just pretend that none of it ever happened."

I run to class completely freaked about Nelson. My mind's going at top speed, all my thoughts piling up on top of each other, like in that Virginia Woolf novel Mrs. Huggan tried to get us to read last year.

*This is crazy. This changes everything. No it doesn't. This changes nothing.*

I don't know why Nelson did it. Hell, I don't know why I did it. I think crying screws up your whole system, makes you a little nuts. Something about endorphins. And seeing someone cry does the same thing. I mean, I bet if I saw Tori Thompson cry, I would feel bad and want to hug her.

Or not.

Point is, Nelson wanted to make me feel better. And I wanted to feel better. Period. We just went about it all wrong. Because we're great friends, and kissing ruins friendships. I don't want to ruin my friendship with Nelson.

Besides for me it's always been Kevin.

Always, always.


"Whoa, Psycho. You're really looking the part. You just need to file your teeth and you'd pass for the living dead," Tori says as I walk into Morality. That gets a laugh out of most of the class. Even Cassie smirks.

It's true I'm looking a little pasty. And I feel vaguely like a zombie after the…kiss…with Nelson.

"Hey, feel like reminiscing about old times?" She holds up her iPhone and the YouTube video of me that she recorded is playing. I watch my body droop while she laughs, "It's classic!" How many people in the world have watched me wilt?

I'm so sick of Tori twisting the knife.

*Time to get even.*

About ten minutes into class, Tori asks to go to the bathroom. *This is it.* It's Tori's usual trick. She smokes a whole cigarette during Mr. Walker's class. Because his B.O. is so bad, he doesn't seem to notice when she comes back reeking.

A minute after Tori leaves, I get up. "Mr. Walker?" I whisper when I reach his desk, trying not to breathe in the stench of his sweat. "Can I use the bathroom?"

"Wait until Miss Thompson gets back." The class is quietly reading chapter four in *Morality Today*. He's reading *Slaugh-*

*terhouse Five*, Kurt Vonnegut's name in bold on the spine. I wonder if something with that title is really appropriate for the Morality teacher to be reading in school.

"Please?" He has to let me go or my plan is a no-go. I hop from one foot to the other for effect.

"Oh, fine," he says, sighing and pulling an orange bathroom pass from his desk drawer. "But only because you never usually ask." I take the pass from him and suppress a desire to cheer.

I pass the girls' toilets and head straight for the back doors instead.

Tori's purse is there, holding the door ajar. If I take it and let the door swing closed, she'll be stuck outside. It's impossible to get back in without ringing the bell, and being caught outside during school hours is automatic Saturday detention. As long as her cell phone is in her purse and not on her, she can't text a friend and will have no way to sneak back in.

I look down the hall. No one.

I get close enough to smell the cigarette smoke, then I bend down and tug at her purse.

The door shuts with a satisfying click.

Right away, her panicked face appears in the window. Then she spots me. Her voice is muffled behind the pane of glass. "You little bitch!" She yanks on the handle, and when it doesn't give she swears some more. "Open that door right now or I'll rip you to pieces, you mother—" There's a THUD as she kicks the door. In the window, her face is red with effort.

I look in her purse, see her cell phone, then leave it there in front of the closed door. I smile my best smile at her and walk nonchalantly back to Morality class, her muffled screaming getting fainter the further I go down the hall.

When I hand Mr. Walker the pass back, he looks surprised to see me before Tori. "Where's Miss Thompson?"

"No idea," I say, slipping back into my chair. I know Tori will make me pay, but for the next few minutes it doesn't matter. I smile to myself.

For once I feel like I've won.


Nelson and I are overly-polite and stiff with each other in Art. The conversation is strained until I finally tell him what I did to Tori.

He laughs so loud Melissa Scott asks what's going on. And he tells her. And she laughs and tells Cherie Borges. And so on.

I guess not too many people like Tori Thompson.


After school, I quick gather my things, worried Tori will flatten me but she's nowhere to be seen. Kevin, however, comes right up to me.

"Hey," he says. "I heard. Actually the whole Geography class heard. Tori was yelling so loud she drowned out the *Violent Femmes*."

I hold tight to my locker door.

"She had it coming." He grins. "Way to go." Relief rushes over me and I smile at him in gratitude. He musses my hair and punches me in the shoulder like I'm one of the guys. I briefly remember the warm feeling of Nelson's hands on my hips, and wonder if I'm not stupid to be so caught up with Kevin.

But then Kevin shakes his head at me like he's impressed. "I knew you were okay. More than okay."

Cassie's further down the hallway, watching us. Kevin glances at her then says, "See ya!" to me.

I watch him stroll up to Cassie. They kiss right there in the hallway, a long, drawn out thing. I can even see their tongues come together. My boots are cemented to the floor, fire roaring in my cheeks. When they pull their lips apart, Cassie looks directly at me. I turn away.

Sam and I walk home. When we get to our block, I see Cassie sitting on her porch steps waiting for me, hugging herself in the cold, her car still ticking in the driveway.

Sam scuttles home. But I hold my head high, and refuse to look Cassie's way as I pass.

Then she says something that gets me: "Hey, Psycho!"

If I was thinking about being friends again, all my warm fuzzy thoughts are sucked away with that one word. I stop just before my own house and turn around.

She stands up, but still has her arms around herself. Her hair blows in the wind, a shiny copper flag. I expect her green eyes to be a kryptonite-like shade, wild with anger. But instead she looks confused and even a little sad. "Stop trying for Kevin!"

"Oh get off it. I only talked to him for a minute," I say with as much loathing as possible. "But that was a nice display in the hallway after school. You make Keri Nielsen look like an angelic little virgin."

The kryptonite shows up after all. "I hate you," she says.

"Not as much as I hate you," I say, and stride to my back door.

Once in my room, I hear a car pull up next door. I look out the window: Kevin's Camaro. Cassie is down her front steps and pulling open the passenger-side door before Kevin even fully stops. I watch as they take off. A rotten feeling rocks my stomach.

I swear and kick at my beanbag chair, splitting the seam and sending hundreds of little Styrofoam balls rolling onto the floor. I kick it again and again, beating the dumb thing flat until Mom bangs on the door and calls me to supper: three bean soup, vegetable loaf, and tofu cottage cheese. Ugh.

If there ever was a moment to be someone else, it's right now.

## *October 28th*

*I watch as my parents wrap their hands around warm drinks. As Sam bites his thumb bloody. As Cassie and Mr. Sanders try cooing reassuring words to them. I watch and I wish I could go back one day. Two days. Two weeks. Hell, when did my whole idea really start? I wish I could go back to then and blot it all out.*

*I move quietly out of the waiting area and turn down a couple hallways into the emergency section. Half the doors to rooms are wide open. There's a little blonde girl screaming in one, and an elderly man covered in blood in another. The doors that are closed, I open. But I don't get far before a woman in pink scrubs comes up to me. "Hey, you can't be back here," she says.*

*"I'm looking for...for Sylvie Sydell?"*

*Her voice softens a bit. "Look, you can't be back here until we call you. Go back out and wait with the rest of the family. Don't worry. We'll let you know what's going on."*

*But I don't even want to know anymore. I just want to change it.*

*What was I thinking? What the hell was I thinking?*

*"Young man,"* the woman says. *I realize she's talking to me. To him. To me.* *"At this point, there's nothing for you to do but wait."*

*Wait. No.*

*At this point, waiting is the only thing I won't do.*

# twenty-three

## October: The Plan To Change Everything

"Pity party's over. I'm officially finished. And tonight we are going to celebrate and have an evening together," Mom says as she's cleaning off the table after dinner.

"What, did you meditate while we were doing our homework?" I'm surprised at how solid she sounds.

"I've realized I'm not so good at meditating when things are going poorly. But I ate some more Ben and Jerry's. And ice cream always brings clarity." She puts her hands on her abdomen. "I'll just have to pay for it later."

"Okaaayy." I share a look with Sam. "TMI."

Mom's still attempting joviality. "Let's watch a movie tonight. There's always something on TV. I'll even make some popcorn!" It should sound good, but instead of butter and salt, Mom sprinkles flaxseed on the popcorn. The movie treat in our house tastes vaguely like Styrofoam topped with powdered cardboard.

But Sam and I know when to humor her. And now's a good time.

Ten minutes later, we take our bowls with us and sit down in the living room—Sam and Mom on either end of the couch and me in the big brown armchair.

Sam has the remote and flips through the channels, which doesn't take long since we don't have cable. Mom opens the TV Guide and scans through it. "Hmmm. Looks like there's *Harry Potter* or *The Exorcist*.

Both Sam and I say, "Exorcist."

Mom's appalled. "You're kidding me?"

The film is an old one, really old. "I remember watching this when I was a kid," Mom says, pointing to the description in the TV Guide. "You're sure you want this? I was terrified when I saw it."

"We want it," Sam says as the film starts. "Even though it's so ancient the special effects will be lame."

I go from watching the movie to thinking again about how Cassie and Kevin kissed. Here I am, watching some horror film with my brother and mother, while Cassie is out with Kevin. She's probably watching a romantic comedy with him right now, eating Sugar Babies instead of flaxseed flavored popcorn.

I think of her at the lunch table, pursing her lips and looking at me like I'm a leper. I think of her sneaking to meet Kevin behind my back. And I think of her on her porch, screaming, "Psycho!"

Hatred, sticky as tar, bubbles inside me. She has the beauty. She has the boy. It's not fair.

*Make it fair*, says the voice in the back of my head.

*But how?*

I hear my mom gasp and focus my attention once more on the film. On the screen, a priest is holding up a crucifix over the writhing body of a girl and chanting, "I cast you out!"

My breathing quickens. I feel dizzy. My head starts to buzz.

"Be gone! From this creature of God!"

I stand up, staring at the screen but no longer seeing it. My bowl of powdered popcorn slides to the floor.

*That's it.*

"Sylvie? Are you okay?" Mom asks.

"Be gone!" says the priest on the screen.

*That's it. That's it.* My head is reeling.

"Sylvie!"

I sit down again. Both Mom and Sam gape at me.

"I'm fine," I choke out. But I'm not. I'm hyper-ventilating, my heart pounding and pounding inside my chest. No matter how much I try, I can't seem to suck in enough air.

"Oh my Lord!" Mom yells. She runs into the kitchen and comes back with a paper lunch bag, shoving it over my mouth. I try to slow my breathing.

But Cassie, *The Exorcist*, and astral projection are rolling furiously through my brain.

Inhale. Exhale. Inhale. Exhale. The bag crackles as it deflates and inflates. Once I catch my breath, Mom hugs me, her eyes rimmed with tears. Sam's stopped watching the movie and is watching me instead. I try giving him a smile but my brain's going ballistic and I seem to have forgotten how.

Mom gets up and turns off the TV. "No more scary movies for you."

It takes a moment, but I pin down my thoughts.

Cassie. *The Exorcist.* Astral Projection.

*Make it fair.*

That night the shadows stroke my face until I fall asleep. I dream about Kevin.

We're sitting together on the large expanse of lawn in front of the lighthouse, the crash of Lake Michigan background noise for our conversation. It's foggy and damp, but Kevin's thigh is warm against my own, even through our jeans.

"I hate the whole divorce thing. It's like I've got two strangers for parents," I say.

"Hey." Kevin tries a little smile. "I understand. I really do."

His fingers stroll quietly up the inside of my forearm. His coffee eyes catch my gaze and he pulls my left hand into his right one. My skin goes wild. Like every nerve in my body startles to attention and sighs with longing each time the pad of his thumb draws a circle on my palm.

I lean into his shoulder. He smells like Polo cologne and clean sweat. I breathe in the scent of him and close my eyes. His arm goes around me in an embrace. I feel his lips on my forehead and a hand in my hair.

"You're so beautiful," he says.

"What? What did you say?" It's like a balloon inflates underneath my ribs. A happy balloon.

I want it. So badly. For him to think I'm beautiful. For him to see me as someone other than Psycho Sylvie Sydell. Psycho Pathetic Skinny Sylvie Sydell.

"You're gorgeous." He laughs. The sound of it cuts sunshine into the fog. "You don't believe me?"

Pffft. Pfft. The balloon is getting bigger and bigger. Something's wrong. Suddenly, the good feeling turns to pain and my ribs ache so much I pull away. "I…I…"

The sound of the waves turns to a low growl, like a huge predator ready to pounce. The sky changes from gentle grey to angry black.

Kevin grabs my purse from the ground and rummages through it. He finds a small, silver mirror and wipes his thumb across the glass to get the lint off. "Here." He pushes it towards me. "See for yourself."

I take the mirror from him and hold it delicately between my fingers. I tip it to my face and look inside.

The face that peers back at me is not my own.

It's Cassie's.

I wake up with a start and can still feel the cool mist of the shadows in the air.

*Become her.*

Hatred and jealousy and anger urge me on. *But it's evil*, I tell myself.

And yet…I want it so bad. So, so bad.

And now I know how.

# twenty-four

## October: Keep Your Friends Close. And Keep your Ex-Friends Closer.

In the morning I'm determined. Any doubts and any moral dilemmas are gone. I spent the night going astral, letting the shadows soothe me. Seduce me. Sway me.

Let's just say I've come to terms with being evil. I am going to possess Cassie. Become her. Simple as that.

As I brush the nasty taste from my mouth with Colgate, I outline my plan: *To Do: make friends with Cassie again.* (The plan won't work otherwise.)

That's my goal for today. *Forget the fighting. Bring on the blood sisters.*

On the way to school, Sam tells me he heard from Bryce and Kevin and everyone else that Tori got detention. Not only that, her parents are so fed up with her having problems at school that they took her car away.

"You're kidding!" Tori would rather die than live without her car.

But sure enough, when Sam and I get to St. Anthony's, the school bus is just belching out its load of students. There, coming out of the yellow bus, is Tori Thompson. She looks mortified.

"Wooo hooo!" I yell, waving my arms. My fear of Tori is overcome by the desire to rub it in. "Have a nice ride?"

Tori's face turns purple and she screams, "I'll kill you!"

"Well, I know it won't be by running me over since you're no longer driving your car!" Sam and I walk up the front steps, laughing out loud.

When we open the front doors, I feel a smack on my shoulder. A girl who's never said a word to me before gives me a big smile and says, "Way to go! Tori needed it."

"Nice one!" another girl whispers as she walks past. I move in a daze as other people congratulate me and give me the thumbs up.

I feel everyone staring at me—in a good way. It's weird. So weird.

Now that I've made my decision to go ahead with my possession plan, everything seems to be a cinch. I've never felt so at ease at St. Anthony's as I do walking through the hallways after school. It's like by just deciding to become Cassie, I've already taken on some of her persona, and people respond. I can't believe people are liking me for me.

Mimi Wilder and her friends ask me to sit with them at lunch. I say yes.

If you ignore the chain of red eruptions on her face, Mimi's actually good-looking. She's got friendly eyes and funky yellow glasses. Her hair is shiny brown and always pulled back into a pony tail.

While we eat, I go from entering the conversation to receding into my thoughts, working out my plan.

"Don't you think so, Sylvie?" Mimi asks, pulling me out of my thoughts.

"Huh?"

"Cassie and Kevin look like Hollywood stars together. The Perfects."

I almost choke on my cheeseburger.

But she continues, oblivious. "I can hardly believe you're sitting here with us instead of them. It's so cool that you…"

I stop listening.

From where I'm sitting I get a clear view of Cassie. She's practically on Kevin's lap they're sitting so close.

The knife she's stuck in my back is killing me.

I stare at her until she feels my gaze and looks up. *Enjoy. Because he won't be yours for long. I'm coming to get him.*


In Art, Mrs. Stilke hushes everyone at the beginning of class and says, "I have an announcement to make."

We all wait.

"Like I said, I entered all of your designs in the yearbook cover contest. And we have a winner right here in this class." Her kohl-lined eyes snap over to me. "Congratulations, Sylvie."

There's a moment of silence when everyone turns and stares at me. I feel my cheeks blaze. "I knew it!" Nelson yells and starts clapping. The rest of the class joins in.

Nelson hooks me around the shoulders in a half-hug, and for the slightest second I close my eyes and feel his closeness and think *I could get used to this.*

After class, Melissa Scott turns to Nelson and says in a smooth voice, "The girls' basketball team is having a dinner at Infusino's tomorrow night. We're supposed to bring a date. Wanna come with me?"

I pretend to be busy stuffing my backpack, but my hands are shaking too much to do it gracefully. I drop a stack of papers to the floor.

Nelson squats down to help me pick them up. He hasn't answered Melissa yet, and he looks to me like I should tell him what to say.

Right then, Mrs. Stilke calls out from behind her desk, "Oh, Sylvie! Kevin Phillips has been making such progress thanks to you. He told me he'd love it if you continued helping him the rest of the year. That the two of you make a good team."

Nelson stands without having picked up one single sheet of paper off the floor. He turns to Melissa. "What time do I pick you up?"

I'm walking down the hall, telling myself Melissa and Nelson don't matter because Kevin's who I really want when *wham!* something hard and pointy smacks me in the ribs and sends me skidding into a row of lockers, my books flying. It's Tori, with the corner of her English book pointed at me like a gun. She's grinning, her eyes wild.

Then a booming voice and a suffocating body odor come from right behind her. "Looking to get detention another Saturday, Miss Thompson?" asks Mr. Walker.

"No," Tori says tightly.

"Then move along. And don't let me see you pull something like that again." Mr. Walker motions down the hallway. Tori narrows her eyes at me, but starts moving. I breathe a sigh of relief and Mr. Walker returns to his classroom.

I'm just finishing picking up my books from Tori's attack when Cassie walks up to deposit her books in our locker. She makes a point not to look at me.

*Here we go.*

"Cass," I start. She still doesn't look. So I say it again and move right next to her. She throws her books in the locker with unnecessary force.

"Look," I say. "I'm sorry. I don't want to fight with you."

"Yeah, well, maybe I'm enjoying not being your friend."

But she doesn't look like she's enjoying it. And she has to be my friend. In order for my plan to work. "You mean it?"

"You make me so mad."

"I'm sorry. I am. I haven't exactly been all sunshine to be around."

Cassie sniffs then finally looks at me. "You can say that again."

"Do I have to?"

A ray of autumn light from the window at the end of the hall shines directly onto Cassie's head. Her hair reminds me of the pans of watercolor Mrs. Stilke got for the class. Something between red ochre and burnt sienna. I feel desire scratch at my insides. Such gorgeous hair. I want it.

"I'm sorry, too," she says. "I shouldn't have said…some stuff." Hatred flares inside of me as I picture her screaming, "*Psycho!*"

"Me neither."

Kids bang into us as they pass us, jostling to get out of the building. But it's almost like Cassie and I are in a bubble. Just the two of us.

Cassie shakes her head in disbelief. "I can't believe we've even been fighting. I miss you. You've always been there for me. Even if my parents weren't there, you always were. I guess you're the only person who really knows me."

I have to say it: "And you know me. I've always liked Kevin. Always."

She at least has the sense to look ashamed. "I know. I never meant to hurt you. I didn't plan it, Sylvie, really. You should know that. "

"So asking you to break up with him…?" *Here's your chance, Cass. Just leave him alone and I won't go through with it.*

"Won't happen." She says, looking both sorry and stubborn at the same time.

I had planned on lying. On telling her that her being with Kevin doesn't matter. Just to get her back to being my friend. But the words won't come out of my mouth.

We stand in silence. Finally, Cassie says, "So now what?"

Ah…I don't have to lie after all. I hold up my index finger. "Let's go back to being friends. Blood sisters forever, right?"

She holds up her finger and hooks it around mine. My heart speeds up. "Forever and ever, Sylvie."

We let go, then give each other a hug.

*Objective number one: completed.*

*Objective number two: get her to astral project.*

We walk out the front doors together, the sunshine making me squint. I glance at her gorgeous face, her filled-out body, and feel instantly ugly. That's when I know that no matter what kind of bull she comes out with about the inside counting, she would never really change bodies with me. I can't do this nicely. I'll have to steal.

Huh. Me the body thief. I've never stolen anything in my life. I smile at that and Cassie says, "What?"

"Nothing." I shake my head. "Absolutely nothing."

# twenty-five

## October: Possession is Nine Tenths of the Law
## (Or...if I get it, it's mine)

Fate is on my side. My dad has to travel for work over the weekend, and so Sam and I stay home.

Perfect. I invite Cassie to stay over as a way to 'renew' our friendship. She hesitates, as she's supposed to go out with Kevin, but in the end she tells me our friendship is worth more to her.

*Yeah. Right. But she won't stop seeing him.*

Mom proposes taking us all to Chicago on Saturday, so we can spend 'quality time together.'

"I've signed the divorce papers," she says. "So I won't have you often on the weekends."

Even though I was expecting it, her signing those things, I have a weird feeling in my chest. Like someone's been digging there. Like its half empty. My family is falling apart for real.

But Chicago is a cool idea. Cassie comes over Friday night, a bright smile on her face.

"I love this! It's been too long since we've had a sleepover," she says, punching her pillow and flipping around on the air mattress. She turns round and round on it, like a kid in a bouncy castle.

"I've got a secret," I tell her, turning away from Twitter.

She stops hopping and throws herself flat onto her back. "Yeah?"

"I can astral project."

She raises an eyebrow. "Which means?"

"I can leave my body. You know, like Kevin's step-mom."

She rolls her eyes. "Kevin says his step-mom has mental problems."

"You think I do?"

"No, that's not—"

I cut her off. "I already told you this, Cass. Three years ago. Remember? *Truth or Dare?*"

"Yeah," she says slowly. "But…"

"But what?"

"I thought it was just a—" she waves her hands, searching for the word "—euphemism for blacking out."

Oh. My. God. She really didn't believe me. It feels like the bottom just dropped out beneath me.

It's hard to keep the anger and sense of betrayal out of my voice. "It wasn't a euphemism. It was true. And still is. Only now I can control it better."

She still doesn't look like she's ready to believe me so I suggest a test. "Take a piece of paper and write anything you want on it. Something I won't guess. Then go put it downstairs on the table."

Cassie laughs but agrees to do it. When she comes up, I relax and go astral. I'm downstairs and back within seconds, so fast now with the shadows' help.

"*Sally sells seashells by the seashore?*" I tease when I'm back inside myself. "That's original."

"No way." Cassie turns pale.

"Yes way. And if you still have doubts, I can do it again."

We set up the test three more times, putting a new paper somewhere else each time. I tell her all about going astral—how everything looks, how weightless I feel. Cassie keeps swearing under her breath in amazement. "This is so damn cool."

"Wanna learn?"

"Anybody can learn?"

"Yeah. Sure. It just takes some major concentration."

"I don't know…is it scary?"

"It can be freaky because it's something you've never done, not scary, though. Anyways, it's so worth it. Like being invisible. Or having wings. You could go anywhere, you know. Rome, the North Pole…"

I don't look like I'm convincing her. "Or you could just stay on our street," I say. "Check out how your parents are doing without you home."

That gets her. "What?"

"Cass, if you learn how to do this thing, you wouldn't necessarily have to be home to make sure your mom's okay."

She's silent for a long time. Then she looks at me and says, "So how does it work?"

I teach her to relax. To concentrate on slipping out of her body. The whole time, excitement percolates in my stomach, excitement and the strangest kind of detachment. Like I'm preparing an assignment for Chemistry class, not a plan that goes against every moral code I know. It feels just like the separation that happens when I project—there's a warm tingly sensation and a squeeze and then I'm weightless. Only this time I'm weightless of my ideas of what is right and what is wrong, I'm weightless of every emotion besides anger.

Anger and revenge are my anchors. They keep me grounded to my plan.

Cassie's good at it. The relaxing. Almost too good. A few times she falls asleep and I have to wake her up. "Stay alert while still relaxing. Think you can do that?"

We spend the whole evening trying. Cassie's starting to get discouraged, and I'm worried I'll lose her. If she doesn't project, my plan can't work. "Let's give it one last try," I say. I turn out the lights and stretch out on my bed. The moon has waned into a lopsided circle. It lights the room with a dull glow.

By now, I know I can relax and leave my body within a few minutes. So I'm not really trying to do it myself yet. I'm listening, waiting for some clue to tell me Cassie's done it.

It's going on half-an-hour when Cassie's breathing slows. Significantly. I slit open one eye and glance down at the shadow on the air mattress. Cassie's completely still.

Is she doing it? Or is she sleeping again? I'm about to move in for a closer look when I hear Cassie gasp.

"I can't move!" She yells. "I can't—"

I jump off my bed and go to her, putting a hand on her arm. "Yes, you can, Cass."

"No, I—" But then she sits up. Her eyes are wide, shining in the dark. She says, "Turn on the light."

I do. There's a look on Cassie's face somewhere between terror and elation. "I…something happened."

My throat squeezes tight with anticipation. "What?"

She shakes her head. "I'm not sure. But I felt...funny. I was in this room, I could see the walls, out the window to the ground."

"Yeah?" My heart is pounding. Ba-boom. Ba-boom. *This is it.*

"The thing is, how could I see to the ground when I'm on the floor? I'm sure I wasn't dreaming. Oh, Sylvie, this is warped."

"It's not. Then what happened?"

Now she frowns. "I can't remember really...I couldn't move and I yelled out to you. That's it. It doesn't sound like much, but—"

"No. It's a lot. You did it, Cass. You actually did it! The next time you do it you can stay out longer!" I bounce onto the air mattress on my hands and knees. "You did it!"

"I don't know."

"No. You did it, Cass. I'm sure of it."

"Really?" A hesitant smile crosses her face.

"Yes!" I laugh and we bounce around on the air mattress like four-year-olds until I think it'll pop. Finally, I stop and say, "You have to do it again, you know. Right now. Try again tonight."

There's a knock at the door. I get up and open it. Mom's standing there in her mint green satin pajamas. "What's all the noise about?"

I glance at Cassie, then turn to Mom. "Nothing. We were just laughing."

"Well, keep it down. It's almost two a.m. Some of us are trying to sleep. You should, too. We're leaving at eight o'clock and not a second later. No sleeping in until noon."

"Okay."

She nods. "Goodnight, girls."

"'Night." I shut my door and turn out the light. "Let's try again."

Cassie's eager to try again, but falls right asleep. Five minutes into her relaxation session, light snores punctuate the darkness.

*It's okay*, I say to myself, frustration building inside me. I take a breath and let it out. *It's okay. Tomorrow. She did it once, she can do it again.*

*And in twenty-four hours everything will have changed. Everything.*

Mom is obviously trying to compete with Dad for the best days out on the weekend. Saturday morning at eight sharp she starts up the station wagon and Sam, Cassie, and I pile in. She takes us to Chicago for the day.

"This is tons better than Dad's bowling outings, Mom," I say as we are on our way.

"It's not a contest, Sylvie. Your dad makes a real effort with you." But despite her words, she puffs up and uses her sweet honey voice that only comes out when she's truly pleased. I haven't heard that voice for a very long time.

We go to the Field Museum and wander through exhibits on ancient Americans and feel dwarfed in front of the T.Rex the museum has named Sue.

"Who do you think is older, this Sue or Grandma Sue?" Sam jokes.

"Sam!" Mom acts shocked.

"Oh, come on, Mom. You have to admit Grandma looks old enough to have come out of the Jurassic. She's all leathery."

"That's because she lives in Florida," Mom says, which just makes us laugh. Even her.

Then we go to Shedd's Aquarium and fight the crowds to see the sharks be fed and watch the Beluga whales from behind glass. We have a late lunch downstairs in the aquarium. But even though it's mid-afternoon by then, there are still so many people that no tables are free. We end up sitting on the floor to eat the avocado sandwiches Mom has prepared for us. Cassie has a small bag of Cheetos in her purse, and she and I sneak some every time my mom isn't looking, trying our best not to laugh and give ourselves away.

I should hate it all. I really should. But it's weird. I forget to feel angry and bitter. Instead, I have fun. Mom isn't too overbearing, Sam doesn't annoy me, and Cassie is just like she used to be. Or maybe I'm like I used to be—before I started resenting my parents and scheming to steal my best friend's most precious possession.

Outside the aquarium, we all stop for a second to look over Lake Michigan. Though the sun is bright there's a biting wind that snaps at our ears and finds its way between the buttons on our coats. Mom, Sam, and Cassie start back towards the car to get out of the wind. I hang back, watching the grayish-brown waves crash into each other, a churning in my stomach mirroring the violence of the lake.

"Come on, Sylvie!" Mom calls to me from across the expanse of concrete in front of the aquarium.

"Coming!" But I'm almost afraid to leave. I kind of liked being me today. And I liked spending time with my brother and my mom. I liked being friends, real friends, with Cassie again. Knowing what I have planned for tonight keeps the storm in my stomach alive and my feet plastered to the ground.

"Sylvie!"

I turn and start walking towards the car, my steps slow. I don't have to project tonight. I don't have to possess Cassie's body. I could just leave things as they are, and learn to enjoy life, my own life. I could. Things are already better at school, I'm not normal but I've got friends again. Cassie especially. Nelson's with Melissa Scott, but he's still a good friend. Home's not the best, but at least there's a sort of routine now, going to Dad's on the weekend.

And then there's Kevin. We have weeks more worth of tutoring sessions planned.

I get into the car.

Here is my chance to accept myself and my life as it is.

I buckle myself into the back seat next to Cassie. She turns to me, her smile self-confident, her skin lovely as silk in the sunlight.

And that's when I feel it. The hot tingling, slowly squeezing out the doubts. The voice that says, *But you could have it all.*

I don't want my life as it is. I want to be someone. Someone like Cassie. To be liked. To be with the boy I like. To have parents who like each other.

*Besides*, I think as Mom pulls out onto the road, *I've made all these plans.* It's too late to back out now, isn't it? Isn't it?

I can't back out. I can't. I'll give Sam a normal sister. I'll finally have Kevin. I'll get to *be* my best friend. And, if I'm completely honest, being Cassie and having Kevin is what I've secretly dreamed of for a long time.

I glance at Cassie. She's reading a text message on her phone and grinning. She passes the phone to me and I read what's written on the little screen: *"I keep thinkn bout u."* From Kevin.

*And Cassie*, I think. *What about her becoming me? How would she feel about that?* I swallow hard then force myself to give her back her phone with a smile.

*She'll just have to learn to live with it.*

We go back to my house and have a perfectly normal evening. Like old times. Mom even forgoes the flaxseed on the popcorn and lets us sprinkle it with salt. We rent a movie, one of those laugh-a-minute ones. Only I can't seem to get a smile to stick on my face. My resolve to possess Cassie comes and goes in waves.

I get up in the middle of the film and head to the bathroom.

I can hear Cassie, her velvety laugh coming from my living room. I shut the door and the sound abruptly stops.

*You can do this*, I tell myself and move over to the sink.

I'm stretched tight with anticipation, like a canvas on a frame, a dribble of fear marring the surface. I clutch the edge of the basin, dry heaving, and wait for the fear to pass. Putting my wrists under the tap, I run the cold water until I feel like myself again.

Myself. If I weren't so scared, I'd laugh at that.

Because after tonight I hope I won't feel like myself at all.

# twenty-six

## October: Untethered

The lights are out. Cassie is on the air mattress on the floor beside my bed. She's breathing deeply, printouts from the net on astral projection across her belly. This time she has to succeed. She just has to. I'm not sure I'll have the guts to try this another time.

I close my eyes and allow my body to sink into the mattress. *Relax my toes, relax my ankles, relax—*

All of a sudden, an electronic cha-cha-cha fills the air. I sit up and glare at Cassie, who's groping for her purse in the dark. "You didn't turn off your phone?"

"Sorry. Where—oh! Found it." The tiny screen glows green in the palm of her hand. "It's Kevin. Hello?"

My palms start to sweat as I wait. My eyes adjust to the dim light. Cassie's twirling a strand of hair around her finger while she talks. "Nothing. We were in bed…Shut up," she giggles.

Ugh. I make a vow here and now not to giggle like that when I'm Cassie.

"What?" Cassie says into the phone. "Already? All right. Yeah…tomorrow. 'Bye." She hangs up.

"What'd he say?"

"He's already home. He's wiped out from his first week of swimming practice. We're gonna meet for lunch tomorrow."

"That's kind of odd, him coming home early on a Saturday night."

She shrugs. "It's not *early*. Besides, he's tired."

"Or he's up to something," I challenge with a smile.

She looks at me, her eyes narrowed, somehow glinty in the darkness. But she turns off her phone. "All right, detective. Let's find out."

I grin and lie back, my eyes on a patch of moonlight on my ceiling. This is it. This is the last time I will be me. I can feel it.

I wait for Cassie, sensing her grow more and more still, then allow myself to relax and work on leaving my body. *Go ahead. Slip out.*

Right away the shadows surround me. The noise is deafening. Hoarse, high-pitched hissing that hurts my ears. I'm half-out of my body and they're pulling at me. My reflex is to resist, and so I stick there, half-in-half-out, feeling like I'm a balloon flying in the breeze while its string is stuck in cement.

I concentrate as hard as I can and finally I'm out. Out of my body. The noise gets louder and louder, like oddly monstrous, jubilant cries. Like the inky stains just won the out-of-body lottery.

It's impossible to think with that going on.

*Stop!*

They do. They slip back, almost invisible in the dark so it seems like just me inside my dim room, hovering over my and Cassie's bodies. Just the cool glow of the moon and an inviting, velvety night. Just the calm sense of power I get when I project. It spreads through me like a balm.

I hear the gentlest hiss. *Go on. Do it.*

That's exactly what I'm determined to do.

If Cassie's out of her body and near me, I should be able to see her, or sense her at least, shouldn't I? Maybe as a slight glow, or an outline or something. I think of the shadows, would they know to tell me she's near? Is that what they're trying to tell me? Did I miss her? Is she not out, or is she somewhere else?

I look down on Cassie. Her breaths are slow and shallow, almost difficult to discern. If she hasn't left her body, she's not far from doing so.

There's no taking her body until she's out. But the second she *is* out I have to rush in, or I could lose my chance forever.

I hover over Cassie, listening to her breathe. What should I do? *Kevin's.* Maybe she's already there, spying on him, seeing if he's really home. I have to check. Quickly.

I find myself in Kevin's bedroom. It's familiar to me now: the mess of clothes and empty bags of chips on the floor, the posters of women in bikinis, the numerous medals and trophies on the shelves. And Kevin, there on his bed. Asleep.

Cassie isn't here. I have to get back. I can't wait too long. But…I move closer to Kevin. I just want to see him one last time as myself before going.

Like almost every other time I've come to find him like this, he has a notebook face-down on his chest and is still in jeans and a sweatshirt. The room is dark, but I know his eyelashes are copper and that he has a slight bump on the left side of his nose. I move closer to him, remembering the scent of him, amazed at how still and calm he is in sleep.

I try tracing a finger along his cheek, but my hand goes right through him. *Can you hear me, Kevin? Can you? It's because of you, I wanted to become Cassie. Ever since fifth-grade, I've loved you.*

I move above him, my face so very close to his. My desire to be a part of his life makes me ache. *And all of this, all of my planning to become someone else was to get to you. I'm giving up my self, all for you.*

Suddenly I feel a presence next to me. I *know* someone's there. Oh, my God! She's out. She's here. *Now!* I think, *Get the body now!*

There's a flash of golden light, then like a lassoed rodeo calf I'm jerked back into my body with such force I can't even cry out. Pain sears through me, forcing my eyes to tear up. I blink and wait, my nerves on fire. Like frozen fingers plunged into hot water, there's agony before the relief.

Something's different this time. Almost alien. I don't know which sinews to settle into, which areas to embrace.

My body. It's not the same. It's heavier, warmer, and longer than before.

I move to sit up and hear something like papers drop to the floor. My body tingles. Papers. Cassie had the printouts on astral projection with her on the mattress. I put a hand in front of my face. It's too dark to see clearly, but from the shadow in the moonlight I make out the long fingers. The strong wrist. I can tell they're not my own.

*It worked. Freakin' hell, it worked.*

It worked.

I let out a gargle of a laugh. I've done it!

I struggle to get out of bed, then move to turn my light on. But in this new body I'm confused. Isn't the light switch here by my door? Everything seems backwards. My bedroom door isn't where I thought it was and I trip over my shoes on the floor. Finally, I find the door and the switch. But when the light comes on, I panic.

Something's wrong. Very wrong. My heart pounds faster and faster as I look around the room, recognizing the posters of women in bikinis, the trophies on the shelves. The bed, though. The bed is empty. *Oh, no. Oh, please, no.* I don't dare look down at myself. But there's a mirror across the room that I'm drawn to. I wade through the mess on the floor to get to it and stare at my reflection. Only it isn't my reflection at all. And it isn't Cassie's. It's Kevin's.

I reel back and sit on the bed, swallowing bile. *This isn't happening. This can't be happening.* I can understand taking over an empty body, but how could I have pushed Kevin out of his own?

My heartbeat, Kevin's heartbeat, is loud and fast. I can taste more bile working its way up my throat. I swallow again and then something on the floor catches my eye.

The corner of a book is sticking out from under the bed. I pick it up. *The Road to the Out-Of-Body Experience.* Another one, between the bed and the nightstand is called *Practical Tips on Astral Projection.* Then I notice the notebook that was across Kevin's chest and fell to the floor. I open it. The pages are covered in blue ink with Kevin's left-handed scrawl. The first page reads:

*Butterflies. Her walls, butterflies. Books on shelves. Butterfly chat rooms!!!! Get her with this?*

*Parents don't pay attention. To do: Make her feel wanted.*

*Loves Sugar Babies. Every night and more.*
*Takes baths.*
*Sylvie like her sister. Sylvie the road to getting Cassie?????*
*Has to be serious. Parents always loaded. Wants to have fun.*
<u>*But definitely not easy.*</u>

I stop reading and put a shaky hand to my mouth. No wonder Cassie said Kevin seemed to know her: he's been doing to Cassie exactly what I've been doing to him, only for him it's worked!

And tonight…tonight he must have gone out of his body again, just in time for me to screw up and fall in. The presence I felt…that wasn't Cassie. That was him!

*I'm supposed to be Cassie, not Kevin!* I want to scream, but I bite Kevin's tongue instead.

I drop the notebook. *Don't panic. It's okay, Sylvie. You can still do it. Just get out of him. All you have to do is relax and leave his body. You've left your own tons of times. All you have to do is get out. It's simple.*

Closing my eyes, Kevin's eyes, I lie back on the bed and begin my relaxation technique. *Relax your toes…Relax your toes.*

They're stiff and crampy. *No worries. You'll get it.*

*Relax your toes. Relax your ankles…*

Suddenly, a loud ringing breaks my concentration. The ringing continues until I realize it's coming from Kevin's cell phone on the night stand. I pick the phone up, wondering if I should answer. Then I see Cassie's number on the screen. *Oh, no.*

"Hello?" The voice that comes out is Kevin's.

"Oh, God, Kevin. Oh, my God!" Cassie sobs into the phone. Dread crawls through my limbs. "It's...it's Sylvie. We were...I can't...can't wake her up."

I grab the phone tight. "Don't try," I say, my voice Kevin's but sloppy. "Look, I can't explain, but I know what you were doing. You just need to leave her alone long enough for her to get back in her body."

"But how? Oh! Mrs. Sydell! I... don't know what to do. I can't wake her up!" I hear a commotion and the phone jiggling. I yell as loud as I can, "Cassie! Cassie!" but she's no longer there.

*I have to get back to my body.*

Outside Kevin's room, a baby cries. There are footsteps then a loud banging on the door. The knob turns, but the door's locked. A woman's voice swears, then hisses, "What's going on? David was sleeping!"

I freeze and keep quiet. Eventually, I hear footsteps going back down the hall. The baby's still crying.

*Get out of Kevin's body, Sylvie. Now.*

So I try to relax, to no avail. I turn out the lights and try again. Impossible. I try again and again. My body, Kevin's body, shakes with the effort of it. I am sweaty and worn out. But I keep on. Yet no matter how many times I try it doesn't work.

I'm in Kevin's body. And I can't get out.

part two

# twenty-seven

## Stuck (And, man, does it suck)

I look down at Kevin's watch. *OCT 28 2:50 a.m.* I've been wandering around the halls for half an hour now, trying to find out where my body is. My hands are shaking like I've got delirium tremens. My head still isn't clear; the same four-letter word fills it over and over again.

I've been in this body for almost three hours. It feels like three years. It already feels like that was another lifetime when I thought I could possess Cassie's body.

*Really good idea, Sylvie. Great one.*

What the hell was I thinking? I mean, everything went wrong, but even if it had gone right. Even then.

Where is my damn body? Where is Kevin? He's got to be in me. Has to be. Otherwise...

"Hey! Kevin!" Cassie is in the hall hurrying towards me, getting my attention with a hard whisper. "What are you doing?"

I think of how she reacted when I told her the truth. I don't want to make her angry again. "I'm looking for Sylvie,"

I say as I open a door. A couple stands on either side of a bed, looking over a little boy. I let the door close silently.

"What is wrong with you?" Cassie stops dead in her tracks. "Why are you acting crazy?"

"It's complicated," I say. This time I look her directly in the eyes. Those evergreen eyes. Bitterness shoots through me like an arrow. And so does something else. A sort of swooping, like I'm in free-fall.

*Whoa.*

"The waiting area is that way." A man wearing a paper shower cap points us down the hall.

We end up in front of some beverage machines. There's a whole crowd here, families pacing the linoleum and downing Pepsi. Cassie punches in some numbers and a couple bucks for tea and coffee. "I'm the beverage girl," Cassie mumbles. "I don't know what else to do."

Sadness and guilt and anger and regret all swoop over me at the sight of her getting drinks for my family. I feel for a second like I might pass out.

"Please," I start and put my hand around Cassie's upper arm. She looks up at me, but doesn't say anything. Her teeth rake across her bottom lip and her eyes get greener the longer she stares at me. All of a sudden, the swooping I'd felt before comes back, along with a tingling in the core of me. What the…? I know this feeling…what *is* it?

*Oh. No.*

*No. No, no, no. Not possible.*

There is no freakin' way in hell I am attracted to Cassie! I jerk away from her, accidentally knocking the tea and coffee from her hands. They spill onto the shiny floor. "I'm sorry…"

*Oh, God.* I need to get it together. I run to the restroom.

An obese woman with tangerine colored hair is in front of the mirror putting on frosty pink lipstick. I move past her and to a stall.

"Hey! You can't go in there!"

I stop. "It's plugged up?"

"No, you idiot! Can't you read?" She points to the door of the restroom. "This is the LADIES room!"

"Oh…yeah, oh…sorry!" I say, backing out of the room, suddenly very aware of the package hanging between my legs. With all that tingling going on, how could I have forgotten?

The men's room is empty. I avoid looking in the mirror as I pass it and lean against the brown tile wall, counting to keep my head on straight. *1, 2, 3, 4, 5, 6, 7, 8, 9, 10…1, 2, 3, 4, 5, 6, 7, 8, 9, 10…* What the hell is happening? Kevin's not in this body anymore. Could his body, even without him in it… remember certain things? Like Cassie turning it on.

*Freakin' hell.*

Well that's one thing it's going to forget ASAP. It's called mind over matter.

I take deep breaths and tell myself to calm down. *Keep it together, Sylvie.* But suddenly, I'm totally aware of a different weird feeling below my waist. My bladder. Kevin's bladder. It feels almost ready to burst.

There's no way I'm going to pee as a boy. *Hold it.* I try to will the feeling away, but can't.

The door to the restroom swings open and a middle-aged guy with dark hair and a Green Bay Packer jersey stands in front of a urinal. He spreads his legs a bit and lets out a long, satisfied sigh as he unzips his zipper.

I go to the sink and run the hot water, sudsing up, staring down at my hands. Kevin's hands. I hear the urinal flush and then the whoosh of the door opening. Didn't even wash up after. Typical guy. How disgusting is that?

Alone again, I stand in front of a urinal, staring down at the zipper on Kevin's jeans like it's a death trap. I've seen guys pee often enough—who hasn't? I mean, I just had a perfect demonstration. But actually having to do it myself…having to…ugh. Even it being Kevin's doesn't change the fact that I'm grossed out.

I try to unzip Kevin's jeans, but can't grasp the zipper because my hands are already slick with sweat. I blow out two quick breaths, wipe my hands on my legs and try again. The noise of the zipper going down echoes in the empty bathroom. *Oh, crap. Here we go.* My fingertips get as far as the rough edge of Kevin's briefs when I actually touch *it* through the cotton. "Agh!" I pull back and dance around shaking my hands like they're on fire.

*Okay okay. Calm down.* Maybe I don't have to touch it. Forget the urinal. Pee like a girl.

I head to a stall and turn the lock. *Deep breath. In. Out.* I undo the button on Kevin's jeans, shove down his pants and underwear and sit down on the toilet like I normally would (well, except with my legs wider apart). *Whatever you do, don't look down*, I tell myself.

I pee. I can hear it splashing in the bowl and all is well until the tinkling noise changes to the sound of liquid being poured onto material. I glance down and see a yellow stream splattering out of the bowl and hitting the waistline of Kevin's jeans. *No!*

There's no getting around it. I'm going to have to guide the thing.

*Oh, God, oh, God.* I barely touch it with the tip of my index finger, but it's enough to keep the peeing in the bowl, at least. And that's when it hits me: I'm *inside* Kevin. Stuck inside him. For real. My breath starts to come fast and quick and the stall tilts. I'm on the verge of hyper-ventilating so I hang on to the toilet paper dispenser for dear life until my breathing slows. And then a low whimper leaves my mouth and I start to cry.

*Get it together, Sylvie, or there's no way you'll ever get out of him.*

I wipe my eyes with toilet paper and pull up my pants. I hear the door to the room open again. I decide to wait in the stall and just peek through the space in the door to see when it's clear.

That's when I see Sam.

I quickly look away. I actually think I'd rather die than watch my brother take a leak. When I hear the urinal flush, I say loudly, "You've always got your hands in your mouth. If you don't wash them, I'll puke."

"Kevin?"

I come out as he's pumping orange soap from the dispenser into his left palm. The sight of the back of his head relieves me. He's here. He's real.

"How're you holding up?" I ask, moving to the sink beside his, turning the water to HOT.

He looks at my reflection in the mirror. His glasses are crooked and his eyes are an angry red. "All the times I was ticked at her, wished she'd just go away…She can be a pain, but the thought of her *not* being…" He swallows hard. "It sucks, Kevin. Really, really sucks."

And here I thought his life would be better without me.

I hug him and kiss his gelled hair. He seems a little embarrassed, but doesn't pull away. I want to make him feel better. But he's my brother, so I also feel a twisted desire to rub it in. I say, "You like having her as a sister, then?"

Sam nods.

"She's pretty talented, huh? Great person?"

Sam nods again, but gets really pale. "I'd better get back." He starts to move.

"Wait!" I say. Sam has to believe me. Just has to. He's my brother. And I need help. I need to find Kevin and my body. "I've got to tell you something, Sam. It's going to be hard to believe, but you have to listen all the way to the end. Okay?"

Sam shrugs.

I keep my voice even. "This sounds crazy, but it's true: I'm not Kevin. I'm Sylvie stuck inside Kevin's body. I need you to help me get out."

Sam stares at me in the mirror, then slowly turns to face me. "They've just told us Sylvie's in a coma."

"A coma!" That means Kevin's not in my body! That means...*oh, God, what does that mean?*

"Yeah. And they don't know when or if she'll come out. So I don't need any games right now, Kevin."

"No, this isn't a game, Sam. I'm Sylvie. I can prove it. Look. I know you had a stuffed pea pod instead of a teddy bear when you were little. You—"

"This isn't funny, you jerk. I thought you were okay, but you're not."

"Sam! Just listen! You have to listen to everything. You'd know—"

But all of a sudden Sam punches me right in the gut. I feel the breath shoot out of me, both from pain and surprise. I don't think Sam has ever, EVER hit anyone in his life.

"Shut up, Kevin," he says, and leaves.

My stomach is killing me, but I straighten up and follow him. He practically sprints to where our parents are waiting. "Get Kevin out of here," he says to Dad. His voice is full of hatred.

"N-no, look, Sam," I stutter.

"He's wasted, I think. I don't know. But he's making jokes about Sylvie, and I don't want to hear it."

"No, I'm not!" I yell, but it doesn't matter—my mom's face gets blotchy and my dad swears.

"Get out of here," my dad growls. "Or I'll throw you out."

Mr. Sanders shakes his head at me. Cassie looks like she's posing for Munch's *The Scream*. Sam's eyes are even more angry. Even more red.

They won't listen to me. Not now. I shouldn't have said a word. I smother a sob that makes its way out. I grab my stomach and run down the hallway and out the front doors.

And then I'm alone. In front of the hospital at almost 4:00 in the morning. It's dark, the dimmest color on the watercolor palette at school: Lamp Black. I don't know what to do or where to go, so I grimace in the cold and walk. I walk and walk until my stomach no longer hurts, but my ears and nose are numb with cold. Luckily, I'm near the 24-hour Kimmy's Kafe. The bitter smell of coffee greets me as I open the door. My ears and nose tingle in the newfound heat.

I sit down at a cracked Formica table and feel in Kevin's jeans for his wallet. He's got $34.77 and his dad's VISA. Good. I'm suddenly starving.

I order eggs, bacon, sausage, French toast, and hot chocolate with extra whipped cream. No All-Bran in sight. When the food comes, it looks like there's enough for three people. But I crave the fat, the grease, the sugar. And this body seems to want anything, as long as there's a lot of it.

I poke a piece of French toast. The fork feels tiny to me in these big hands. I'm a bit clumsy, but manage to get it to my mouth and chew.

*Think.* Kevin's not in my body, or I'd be walking around. So we can't talk this over, figure out a way to switch back.

*What happened to Kevin?* If I can't get out, he can't get in.

I sit thinking forever and order a Coke. The sun comes up as I'm finishing off the last of it. That's when Kevin's cell phone beeps. I take it out of his jeans pocket. It's a message from Bryce: *"Jst got bck frm wiiiiiiiild nite. 3 dys left. U screw u win. No screw I win. Get on it, derp."*

He might as well have written in Sanskrit. I don't get any of it.

*Ugh. Who cares?*

I pay for my breakfast and walk back outside. The wind has kicked up. Now what? Where do I go since I can't go home?

*My body is in a coma. And I can't get back to it.* Terror scuttles through me. I'm freezing, tired and my head feels like it's been bashed in with an axe. The wind zaps my ears and I hunch down into Kevin's sweatshirt. I put one heavy foot in front of another and trod on for a good hour until I get to Kevin's house. I stop in front of it.

Hoping to sneak in, I go around and try the back door knob as quietly as I can. It's slick black metal, really cold. I turn it left, then right. I even tug and push hoping I'm not making too much noise. But it doesn't give. I blow on my hands. The wind makes my eyes tear up. I trudge back to the front. My legs are stiff as I climb the porch steps. I step over a rolled-up copy of *The Journal Times* shoved into a sleeve of thin, orange plastic. The storm door opens, but not the inner one.

*Come on, come on.* I push and pull on the polished gold handle. Panic is like an itch under my skin. I search Kevin's pockets but find no keys. A dark cloud passes over and I feel pricks of freezing rain on the back of my neck. It's the last straw. A tremor starts somewhere in my lower spine and takes hold of me entirely. My teeth chatter. My whole body spasms. I take deep breaths and wrap my arms around myself. That's when the front door is yanked open and Kevin's dad stands in the doorway.

"Where on God's green earth have you been! We've…" But I can't concentrate on his words my teeth are chattering so badly. I just watch his face turn different colors and hug myself tighter hoping to stop the shivering. Finally, Kevin's dad stops talking. He stares me down like he's waiting for an answer.

"I…she's…in…a…coma," I say, barely getting the words out for all the teeth clacking.

"Huh? What're you talking about?"

"S-Sylvie. Sylvie S-Sydell."

"Who's that? The girl you've been dating?"

"N-no. She's… she's…at the hospital."

"Oh, Christ. Why are you telling me this? Bryce put you up to something again, didn't he? What happened? What did you do?"

"N-Nothing."

That's when I hear a low voice somewhere behind me say, "*That's bull! You did everything!*" My lungs are squeezed flat with fear and I turn around. But no one's there.

"Look at me when I'm talking to you! Was there drinking and driving? Drugs? You leave sometime during the night, stay out and don't tell us where you are, and then you come back to say some girl's in a coma? Jesus! What the hell were you up to?!" Kevin's dad's voice reaches decibels I didn't realize were possible.

"No," I say. "I wasn't with her. It…it w-wasn't me."

But the voice says, "*Yes, it was. It was you.*" A cold gust of air reaches into my collar. I stiffen but I'm too scared to turn around.

Mr. Phillips studies me, then opens the door wider. "Get in here." In the living room, Kevin's step-mom glares at me while she rocks Kevin's baby brother in her arms. The hatred in her eyes makes me take a step back toward the door.

Mr. Phillips questions me some more then finally says, "I'll call the hospital to see what's going on. But after what you've pulled, you're grounded for a week. The only time you will be out of your room is for school and swim practice."

I run up to Kevin's room and, once inside, I lean against the door, trembling. My body spasms so much, my head and elbows knock audibly on the wood. Hot tears run down my freezing cheeks.

*That voice. That voice.* It wasn't in my head, I know that. It also wasn't the voice of the shadows. The voice…was like it was coming from the air and not…from a body. It was low enough to be Kevin's. I wobble over to Kevin's mirror and look directly into the face I know so well—the seven freckles, the copper eyelashes, the bump on his nose. It is Kevin's face, but the expression behind his dark eyes is not one I've seen him wear. It's terrified, lost, and even feminine. That's my expression. Not his.

Tremors take hold of my body again. I grab onto Kevin's headboard and whisper, "Where are you?"

No answer. There's no sense of anyone but me. *Get a grip, Sylvie. You're going psycho, here. Psycho Sylvie Sydell.* I breathe in slowly and wait for my fear to dull down into something I can try to ignore.

I have to get out of him.

I want my mom. My dad. Sam. Cassie. Nelson. I need someone to be my friend right now.

Kevin's phone beeps.

Cassie's name is displayed before me, and I stare at it until my throat goes raw with unshed tears: *"Sylvie is my BFF. U bettr hav n explnation or it's OVER."*

Oh, yeah. Do I have an explanation. Just not a believable one.

*"Talk 2 u bout it 2morrow,"* I write.

Because I hope by then I will be back to being me.

# twenty-eight

## Watch What You Wish For (Because you'll get something else altogether)

I'm so tired I'm dizzy, but I try to project over and over until I know it won't work. I call to the shadows, but all is eerily silent. I spend the rest of the day on the computer, pleading for help in astral projection chat rooms. With no luck.

Kevin's dad knocks on the door. "We're going out to eat. There's Macaroni and Cheese to make if you want it." He walks away without waiting for an answer. A few minutes later I hear the back door slam and a car engine starting. Kevin's parents haven't talked to me all day. I mean, I come home really shook up about me –well, Sylvie—being in a coma and I'm ignored?

Let them go out to eat. At least that way I don't have to pretend to be Kevin.

I try projecting some more, then when that fails, I try to sleep and fail at that. I hear Kevin's parents come home. Baby David cries for a while then the house is quiet. Despite being wiped out, my eyes don't want to stay closed. Every creak and moan in the house keeps my body tingling with both fear and anticipation. Maybe tonight is when Kevin will come and take back his body. Maybe he'll come and I can slip out sometime during my dreams.

When I do finally doze off, I hear the low-pitched hissing of the shadows. Their voices join up in rusty laughter and I see them, their fingers stroking Kevin's arms. Kevin stares at me, his eyes burning hatred. A silver cord slips tighter and tighter around my neck.

I wake up sweaty and shivering. I flick on the bedside light in panic. *Just a dream, Sylvie. Just a dream.* Yet I can't shake the nightmare.

The sky is still pitch black at 6:00 a.m. and everything seems blurry. My eyes burn. I blink. I blink again, and the room goes in and out of focus.

What the...?

I rub my knuckles against my eyelids and something falls out of my right eye. It's tiny and wrinkled and translucent. Kevin's contact. Oh, crap. The damn things have been for two days straight.

No one else is up, so I lock myself in the bathroom. It takes me a good long time to get the left contact out of my eye. When I wash them off and try to put them back in they sting so much I can't keep my eyes open. Forget the contacts. I'll have to find Kevin's glasses.

But the smell coming from my underarms is overpowering. First things first.

I undress myself without looking, but once I'm in the shower scrubbing up, I peek. I glance down at the muscled chest, the strong legs. So beautiful, so solid. I pass my soapy hands over the hard planes of Kevin's body, rough with hair and then quickly over his...penis. And then I stop. The skin on it is soft. I mean, I wasn't expecting sandpaper or anything, but still…

Suddenly, I feel the thing grow firmer in my hand and I jump. "AHH!" I just catch myself before I skid on the soapy shower floor.

*This is soooooo wrong. So, so wrong.* I mean, I've imagined putting my hands on Kevin's body before, but I wasn't wearing it! My head starts to buzz like it'll explode. I lean against the slick wall tiles and wait for the sensation to pass. Then I finish the shower staring intensely at a spot of mildew in the grout.

I sneak out of the bathroom and back to Kevin's room. Everyone is still asleep.

All of Kevin's clothes are on the floor. I can't tell which are clean and which are dirty without putting my nose to them. I finally put on his green cable knit sweater and a pair of jeans. I find a clunky pair of old glasses, his keys, phone, and wallet and hurry as quietly as I can downstairs.

I slip into Kevin's Camaro, his heart pounding inside me. I've barely driven in the six months I've had my license, and most of that wasn't in a stick shift. Is it stomp on the clutch and then put it in gear or the opposite? I turn the key and manage to get out of the driveway and into the street without a problem. The car shakes every time I change gears, but I don't kill it. I get to the hospital in one piece.

At the front doors I realize I'm four hours too early for visiting hours. But then I think that might not be bad. That Mom won't be there yet, that I might be able to slip in without anyone noticing. If I had the room number. I think about texting Sam. But there's no way he'll give me –Kevin—that info.

Kevin's phone rings and I answer it without looking at the screen. "Yeah?"

"Where the hell are you, dude?" It's Bryce.

I sigh. "I—"

"You won't believe it. Sylvie, Sam's sister, she's in an effing coma. Like, lights out."

"Yeah, I know." It's only 7:00 a.m. and the word has already hit school. I feel my throat tighten.

"You knew?" Then Bryce's voice turns devilish, teasing. "Ah-ha…Been consoling Cassie, huh? But she still didn't put out, did she? Two days left, sucka."

I clench the phone tight and try to keep the shock out of my voice, "What are you talking about?"

Bryce laughs like I've just told a joke. "Nice try. Hey, don't forget we've got extra practice tonight. Coach'll string you up if you're not there."

After hanging up, I stare down at the phone. I don't believe it. I *can't* believe it. Kevin's a decent guy. He wouldn't have made a bet to…*No. Not possible.*

I look at my reflection in the glass doors of the hospital. Kevin looks attractive and honest. Even doubly honest with the glasses. But if I think about it, with that face, I could dupe anyone. I just hope Kevin didn't dupe both me and Cassie.

I step inside the hospital and ask the lady behind the desk for Sylvie Sydell's room number.

"Visiting hours don't start until eleven." She snaps her gum and stares at me.

"Yes," I say, trying to milk my attractive and honest look. "I realize that. But I was on my way to school and she's in my class. I just thought if I knew the room number we as a class could send her flowers or something." *Yeah. Right. That'd be the day.*

It works. She softens and types something on her computer. "Sydell. 216." Now she looks up at me, her eyes hard again. "But says here NO VISITORS. Clear?"

"Crystal."

She nods and tells me to have a good day. I walk out the front doors and follow a path until I come to a different entrance. *All right. Act invisible.*

I get a few strange looks, but no one says anything to me until I get into the patients' wing.

"Too early for visitors," says the nurse behind the counter as I try to walk past unnoticed. She's short, round and has glasses that look like they're about to fall off her nose.

"Oh, uh, no, I'm not a visitor. I've got a physical therapy appointment." I rub my shoulder for effect. "I'm on the swim team."

The nurse pushes at her glasses and smiles at me. "Have to get your appointment in before school, huh? It's a big complex. You're in the wrong building." She gives me directions. I nod and pretend to leave, but round the corner and wait for her to abandon her post instead. It takes ten minutes, but finally she disappears into a room down the corridor. I sprint after her, keeping an eye on the room numbers as I make my way down the shiny white hallway. *210...212...214...216.*

I push open the door as slowly and silently as I can. A green curtain is drawn partially around the bed, so I see nothing but a lump underneath the blankets. I'm expecting to find myself alone with my body, but opening the door an inch further I see my mom. She's wearing a rumpled pink sweat suit and looking out the window. There's a hospital pillow on the only chair in the room and right away I know she's been here all night. An ache twists my lungs inside out. How many times has my mom tried to touch me lately and I've pushed her away? If only she'd turn around now and hug me, tell me everything's okay....

She does turn around, but I can tell by the way her eyes flash that she won't be taking me in her arms. She stabs the call button at the side of the bed and barks, "You're the boy who made jokes about my daughter! Who do you think you are, coming here? Get out! Now."

"No, look! Sam was wrong. I wasn't making jokes—"

"Out!"

I make a lunge for the curtain around the bed—I just need to see for myself—but Mom's suddenly Superwoman. She's faster than a speeding bullet and is blocking my way before I even notice she's moved.

"I just need –"

"OUT!"

Yeah. She's stubborn. She won't listen if I try to explain any more. And there's no way I'll fight her. So I slip back out the door and run down the hallway past the same nurse that gave me directions earlier. "Hey!" she says as I pass, but I don't stop until I'm back at Kevin's Camaro.

The only place to go is school. I start the car and make my way there. Okay. Kevin's schedule...*think, dammit!* Chemistry, math, free hour. That means working in the office. His locker code...God, I've watched him so much I should know it...*15-35-2. Or is it 35-2-15? Oh, crap.* This is so freakin' unreal. Can I do this? Can I pull off being him? I'm going to have to because I am him. Or he is me. From now on, what I do, or think, Kevin does or thinks. Sounds like a fantasy—

three days ago I would have thought that'd be great—but I never would have meant it all so literally.

The car rattles and kills as I let up too quickly on the clutch at the stoplight one street before St. Anthony's. Dwayne Fischer pulls up next to me in his truck, and yells out, "Hey, Phillips! You drive like a girl!" He laughs and punches it to get ahead of me.

*What? I can't even catch a break in a different body?* I start the car again and wonder how Kevin would have responded to Dwayne. Except Kevin never would have killed the motor in the first place.

All of a sudden a scene flashes in my head, so vibrant, so real, I wrench the car over to the right and slam on the brakes to catch my breath. I see Dwayne in his truck after school. It's the day he embarrassed me in the cafeteria, I know it. I don't know how I know but I do. Dwayne's laughing, then yelling out the window at Nelson Strange when I walk up. Only I'm not me. I'm Kevin. And I watch Nelson bang on the hood and say, "You're a prick, Fischer!" which only makes Dwayne laugh even more.

Then the scene is gone and I'm blinking at the road in front of me. *What the hell was that?* Breathe in. Breathe out. I shake my head. *Weird. Really weird.*

I drive the block to school.

There are only about two minutes to spare before classes start, so luckily I don't have to chat with anyone in the hall. But as I slip into a desk in Kevin's chemistry class, Tyrone Dickson punches me in the arm and motions to my glasses. "Stylin'." He whips them off my face and puts them on his own. "God bless America, you're blind!"

I take the glasses back.

"Hey, that Sylvie chick's in the hospital," he whispers.

"I know."

Over the loudspeaker during the announcements, I'm mentioned. "Say a prayer today for Sylvie Sydell, hospitalized over the weekend," says Sister Catherine in her high-pitched voice. I feel like I'm at the wrong end of a telescope. Like even though everything around me is close enough to touch, it's strangely distant. There are a few whispers, but then class starts.

Mr. Paige complains about how little he's paid to deal with walking hormones, but then manages to give us a few instructions for our chem experiment. It's called *Genie in a Bottle*. We create a cloud of smoke in a bottle and let it free. I drop the tea bag full of potassium iodide into the hydrogen peroxide and watch a cloud rise up and out of its prison. Just like that. What an easy escape.

Suddenly, my throat tightens and tears sting my eyes.

Tyrone's talking about the swim team's next meet. I swallow and blink and forget to listen. He flicks me on the forehead with his finger and says, "Yo, Kev. Wake up!"

"Yeah. Still half-asleep." I fake a laugh. From then on, I grunt from time to time, doing my best to act like I know what the hell is going on. But I guess I sound as much like a Neanderthal as Dwayne Fischer because Tyrone squinches his eyes at me and says, "Man, you got brain damage?"

That's how the whole morning goes. With me just trying to make it through. With me wondering why I'm still stuck in this body. Wondering why I can't make an easy escape, too.

I feel people's eyes on me as I walk down the hall, and hear giggles in my wake. When I turn around, everyone makes a point to pretend to be busy. It happens all morning until Ryan Witteck practically kills himself laughing. "What'd you stick up your ass, Kev?"

I watch how I walk from then on.

Before lunch I head to the boys' bathroom. Some idiot's blocked up all the toilets with entire rolls of toilet paper, so I wait until I'm alone and try peeing at a urinal. I manage it without splashing on my shoes. If it weren't so twisted, it'd be a major victory. The handle to flush the urinal is sticky. I wash my hands so thoroughly I could be scrubbing up for surgery.

I go to the cafeteria and head towards the table where Cassie's sitting with Kevin's regular crowd. Except Sam isn't there. I wonder if he's stayed home until I spot him sitting by himself in the far corner. I change direction and head his way.

All sorts of guys from the swim and baseball teams smack me on my shoulder as I cross their paths:

"What's up, Kev?"

"Hey, Phillips!"

"Yo, how's it hanging?"

I nod and keep going, wishing for a second that Kevin wasn't so popular. A group of sophomore girls giggle like idiots as I pass their table. Keri Nielsen comes up behind me and grabs my butt. I practically squeal like a little girl at that, but I continue towards Sam. He sees me approach him. The dark eyes behind his glasses turn black.

"How come you're sitting here?" I try to give him Kevin's winning smile. The one that melts everyone. I hitch my right side of my lip up a little higher than the left and lift my eyebrows. But I can't do it right. It feels like a palsied twitching, not a mastered movement. And Sam isn't melting at all.

"I don't want to be near *you*, that's why." His eyes are bloodshot and he's got Band-Aids over both thumbs. He hasn't taken a bite of the hamburger in front of him, but the bun is riddled with holes where he's picked off the sesame seeds. The sight of him is gut-wrenching. I can imagine he's all alone in our house now, with Mom at the hospital all the time. Or maybe he's sleeping at Dad's on the air mattress until things are back to normal.

If they get back to normal.

Guilt and fear coat my tongue; I say thickly, "Sorry, Sam. But it's not what you think. I'm trying to get things right."

"Leave me alone, Kevin."

I want to tell him everything, but I can't seem to say any more. So I leave him, buy some limp french fries and a Coke and walk back towards Cassie's table. Tori Thompson is there. There's no good reason for her to be there—lately she's been sitting by Dwayne at lunch. She's just there for dirt, that's it.

They've been talking about me—the Sylvie me—I can tell by the hot pink spots on Cassie's cheeks, by the way Sarah is rubbing Cassie's shoulder and kind of holding her back. There's a twinge, and a longing washes over me. Like I want to touch Cassie, run my hands over the thick curtain of her hair.

*Argh!* I grit my teeth and force the feeling to pass. Force myself to look at her like *I* always have—not like Kevin has. Cassie glances up and her eyes are wary. She's still waiting for an explanation for my behavior yesterday.

I sit down at the table, feeling awkward and out of place. I push my tray forward and almost knock over the Coke. I let out a little yip and catch the cup right before it goes over. Everyone turns to look at me.

*You're Kevin, Sylvie. He doesn't yip. He doesn't feel awkward. He's always at home.*

*And people listen to him.*

Tori looks at me and raises her eyebrows as she sees my thick glasses. She smirks. "The nerds' table is over there, Kev. Go work out some algorithms."

"I'm glad for the glasses, Tori." I point a french fry at her. 'Cuz now I can see what a skank you are."

"Ha!" Tori narrows her eyes at me, an uneasy smile on her face. She doesn't seem to know if I'm joking or not. She puts a hand through her frizzy hair and squares her shoulders. "My parents are letting me have my car back…" she starts.

"Go tell someone who cares," I say, thoroughly enjoying bossing her around. "And take your tray with you."

Tori's eyes get wide then narrow again. "Don't tell me what to do," she growls, but she flips her hair and leaves.

"Don't bother coming back," I yell to her back.

"Well," I say to the table at large. "So, I guess Tori's happy. That I…uh…Sylvie's in a coma."

Sarah shakes her head. "Actually, when she heard Sylvie was in the hospital, she seemed pretty upset."

"Yeah," I say. "Upset she wasn't the one who put her there." That gets some laughs.

"I like Sylvie," I continue. "I mean, she seems a bit weird at first, but she's cool when you get to know her. And smart."

Cassie stands up. "I'm gonna eat with Sam."

I stand up, too. "Uh…okay."

"Alone." She takes her tray and crosses the cafeteria. I watch, wondering how I'm going to get her to listen to me. But Bryce says, "Phillips, take a chair."

Everyone kind of grunts and I shrug, sitting.

Michelle sucks on her Diet Coke with a big slurping noise. "What's up with you and Cassie?" The smug look on her face gets my claws out. She and Sarah turned their backs on me the minute they could move to this table. And the only reason they're here is because Cassie was with them. Now Michelle's feeling a little too comfortable for my taste. I don't know if it's the testosterone or what, but I am so, so ready for a fight.

I shove Michelle's tray closer to her and motion towards Cassie and Sam's table. "Why don't you go find out?"

Her eyes flit around to everyone and her face is bright pink. "Oh, that's okay."

"Thought so."

No one says a word. I guess I'm a pretty bitchy Kevin. Actually, with the testicles and the underarm jungle, I'm surprised more guys aren't. Bitchy, that is.

"Better wax her for me, Phillips. And I want her on a full tank, too," Bryce says to me.

"Huh?"

"Don't play dumb, dude." Bryce lifts his eyebrows at me and gives me a malicious smile. I look around the table to see if anyone else knows what the hell he's talking about, but everyone else looks just as confused as me. "You got 'til Halloween. But the way things are going…" He shakes his head in mock sadness.

"What're you talking about?" But my stomach feels tight, and I involuntarily glance over to where Cassie's sitting. *A bet. He and Kevin had a bet.*

The bell rings and Bryce punches me in the arm, "See you at practice."

Kevin has Art next. I get through it without much trouble. Kevin's hands feel like paws, they're so big. It's not easy to work with any delicacy, but my artistic sense keeps me from making a mess of things. Mrs. Stilke looks at me funny when I finish my collage and it's not a disaster. Art's the one class I love—I can't just blow it off completely.

"That's...that's wonderful, Kevin," she says, blinking like she's trying to clear her vision. "I knew if you put your mind to it you could find the artist inside you."

I almost laugh out loud. "Yeah, there's an artist inside me. Just a little stuck."

In English, Mrs. Huggan has moved on to *Twelfth Night*, by Shakespeare. "Guess what?" Mrs. Huggan announces to us all. "It's not a tragedy!"

No, the real tragedy is I can't focus on anything Mrs. Huggan is saying because the desks in this room are suddenly too small and too tight for me. I can't spread my legs apart. And...*it*...is getting crushed. *Oh, come on.* Mrs. Huggan continues talking. I tune in and out as I squirm and suffer. "Shakespeare wrote for all male actors...Viola's part...played by a boy...pretending to be a woman...disguised as a man!" *Ow, ow.* Finally, I shift in my seat and do the unthinkable—I grab between my legs to move things around. *Ugh.* How can guys stand having all this equipment hanging off of them? It's always getting sweaty or pinched or just in the way. I glance around the room, my cheeks pink with embarrassment, right when Mrs. Huggan says. "What do you think, Kevin, of all this gender-bending? Of appearance versus reality?"

"Well, Mrs. Huggan. I have absolutely no experience in that."

In Morality, we're expected to have small group discussions on "What is sin?"

"I can tell you what sin is," says Mitch Scholes. "It's a sin to force us to sit in this room without gas masks. Doesn't Mr. Walker ever take a shower?"

"Did you say gas masks?" Dwayne Fischer leans to one side and blasts out a long fart, right in my direction.

Mitch and I scrunch up our noses and moan protests. Mitch fans the air with his hands. "Come on, Dwayne! What the hell did you eat?"

Dwayne takes a long whiff. "Mmmm. I kinda like it. Admit it, Mitch. When you let one rip, no matter how ripe it is, your own smells pretty damn good. Like home-cooking." He smacks me on the arm. "Ain't that right, Kev?"

I do *not* want to enter this conversation. So I point to my throat. "Sore," I whisper. "Can't talk."

Dwayne and Mitch both look at me with slitted eyes. "Yeah," Mitch says. "I thought you were acting funny."

Instead of discussing sin, Mitch and Dwayne make jokes about the football coach's sex life, the swim coach's balls, and then move on to discuss who was inebriated at the last party.

*Why are we girls attracted to boys again?*

I tune out Mitch and Dwayne and instead listen to snatches of discussion coming from the other groups. "Selfish."…"Not caring about the other person's feelings."…"Murder, for sure. Hey, what about suicide?"…"Greed."…"Stealing."…"You know, oh, what's the word? Manipulation! That's it. Being manipulative."

*What if my plan had worked? What if I'd pulled it off?* Suddenly, it's like there's liquid fire in my veins, hot, itchy, horrible. I can't believe I even tried to take over Cassie's body. The idea seemed to pop magically into my head and it sounded just right. *Sounded right how? What were you going to do, forget your entire family? Your best friend? What did you think? You'd be Kevin's wife?*

I *am* a freakin' psycho. A complete head case. Taking over my best friend's body? Really? What the *hell*?

For the first time I feel something other than regret or guilt over what I'd been trying to do this past weekend. For the first time, there's shame.

Real shame.

"So." Mr. Walker asks us all for our opinions on sin and writes a long list on the blackboard. He nods his head and says, "It needs more discussion, but for today I think we can sum it all up like this." And then he writes: "Hurting others or yourself."

I look down at Kevin's hands, in place of my own. *And what if you hurt others* and *yourself? What kind of sinner are you then?*

After school, I see Nelson in the hallway and I wave to him, "Hey, Nelson!"

He turns and looks behind him, as if I'm talking to someone else.

It's fantastic to see his blue head amid the beige walls. Like water in the middle of a desert. A normal boy, not a tool like the one I've been inhabiting (uh, the bet?) or a complete dumbass like the others I've been frequenting today.

"Hey, how was Art class? Did Mrs. Stilke give out a new assignment?" I follow him to his locker.

He throws a huge binder inside and yanks out his leather jacket. He keeps his eyes down as he says, "Art class blowed, Kevin. Sylvie Sydell sits right next to me normally. And now she's…" He lets the sentence die out.

Right then Melissa Scott comes up to us. She gives me a sly smile but focuses on Nelson. "What's the address of that haunted house?" She wraps a long tendril of hair around her index finger as she's talking.

Nelson gives her the address, slamming his locker shut.

"So I'll come and see you. And then afterwards…we can… have fun."

"Except that I go out with the whole staff afterwards. It's kind of a tradition. I'm sorry." But he doesn't look very sorry.

"'Kay. We'll see." Melissa gives him a little peck on the cheek and waves to us both.

"So," I say, my voice bitter. "Looks like the basketball dinner went well, huh? You together now?" Nelson eyes me like I've just sprouted antennae then walks away without answering.

Something about that little kiss gets my stomach roiling. The fact that Melissa put her lips to Nelson's face shouldn't bother me, but it does. It really does.

The whole thing throws me for such a loop, I almost forget to sneak out before seeing Bryce, in order to avoid swim practice. I know if I skip practice Kevin's dad will want to kill me, but it's that or basically kill myself by drowning. I try to skim along the hallways like I'm invisible. I don't get far. I'm not even into the parking lot when Bryce comes up next to me and says, "Coach is gonna ream you out for missing practice yesterday."

"I'm sick," I say. "I'm not going to practice."

"Ha. Yeah."

I take a breath and let it out, not sure I really want to ask, but knowing I have to. "Remind me again what the bet's about?"

Bryce laughs, wraps his arm around my neck and grinds his knuckles playfully into my skull. "No more trying to get out of it, dude. A deal's a deal. Just because you screwed up and Cassie got pissed off doesn't mean the bet's off. Get into her pants by Halloween or the Camaro's mine."

I pull away from him, suddenly feeling dizzy. "That's horrible!"

Now Bryce laughs even louder and mimics *that's horrible* in a feminine voice. "Hey," he says. "Not for me!"

But Kevin loves his Camaro. It was a piece of junk when he bought it. He took it apart piece by piece and rebuilt it. For his sixteenth birthday, he got his license and a paint job for the car. Sparkly silver. Every time he's in the driver's seat, he acts like some hot-shot celebrity. He radiates pride. He must have been real sure of himself, sure he'd win the bet, or he'd never have risked losing that car.

*Oh, man. Oh, hell.* Kevin's a creep. A cretin. A low-life, grade A wad who makes bets on bedding girls. And I liked him? *Loved* him?

I bend over. "I think I'm gonna hurl."

"We're gonna be late, Phillips." Bryce sounds like he's had enough.

I stand and start towards Kevin's car when Bryce says, "Whoa. Where you going?"

"Home."

"What's your problem, dude? You've been acting stoned all day, completely out of it. At least say something to Coach about missing or you'll be off the team."

That doesn't seem so awful to me, but I know it would be to Kevin. And I'm supposed to be him. So I go and tell Coach I'm too sick to practice.

"WHAT???" Large globs of frothy, white spit fly from his lips as he lets off a string of swear words that probably shouldn't be said within half-a-mile of any Catholic school. I let him rain profanities on me, while, despite myself, I glance down at his pants. In Morality, Mitch and Dwayne had joked about him having only one—

"Phillips!" I start at the sharp tone in his voice and snap my eyes back to his face. *Oh, my God. I cannot believe I was just looking at his crotch!* "Go," he says. "But you show up for the meet Thursday even if you're half-dead, you hear me?"

"Don't you think since I've missed already that maybe you want someone else—"

"Be at the meet, Phillips, or don't show your face here again."

Like I'd want to.

# twenty-nine

### Still Life (As in, this is still my life?)

I drive over to Cassie's. At every red light I look at myself in the rearview mirror and practice Kevin's smile. At first it looks hideous. My lip kind of snags on my teeth and my gums are exposed. All I need is some foaming at the mouth to complete the look. No wonder Sam wasn't susceptible. But after five red lights and one stop sign, I get it right. Right side up. Left side tilted. Eyebrows pleading, but with pride.

I glance over at my house, dark and lonely, as I walk up Cassie's porch steps. When she opens her front door I beg, "Let me in, please."

"Look, Kevin—"

"Please." I give her the special smile, praying it'll work. Praying I nailed it.

I must have. Because Cassie sighs, but opens the door wider. And as I make my way inside she looks me up and down and says softly, "You look good in glasses."

*Yikes.*

We sit in overstuffed chairs in the living room, listening to the grandfather clock tick. Other than that there's no sound in the house; her parents are still working. She sits looking at me, waiting, twisting her hair into a loose braid. She looks tired, like she hasn't slept, and the life has gone out of her eyes. The friend in me wants to beg her forgiveness for ever having tried my plan. The body surrounding me wants to run its hands over her hips.

I shake my head and try to think clearly. "So I know I owe you an explanation, but you have to promise you'll hear me out to the end."

She lets out a low chuckle. "Whatever."

"Just listen. Carefully." And then I start. I start with the weekend and how we went to Chicago and how we decided to project that night. "You and me were trying to project when this happened. I went astral...I left my body and... and..." I stumble, knowing I can't tell the truth, knowing she'll never forgive me if I do. Knowing I need her more than ever right now. "I don't know, I just ended up inside Kevin. Please believe me, Cass. I know it's unbelievable but you have to believe me. I'm Sylvie."

Her eyes darken and I try to think of something that will convince her. "I know just about everything about you. You can lift one eyebrow, you've always been able to do that... your mom gets drunk when your dad works late...My...my mom serves lentil lasagna on Fridays...When I eat watermelon, I break out in hives..."

I take a big breath and realize I'm crying. "Please believe me, Cass. No one else will and I'm really scared."

She stays quiet, watching me cry. She's stopped braiding her hair, and her fingers are there in mid-twist. *Cassie is still here. She's still her. Still perfect. While I'm...I'm...him.*

"Okay," she says slowly. "If you're Sylvie what's our oath?"

Kevin's heart jumps in my chest. I look into Cassie's eyes. "Blood sisters, blood sisters, as long as we live. Always together. We always forgive."

Suddenly her eyes fill with tears. "Sylvie."

Yes, Cassie's still here. Still perfect. Still my friend.

Even now.

I reach out and pull her to me. We hug for a long time.

Suddenly, she lets go. "But...what happened to Kevin? If you're in him, where is he? Where'd he go?" Her voice is crackly, full of worry.

I think of the disembodied voice I heard before, and feel the prickle of goose bumps rising on my skin. "I don't know, Cass. I have no idea where he is."

"He can't just be gone!"

There's nothing I can say. There's just a sick feeling growing in my stomach. Where *is* he?

"So, why can't you get out? Why can't he get in?" Cassie's voice is high and loud.

I keep saying the same thing over and over. "I don't know! I don't know why!"

Both of us stare at each other with tears in our eyes. We're silent for a while and then I say, "I have to get back to my body. I've been out for two days. I don't know how long I can be out before..." But I can't finish the sentence.

"They won't let anyone but family near...uh..."

"My body," I say for her, the words rough as tree bark.

"Yeah. At least for now."

"I don't know how much time I have." The inside of my throat feels like I just swallowed sand. "How much time Kevin has, either."

"Maybe Sam can get you into the room?" Cassie says.

"He's mad at me. Or Kevin, anyways."

We keep talking for a long time, long enough for the clock to chime the hour twice. Then suddenly, Kevin's cell phone rings. I look on the screen; it says *HOME*. "Yeah?"

"Kevin," a woman's voice whines out of the speaker. "You're grounded, remember? Practice has been over for thirty minutes now. If you aren't home in the next ten, I add another week to your punishment."

I hang up and say good-bye to Cass. It's time to go play Kevin for a while.

At Kevin's house, his step-mom is on duty, patrolling, making sure I go nowhere and have no privacy. She glares at me, but kisses little David who's sleeping in a navy blue carrier strapped to her chest. His pale face is ghostly next to the orange surface of her self-tanned neck. She doesn't look like someone who'd get into something like astral projection, but if Kevin said she did it, maybe she can help.

When she pokes her head into the bedroom to see what I'm up to I say, "Uh…" I'm not sure what to call her. Does Kevin call her "Mom" or what? I think back to all the times I went astral and spied on Kevin. *Andrea*. That's it. I think. "Uh, Andrea, can I ask you something?"

She puts her hand on the doorknob and narrows her eyes at me. "What did you just call me?"

And then I remember. *Amanda. Not Andrea.* "Amanda, do you still astral project? You still leave your body?"

She mashes her mouth into a straight line and doesn't answer. When she finally talks her words are hard as a hammer on a nail. "For the last time, I don't follow you. I do it just for me. For myself, Kevin. So let's not hash over this again and again."

"No, that's not it. Really!" I hold out my hands, hoping she won't leave the room. I know she and Kevin aren't close—they didn't talk much whenever I went astral and saw him with her. But she's his step-mom. She probably wants the relationship to work. She probably wants to listen. "It's that project, too. But the other night something awful happened." I take a quick breath. She projects. She just might believe me. "What if I told you I managed to slip inside the wrong body?"

"I'd tell you to stop talking or you'll be grounded two extra weeks." David stirs in the carrier and she pets his head gently. When she speaks to me, her voice is soft, but furious. Her eyes glisten with unshed tears. "Look, Kevin. You can play your little tricks on me. You can call me psychotic or insane or demented all you want. But your father and I are married. We have a child together—your brother. No matter what you do, I'm not going anywhere."

"But you've got it wrong—"

"No, *you've* got it wrong. All wrong. Persecuting me isn't going to make you feel any better about your mom. Your beef is with her, not me. I'm sorry she hardly ever sees you, but it's *not my fault*."

She swipes at her eyes, leaving black streaks near her temples. "Now I don't want another word out of you or your dad will hear about it. Dinner in fifteen minutes." She goes out the door and slams it behind her.

*Oof. That was a disaster.* My stomach tightens. The one person who could maybe help me isn't open to listening because stupid Kevin's put her off. Why did I think he was so perfect before? I'm already sick of being him. So, so sick of it.

Dinner with Kevin's parents is torture. I try to field all sorts of questions I have no answers to about the swim meet on Thursday and I endure a list of Mr. Phillips' demands and expectations: *I expect you to win, young man. I haven't raised you a loser. You'd better get your ass in gear. You're supposed to be the best. You'd better start acting like it. You'll never get to college on your grades. This is your ticket young man, don't blow it.* And then, pointing to the Camaro, *What the hell kind of park job is that?*

I eat my steak and baked potato with gusto, loving the redness of the meat and the dairy-ness of the sour cream. "Well, there's an improvement," Mr. Phillips barks at me. "I see you've finally taken our advice to use a knife and fork!"

I look down at my hands, Kevin's hands, and the shiny silverware in them. I eye Kevin's parents in confusion. What? Kevin ate with his hands? Every time I've seen him eat, he's eaten just fine. But, then again, it's always been sandwiches or French fries.

"Glad you've given up on your obsession to drive us crazy by eating like an animal." Both Kevin's dad and step-mom talk to me like I'm a nuisance, with an edge to their voice. But they turn to little David when he gurgles and applaud like he's just recited Shakespeare, "Way to go, little champ!" A quick burst of sympathy pinches my chest. Maybe there's a reason Kevin's not shaking Heaven and Earth to come back and reclaim his body.

Back up in his room, I can't sit still. I miss my family. Mom and her Leftover Surprise. Dad and his work addiction.

Even Sam and his chewed up thumbs. I look at the clock. 6:45 pm. If all were normal, my mom would be tidying up right now. Dad would be working—staring at the screen of his laptop like it'd give him the secret to life if he looked hard enough. And Sam. Sam would be up in his room, doing homework or playing with his pet insects or trying some science experiment bound to fizz or foam or fail.

There's a solid pole of pain right straight down the middle of me. It's ludicrous. I can't believe how much I miss Sam.

I sit in front of the computer, entering more chat rooms on astral projection, hoping someone, somewhere can help me. I get kicked out of one group and get sarcastic remarks from the next. I try a third site and hope for the best, but it seems like I'm the only one online. I close my eyes and rub my hands down my face, the way my dad does, startled by the feel of stubble on my cheeks and chin.

All of a sudden I hear a long sigh behind me.

I turn around, expecting Kevin's step-mom with her hands on her hips. But no one's there.

*You're imagining things, Sylvie,* I tell myself.

Looking back at the screen, I see someone's responded to my plea: *I know how you can get out,* it says.

My fingers stumble over the keyboard as I write back: *How?*

I watch the cursor blink and then the letters appear one by one: *The truth.*

*What?* I write. *Like "the truth will set you free?"*

The answer comes quickly: *Exactly.*

Disappointment drops like a boulder in my chest. It figures I'd come across some religious freak rather than someone serious about astral projection. I'm ready to exit the chat room when I look at the username: KEV.

Goosebumps pop out on my arms and neck. It's a coincidence. It can't be him. But I need to know. *Kevin?* I write.

The cursor blinks endlessly until finally I get a response: *Listen to me. Tell the truth and GET OUT!*

*Who are you? WHERE are you? What do you mean?* I pound out. But KEV has left the chat room.

I don't like it. I don't like any of this. I don't scare easy, but right about now my heart's racing like a Grand Prix car.

*Calm down*, I tell myself. There's got to be a way to make sense of it. Of everything. This isn't some ghost story. All these voices and stuff, it's just me, going stir-crazy in this body.

Isn't it?

I say out loud, "Where *are* you?"

No response. Not a sigh, not a whisper. I take a shaky breath and try to get my bearings. Okay. KEV. Just a coincidence. So what did KEV mean with *Tell the truth*? The truth. I've been telling everyone the truth since the beginning: I'm not Kevin. I'm Sylvie. But no one will listen. No one will believe me.

Except Cassie.

*Oh, God*. That's it. It's like I'm on the edge of a cliff, peering over—half terrified, half exhilarated.

Cassie. I've got to tell her the truth. The WHOLE truth. But she'll never forgive me if I do.

# thirty

## Nightmare on Kevin's Street

I dream I'm wearing Cassie's body. The shadows help me pull it on, but their inky fingers are rough and they pinch my skin in the zipper. I stand before a mirror and watch in horror as the reflection before me changes from smooth and feminine to something else. Hair sprouts on my arms, stubble on my cheeks. My limbs pop and protest as they're elongated.

The shadows laugh as I try ripping it all off. I scratch at my neck, my forehead, my toes, but when I find a seam and rip at it, more coverings hide underneath. Dread seeps into my veins as I realize I can't find myself under the layers.

A mask of Kevin's face lays on the floor. Suddenly its lips open and it whispers, "You'll never get out."

# thirty-one

## ICU (Or, I C U don't know what the hell you're doing)

I don't go to school in the morning. I go to the hospital instead. I mean, my mom can't be there 24/7, can she?

I text Cassie to let her know what I'm up to and then make my way to the patients' wing.

This time I know where I'm going and so it's easier to get around unnoticed. When I get in front of room 216, there's no one in the hall. I push open the door slowly.

Mom's not there. I'm relieved and disappointed at the same time. The room is quiet and there's no sign of life except a half-eaten breakfast tray on the roll-out table at the foot of the bed. The green curtain is pulled half-way round, so I can only see the bulk of a body under the covers, but not my face.

I approach the curtain, grasping it with shaky fingers.

From behind it comes a sudden grating breath and the rustle of covers. *Wait a minute. I thought I was in a coma.*

Then it hits me. *Kevin. He's in me!*

I yank open the curtain, my heart skipping, ready to see my own face reflected at me.

"Who're you?" says a sleepy voice. The figure under the covers turns to face me. It's an elderly man, thin and wrinkled. He has a bandage over one eye.

I reel back and knock over the breakfast dishes, sending them crashing to the floor. The old man yelps. I turn around, bang into a chair and then finally make it to the door. I swing it open and run out into the hallway, almost banging into the same nurse with the round glasses from yesterday. "You again!" she yells.

But on Kevin's long legs I'm too fast for her. I get to his car, slam the door and wheeze like crazy until I finally catch my breath.

What the hell happened to my body? That was *my* room yesterday.

I zoom through all the possibilities: Maybe Kevin is in me and Mom took him home. Maybe the hospital just changed rooms on me. Or maybe…maybe my body…died.

No.

Well, there's one way to find out. I go on Kevin's iPhone and search the hospital site for a phone number. Then I punch it in.

"All Saints Medical, can I help you?" I hear the snap of gum and picture the same lady who was behind the desk yesterday morning.

I ask her about Sylvie Sydell and wait while she types on the computer. She snaps her gum a few more times, then answers. "She was moved to ICU last night."

"ICU?"

"Intensive Care Unit."

My scalp prickles and a yawning fear opens up in my gut. "Why?"

"I'm very sorry, but not only do I not have that information, I couldn't give it out if I did."

"But, she was in a regular room yesterday. Is it normal for people to then go to ICU?"

"Like I told you –"

"Okay, fine. Just tell me this: It doesn't mean she's getting better, does it? It means something happened so she got worse?"

There's a long silence on the other end, then a sigh. "I'm sure they're taking excellent care of her," the woman says. Then the line goes dead.

I can't keep my thoughts straight and so I kill the car several times on the way to St. Anthony's. By the time I make it there, it's almost lunch hour. I sit, letting the car idle, while I call my mom's cell phone number.

She answers right away. "Hello?" I can hear beeps and machine noises behind her. She's not at home giving a massage. She's at the hospital.

"Hi. Hello, Mo...Mrs. Sydell. I'm a friend of Sylvie's and...uh...some of us here at school are wondering how she's doing."

Mom mumbles, "Oh, well, good of you to call. She's, well, she's still—" but she doesn't finish because she starts sobbing. High-pitched, wailing sobs that wrench my heart.

"Sorry," I say and hang up, feeling more on-edge than I did before.

Cassie's at Kevin's cafeteria table looking pale and worried. The second she sees me, she jumps up and follows me in line. I scan the place, but don't see Sam anywhere in sight.

"Where's Sam?" I say, grabbing a tray from the pile more out of habit than hunger. I'm not sure I can swallow anything at this point.

"Didn't come to school this morning. I've texted him a billion times, but he hasn't texted back."

I put the tray back on the pile and take a cup instead. Now I really know I can't eat. I'm just going to grab a Coke to settle my stomach.

I tell Cassie about the ICU. Her perfect lips settle into a pout. "We gotta do something."

"I know. And here I am at St. Anthony's acting like Kevin. It's ridiculous. It's just, until I figure out what to do, this is where I can hang."

By now we've reached Kevin's table. I set the Coke down and plop into a chair. Cassie sits next to me.

Bryce shoots his finger at me like a gun and winks. "So you two kissed and made up, huh?"

I ignore him. Everyone at the table starts talking about their plans for Halloween. Someone's brought a ton of bite-sized candy bars and dumped them in the middle of the table. I take a mini Butterfingers and eat it without even tasting it. I don't listen. Instead I look around, hoping Sam will show up.

That's when I see Tori Thompson standing in front of Mimi Wilder's group. There's no way she's up to any good.

Inside, I cringe and automatically glance toward the exit, wanting to flee before Tori makes her way over to me. But then I remember whose body I'm wearing and a surge of satisfaction swells through me. I get up and go to Mimi's table.

"A little early for Halloween, isn't it?" Tori's saying. She puts her hands over her mouth in mock embarrassment.

"Oh, I'm so sorry. That's not a mask; that's your face." She hands her a box of Clearasil. "Here. This'll help."

Mimi's chin trembles and she looks like she's about to cry, but she swipes her eyes and swears at Tori, her blotchy face turning red.

Tori shares her toxic grin with me, and I smile back. "So, *Victoria*," I say. "Pick up any other products at the store? I'm sure the pet section's got some stuff that's perfect for you. Bones for bitches. Or some pomade for frizzy poodle hair."

"Where do you come off—"

"Ah! But what you really need is a muzzle." I wink at Mimi, whose face has brightened considerably, and leave Tori spitting insults behind me.

When I get back to Kevin's table, everyone's looking at me funny but no one bothers to ask what just happened. They're still talking about Halloween.

"…haunted house tomorrow night. Nelson Strange works there every year. I guess it's supposed to scare you shitless." Sarah grins widely.

"I'm in," says Latisha Harper. "Nelson Strange. He's so damn hot!"

"Hey!" Ryan protests.

"What? I can look. Nothing wrong with that."

"Dude's got blue hair!" Bryce laughs.

"Still hot." Now Latisha looks back to Ryan. "Oh, don't worry. He's, like, totally in love anyways."

"Yeah," I say, forgetting to keep the snotty tone out of my voice. "Melissa Scott."

Latisha giggles. "Melissa's been trying to get into his pants forever. But believe me, he's not interested. Everybody knows he's been totally crushing on Sylvie Sydell since freshman year."

When Ashley and Rhea murmur assent, my head starts buzzing and my heart speeds up. "You're kidding."

*They're kidding. Right?*

But they're serious.

And it explains everything. All the times he swept the hair off my forehead, all the times he complimented my work, all the times he smiled at me for no good reason. And the way he got annoyed when I tutored Kevin. And the kiss. *Oh. My. God.* The kiss. It wasn't just to make me feel better.

And here I was too wrapped up in my own plans to even notice. Too wrapped up in wanting Kevin. Wanting to feel normal and pretty and never realizing that Nelson saw me that way all along.

I'm such an idiot.

Bryce searches through the pile of mini candy bars on the table and turns to Cassie. "Hey, Cass? Got something sweet to give my man Phillips? Your Mounds, maybe? That'd give his Almonds some Joy—"

Ashley whaps him on the head. "Don't be a douche, Bryce," she says, but she's giggling pretty hard. "Besides, Kevin's appendage isn't gonna fall off from lack of use."

"That's only 'cuz he's got his hand," Bryce says and the whole tables explodes in laughter with him. Only Cassie and I are completely silent.

Cassie stands up. Bryce says quickly, "It's a joke, Cassie. No hard feelings, eh?"

Part of me wants to curl up in embarrassment and part of me wants to wipe his face across the cafeteria floor. But I'm Kevin. He wouldn't curl up, for sure, but he probably wouldn't hit Bryce, either. So I lean across the table and hiss, "What's your problem?"

The bell rings and we all get up. "Lighten up, both of you. I was kidding," Bryce says, eyeing me. "One more day, dude. See you at practice."

I make my way to Art. Cassie follows me out of the cafeteria and downstairs.

I don't want to talk to her. I know what she's going to ask, and I don't want to tell her that Kevin wasn't the good guy we thought he was. I don't want to have to see the hurt in those green eyes. "You're going to be late to class," I say to her as we enter the basement corridor. It's dimmer here than upstairs. Half of the fluorescent lights are burnt out.

"What was that about with Bryce?"

"I don't know." The lights in the hallway flicker as I say it. My whole body tingles. *Fluorescent lights flicker all the time, Sylvie,* I tell myself. *Keep your cool.*

"He's acting like an ass." Cassie crosses her arms. "I'm glad Kevin's not like him."

In the corridor, it's just me, Cassie and… I turn around. No one else is there, yet I have the feeling we're not alone. Panic seeps into my gut.

"Yeah," I say. "But he's not perfect, either."

Cassie looks like she wants to ask me more, but the warning bell rings. She takes off up the stairs.

"Kevin *is* an ass," I croak out to the empty hallway.

Something as airy and light as a breath brushes my cheek. I rub it briskly and whip around, but no one's there.

*"Boo!"* comes from absolutely nowhere.

The lights flicker and hum once more, and I run as fast as I can to Mrs. Stilke's room.

I spot Nelson in the parking lot as I'm heading out of school. He's at his yellow Nova, a car that's twice as old as I am. I sprint over to him, and poke him in the shoulder as he turns his key in the doorlock. "Hi, Nelson!"

His eyes get really wide and he glides a step further away from me. "Kevin…"

Looking at him, I feel a dizzying warmth, and all I can think is *Did you really like me when I was me?* I think of how softly he kissed me. Of the heat of his hands on my hips. But I don't think I can tell him who I am right away. And I'm supposed to be a guy. So I try some male-talk: "Nice car you got there."

"It's a piece of crap. The floor board on the passenger side is completely rusted out, the gas gage is broken and the window won't roll down."

"But it runs."

Nelson crosses his arms. "What do you want, Kevin?"

I spit it out. "Are you seeing Melissa Scott?"

Nelson pulls open the driver's door. It squeaks loudly. "Why? You interested in her?"

"No, no, it's just…" That's when it hits me. That's when I realize I know nothing about Nelson. We laugh and joke in class, yeah. And I share all sorts of things about my life with him. But I don't really ever ask him anything.

I suddenly want to ask him everything. I suddenly want to know every little detail about who he is. Like what kind of music he plays on his guitar. Or if he likes dogs. Or even why he decided to dye his hair blue in the first place. "I don't know anything about you," I say.

Nelson freezes, his hands gripping the top of the car door. His face turns bright red. "Yeah, well. That's okay, Kevin. You can't know everyone."

"Do you like Sylvie Sydell?"

He turns on his heel and gets into the driver's seat.

But before he can shut the door, I grab it. "I'm only saying that because I know she could use a friend right now. That's all." *And a freakin' lobotomy.*

Nelson's brings his black lacquered fingertips to his temples. "She's not even conscious."

"So, you don't want to be her friend? Or more?"

He looks at me, his mouth twisting downward. "Yeah. I, do. I've always wanted that." He takes a deep breath. "Now, leave me alone."

I nod, but as he takes off I whisper, "No way."

The ICU might as well be Fort Knox for how hard it is to get in. And when I do finally get in, I reach the room where my body is only to see my parents standing outside the door, looking weary.

So I can't get in the room, but I stretch out on a hard love seat in the waiting area. A couple is there, holding hands and watching CNN. I do my best to ignore them and try to relax.

Maybe if I'm close to my body, I'll be able to project. I try my best for a good hour.

Nothing happens. It's like my essence is suddenly super-glued inside. For all my effort, I don't even feel the slightest twitch towards freedom.

I walk back towards my room, fear trickling through me at the sight of all the patients in their beds. Here there are more machines, more tubes, more drips than I've even seen before. In fact, it's hard to see the actual people underneath it all.

I stop outside the room with my name on it, taking deep breaths to calm me down. *In, out, in, out.* Then I push the door open a crack.

My parents are still there. They're blocking the view of my body, but I can make out a myriad of machines around the bed. I hesitate, not sure if I should try convincing them I'm not some idiot guy here to make jokes about their daughter, or if I should just leave and come back later.

Before I make up my mind, my mom puts her hands to her head and says to my dad, "Not pneumonia, Michael."

Dad's voice is strong and somewhat angry. "The doctors know what they're doing."

Mom lets out a strangled laugh. "They don't know anything. They haven't been able to figure out anything yet. Not one damn thing." She sits down in the only chair in the tiny room crowded with medical equipment.

I feel a tap on my shoulder and turn around to see familiar set of hairy nostrils. Dr.Hong. "Visiting hours are over."

"What are you doing here? You don't work in the hospital."

He doesn't seem overly surprised at my familiar tone. "Neither do you. I, however, have the right to check up on a patient." He glances into the room and his voice goes soft, like he's talking to himself. "Someone I hope I haven't failed."

He puts a hand on the door but I stop him. "Wait! Pneumonia? Is that…is that a bad thing?"

Dr. Hong narrows his eyes at me from behind his glasses. Then he sighs. "It's not good. But Sylvie's a spunky one. A fighter. If she finds the strength to fight this infection, all will be okay."

He goes into the room, shaking hands with my mom and dad. The door shuts behind him and I stand there, letting his words echo in my ears.

But how can I fight it when I'm not even in my body?

# thirty-two

## Testosterone Trouble

Back at Kevin's house, I check the internet on pneumonia. Apparently, it's one of the major causes of death in comatose people. Great. Just great. Even without me in it, my body's managing to screw things up. And if I can't get in there and fight the pneumonia, things will be more than screwed up. They'll be over. I was already worried about how much time I had. Now I'm freaking.

If my body dies what happens to me? To Kevin?

I slam shut Kevin's laptop and knock a half-eaten box of cookies off the desk at the same time.

This place is disgusting. I can't even think in this kind of mess. Not to mention something reeks like death in here.

I go downstairs to the kitchen and search for the garbage bags. Amanda is on the couch, feeding David. I can feel her eyes follow me as I open and close cupboards.

"What are you looking for?" Her voice is suspicious. Like she thinks I'm up to something bad.

But I find the bags under the sink. "Got 'em. Garbage bags."

"For what?"

"Cleaning Kev...my room." I run upstairs, but not before I see her mouth gaping open.

I chuck the dirty clothes in the laundry, the food wrappers and peels and empty cans in the garbage bag. I line Kevin's shoes up in his closet and pile his books next to his bed.

And then I pick up the notebook. The one I found when I came into his body. I open it and page through, stopping at a random page:

*I kissed her today. Then Bryce and Ashley came out by the pool and we got distracted. But all the AP is working. I know her like the back of my hand. One remark about parents not paying attention and I've got her. It's easier than I thought to—*

I stop reading because it makes me feel sick.

I need to get out of him. I throw the notebook into his backpack and bring the garbage bags downstairs. Kevin's dad and step-mom are watching the 10:00 news.

I go back upstairs and pace the carpet. Kevin's phone buzzes. It's a message. The number comes up only as UN-KNOWN:

*"rd sum mr"*

What's that supposed to mean? Red summer? And who's it from? I put the phone back in my pocket, annoyed.

*Think.* How am I going to get out of him? I remember the discussion in the chat room and how KEV told me to tell the truth. Fine. I'm willing to try anything. Besides, I've got to talk to someone. I need to get out of this hellhole and see a friend. And I need to tell Cassie the truth. I text her: *"30 min. Your bckyrd."* Two minutes later she responds: *"OK"*

I've heard Kevin talk about sneaking out his window. So I lock the bedroom door, put on a jacket and lift the window screen. The family room adds a slanted bit of roof outside. Just enough to climb out onto. I scoot down the shingles and take a big breath. The jump isn't that far, but it scares me. I land on my feet in the grass, a thud of pain reverberating up from my soles.

It takes me twenty minutes to walk to Cassie's. I pass my own house, my insides a jellied mess when I see the place is completely dark and the car's gone.

I walk down my driveway with a hole in my gut and squeeze through the hedge, the branches clutching at my jacket. In Cassie's yard, the grass is damp and colorless in the dark. Like a rectangle of muck. I sit in a hot pink plastic patio chair instead of on the lawn.

Cassie huffs out the back door, slamming it, and plops down into the chair next to mine. From the glow of light coming though the kitchen windows, I can see her eyes are puffy. She has a can of beer in her hand, and she pops it open with a loud fizz.

"What're you doing?" I say.

"What it looks like: having a beer." She points to her house with her chin. "They can get drunk all the time. Why can't I?"

"Don't be stupid."

"I'm not stupid."

"Cassie," I take a breath. "Drinking isn't going to make your parents notice you."

She stiffens and puts both hands over her mouth. Then she moans and starts to sob, tears coming down her cheeks faster than rain.

All of a sudden, it's like there's a ten-ton machine crushing my chest. "I'm sorry, Cass. I didn't want to hurt you, I just—"

But she cuts me off, her voice choked between sobs. "My mom got fired. I thought she was bad, but I didn't know it all. She even drank at work."

"Oh, no."

"And now we'll need a little money to tide us over, she says. So they sold my car. I mean, I get home from school and they sell it. Gone. They didn't even warn me." She shakes her head and wrinkles up her face until she looks like a raisin. "I don't care about the car. Really. But some of my butterflies are missing. The most expensive ones…You know, it would be nice to have parents who might actually worry about my feelings. Or worry about me. They're in there right now drinking and swearing and blubbering together—like that's not what got them into this mess. They pat my head, tell me to be a good girl and then I'm dismissed. They don't even notice me, really. It's like *I'm* a butterfly in a frame, you know? Just decoration."

A few days ago I would have argued with her, told her that she was nothing like a mounted butterfly. That her parents let her free to fly when and however she wanted. That if anyone was stuck behind glass, it was me with my parents constantly looking over my shoulder. But tonight I understand. I understand that her parents coo over her and dust her off every once in a while, but in general, she's that work of art on the wall no one sees anymore. Her parents are too into each other and too into booze to remember her sometimes.

I've always told myself that Cassie's life is better than mine. But Cassie's parents are inside doing God-knows-what when she's out here in need of a hug, while my parents have practically given up their lives to camp out by my side.

I lean over and pull Cassie to me, hugging her hard. She's bawling, taking deep, trembling breaths every couple of seconds. Her hair is smooth on my cheek and her shoulders shudder against my own each time she inhales. Somewhere in the depths of this body, there's a pull…a fierce desire to run my lips down the length of her cheek and to her mouth. Like I won't be at peace until I do. It's the same feeling I usually get when I'm in front of an empty sketchpad. Like if I don't touch it, I'll go nuts.

Damn Kevin's body. Like this isn't already awkward enough.

With effort, I smooth down her hair and breathe in the scent of her. Desire is replaced by familiarity. She smells like chocolate and Aviance Night Musk. She smells like Cassie. She smells like the girl who, despite it all, has always been my best friend.

She pulls back stiffly, wipes her face with her hands and looks at me. "It's strange giving you a hug when you're him."

*You don't know the half of it.* "You think that's strange, try peeing standing up."

That gets a giggle out of her. Then she looks down at her feet. "I worry about Kevin, you know?"

"Yeah," I say, a knot in my throat, thinking of his bet.

She looks up. "But you were right. I let a boy get between us."

"Yeah, well, I did, too. And I was so jealous I would have done anything to be you." *Hell, I did. I freakin' did. And now look what happened.*

"I should never have gone out with him. Not with how you liked him." Cassie starts sobbing again.

I shake my head and look off into the dark shadows of the bushes outlining Cassie's backyard. They're scraggly and menacing. "Boy, was I deluded," I say, rubbing my hands on my jeans. "You know, I should have listened to you about Nelson. I guess sometimes it's hard to see what's right in front of your face."

We're quiet for a few minutes and I know it's time to tell her the truth. But how can I tell her without it sounding completely evil? *Oh, by the way, I tried stealing your body the other day ....*

Before I can start, she says, "I managed to talk to Sam."

My eyes snap to her face. "What do you mean?"

"I'm trying to convince him you're...you. I think I've got him. Almost, anyways."

An aching pain starts worming its way into me. "You're convincing Sam?"

She shrugs like the whole thing is no big deal, but she looks down to the patio floor and says, "If I were totally alone like you are right now, I'd want a couple people by my side, that's all."

I practically topple her over, I hug her so hard.

"Ow! Watch it! You're stronger now than you were before!" But her voice is amused.

My sobs sound like laughter. "You're the best, Cassie. The best." I swallow a soreness in my throat.

She gently pushes me from her and holds out her index finger, a small smile lengthening her lips. "Blood sisters forever, right?"

I look down at my hands. They're big, with copper hairs curling under each knuckle. There's no minuscule scar on this index finger, but when I hold it up, I mean the words that follow more than I ever have: "Forever and ever."

We lock our fingers together and stare at each other in the dim light. Tears glisten in Cassie's eyes, and I know the same is true for me. And I know I can't tell her the truth. Not tonight.

On the way home, I hear a word come out of the blackness : "Coward."

# thirty-three

## Just Psychotic

Kevin's face is almost touching mine. His coffee-colored eyes are ebony with rage, his breath hot. "You're judging *me*? You think you're better than I am? You're no better, Sylvie."

I try to step back, move away from him, but something tightens around my neck, forcing a gag. The silver cord. My fingers tear at it, but the cord's like vapor and they go right through.

"Get out!" Kevin snarls.

"Please!" I wheeze as the silver cord tightens even further.

"Who do you want to be, Sylvie? Who?"

I can't breathe now. I gasp and claw at my neck.

Suddenly, Kevin's eyes lose their fierceness and his face melts into a soft frown. There is such sadness in his features. "But…maybe…I'm not…"

I wake up with my own hands around my throat and every little hair on my body standing at attention. I'm slick with sweat. I squeeze my eyes shut and massage my neck with my damp hands over and over.

When I open my eyes again, I can see Kevin, illuminated by moonlight, right in front of me.

I scream and knock over the bedside lamp in my hurry to turn it on. Baby David wails. Kevin's dad opens the bedroom door with a *wham* and switches on the overhead light. His voice booms at me, "What's going on?"

"It's, it's…" But Kevin's gone.

# thirty-four

## Who I Want to Be

The next day is Halloween. The whole school is decorated in black and orange and everyone's gone all out on costumes. I don't bother. I figure I'm already wearing one.

Among the sea of monsters and vampires and playboy bunnies, I see Nelson's blue head down at the end of the hall. He's talking to his friend, Mohawk Man.

Suddenly, my stomach's feeling squiggly and it's almost like I'm floating. I push through the crowd of kids to get to him.

"Hey!" I say, tugging on his leather jacket.

He turns to look at me. His face is like something out of a horror film. An open zipper runs from his chin to his forehead, passing through his eye. Where it's open, his skin looks, well, not like skin, but like blood and tissue and rot. It's disgusting. And completely awesome.

"Whoa," I breathe.

Nelson cringes, which doesn't exactly fit in with the disguise. "Kevin."

"That looks…wow."

"Like it?" He points to his face, then his friend's. Mohawk Man has what looks like several bullet hole wounds oozing blood all over him. "Me and Roman help out at the haunted house downtown every year. We've become experts in gore."

"Ah. So that's where Melissa's gonna meet up with you, huh?"

He exchanges a look with Roman and says, "No. Actually not. So go for it, Kevin." He starts to walk away, then turns back. "With Melissa, I mean."

All morning Bryce texts me seriously skanky messages about Cassie. When I don't answer, he sends more, along with instructions for handing over the Camaro and what he plans to do in it. It makes my stomach turn. Just like Kevin, Bryce has an angelic look. You'd never expect he's such a creep. His blond hair is always clean and shiny. And he opens doors for girls.

Unbelievable.

So needless to say, I don't sit with Bryce and Kevin's usual crowd at lunchtime. Cassie is dressed as Cleopatra and she and I find a table in the back corner of the cafeteria. Sarah and Michelle (emo hookers) stand bewildered halfway between Bryce's table and our current one. I make a point to turn my back to them. Just like they turned their backs on me only a few weeks ago. They skitter back to Bryce's table.

Bryce, on the other hand, looks amused. As he walks past from getting a soda, he leans down and unzips the outside pocket of my backpack. He rifles through, then takes out Kevin's keys to the Camaro. He winks and whispers in my ear, his words slurred by his plastic vampire teeth, "The bet's over, dude. Give it up. Don't think you can win now."

And a scene flashes in my brain. So vivid I can smell the smoke from Bryce's joint, can see the blackheads on his nose, can feel the carpet in Bryce's room underneath me. Bryce's voice, hard as cement, says, "So you want to wimp out? There's no wimping out of this. No way in hell." He tilts his head to one side and gives me, Kevin, a malicious grin. There's a challenge in his eyes. "I know why I have a dick, Phillips. Seems you don't."

The scene disappears and I'm back in the cafeteria, watching Bryce walk away. I shake my head clear and whip up out of my chair to follow him.

Bryce is almost to his table, but I catch up to him by the recycling station. It's not Bryce's fault. I know it isn't, but he's the only target I can reach. Besides, I can almost feel the testosterone rushing through me. All those aggressive hormones chanting, "Fight! Fight! Fight!"

"I happen to be sitting with Cassie because I like her. She's a decent person. Unlike you," I say.

Bryce crosses his arms and leans against the huge barrel marked, *Aluminum Only*. "Did you fall on your head or something? 'Cuz you've been acting insane lately." His words are a hard line. "And it's getting old."

"I just want to know…was everything a bet? Sam, too, was he your little practical joke?"

"I don't even know what you're talking about, dude."

"Yes. You do. You're a piece of work, you know that?"

"Here," Bryce says, shoving the Camaro keys into my chest, pushing me back a little at the same time. By now we've gotten the whole cafeteria's attention. The incessant buzz of conversation all around us has stopped. "If you're that sore of a loser go ahead and take them." He calls across the cafeteria to Cassie, "So what's it like, Cassie? Dating *Mr. Nice Guy*." There's a definite sneer in those last words. Then he looks directly into my eyes and growls, "Fuck you, Phillips."

My whole body's pumped, ready to take him down. Break his jaw. But I take a breath, two breaths, to calm down and watch him walk away instead. I scan the cafeteria as he sits down. Pretty much everyone looks stunned.

I go back to sit by Cassie again and let my adrenaline level taper off. I feel people's stares on me, hear the whispers. We don't say anything until the noise level in the cafeteria reaches normal decibels.

"What's going on, Sylvie? Something's up with Bryce and Kevin. Something to do with me." Cassie's eyes are hard. She keeps glancing over at Bryce. "Tell me what it is."

I hesitate. I don't want to hurt her more than I have to. But she has a right to know, I guess. I'm about to tell her when Cassie says, "Look." I follow her gaze and turn around to see Sam approaching us, orange plastic tray in hand. He's not in costume, but looks scary anyways from the way his skin is pale from what's probably lack of sleep. He creeps around the table like we're going to bite him before finally sliding into the chair next to Cassie. He glances at me, then stares down at his mashed potatoes. "If you're who you say you are, what's the worst thing I've ever done?" he asks, not looking up from the grey mass on his plate.

At the sight of him, I feel lighter, more alive. More me. I answer automatically, like I would if all were normal. "You mean besides your being born?"

He stays still.

I get serious. "The celery. Getting me to rub it on my skin before going to the beach. I still have scars. That was a vicious practical joke, you know."

He lifts his head and looks at me. "Sylvie's never forgiven me for it."

I grin Kevin's killer grin. "But I will now, if you believe it's me stuck inside"—I sweep my hands over Kevin's body—"this."

Sam looks back at Bryce, probably going over in his head the likelihood of the real Kevin fighting with his best friend. "But how? Cassie told me you were leaving your body, but I don't get it." He looks ready to cry.

I glance at Cassie. She gives me a little smile, which makes something leap in my chest and tingle down below. *Not again. Mind over matter.* I turn away from Cassie and explain the night the switch happened to Sam. Well, not everything. I skip the evil-girl-wanting-to-snatch-her-best-friend's-body part. Just thinking of it makes me feel like I've swallowed a bowling ball.

"I can't believe it. I mean, I believe it, but…" He brings his thumb up to his mouth, but doesn't chew on it. "You mean this whole time you've been flying around the universe? Where'd you go? South America? Antarctica?"

I feel heat rise under my mound of stubble and I don't meet Sam or Cassie's eye. "Actually, I mostly went to Kevin's."

"To do what?"

I mumble, "Get to know him I guess."

From the way he stares me down, I know what Sam thinks of this. "You mean you didn't even check out the rain forest? That's the first place I'd go."

"Yeah, well, I'm not you, am I?"

He shakes his head in disgust, then changes the topic. Sort of. "But how could you have pushed Kevin out of his body?"

"I didn't. He was projecting, too. So he wasn't in his body at the time."

"You didn't tell me that," Cassie says, startled.

I push a bread crumb around on my plate. I think of the bet and I don't feel particularly sympathetic towards Kevin right now. "I didn't tell you because when he projected he spied on you. He took notes."

"What!?!"

I shrug. "He's not the person I thought he was."

Cassie practically spits fire.

Sam asks, "So you what, *fell* in?"

"Look, Sam, I don't know exactly. I guess that was the flaw in the plan."

"Uh, yeah. You go around invisible, sneaking peeks at some guy like the ultimate stalker from hell and *that's* the flaw?"

I glare at him. Because he's so right. And he doesn't even know the half of it.

"Where is Kevin?" Sam changes the subject.

"We don't know," Cassie says, her voice a pool of venom.

I nod my head, but the back of my neck prickles in memory of the moment after my dream, of actually seeing him.

"What does it feel like? To be him?" Sam draws lines in his mashed potatoes with a fork.

*Tiring. Confusing. Infuriating. Terrifying.* I run my hands along the solid planes of Kevin's forearms. "Wrong," I say.

We sit in silence a moment, Cassie still fuming, Sam trying to digest it all. I lean closer to Sam. "Can you take me to the hospital with you? When Mom's not there? I'm thinking maybe if I get close to my body…I don't know. I'm ready to try anything." *Anything but the truth.* I don't look at Cassie. Guilt, like sludge, seeps into my gut and settles at the bottom. If Cassie didn't like spying, she won't like body snatching, that's for sure.

Sam sighs. "Mom's at the hospital all the time. Dad, too, pretty much." He looks at me. "Sylvie…you…or…" he flails around trying to figure out what to call my body. "Sylvie's got pneumonia. It's pretty serious. " Now he chews on his thumbnail.

Yeah. Serious. I suddenly feel so heavy, it's like someone replaced my blood with liquid lead.

Desperation clutches me. "But isn't there *any* time when Mom and Dad are gone?"

Then Sam's eyes light up. "Today. Mom and Dad have a meeting with their lawyers. They're postponing the whole divorce with, uh, you in the hospital."

Something electric zips through me. A positive amid all the negative. No divorce! "They're not going through with it?"

"Not with what's going on. Not right now, anyways." I know he sees the excitement in my eyes because he says, "But don't get your hopes up too much."

"You sound like me."

"I'll stop, then." He glances at his watch and looks uneasy. "If we do this, we'll have to skip class."

"Let's do it," I say.

"Wait." I hold both Cassie and Sam back as we exit the cafeteria doors. "Wait until the bell rings. Nelson has *B* lunch and I want him to come with us."

"Who?" says Sam.

"Nelson Strange?" Cassie asks in a hard whisper. "He knows?"

I shake my head. "He doesn't know. But…I think I want him to know."

"He won't believe you, you realize that?" Sam says. "I'm your brother and I'm not even a hundred percent convinced. Ninety-nine. Not a hundred."

"You like Nelson now, don't you?" Cassie touches my arm and squeezes it gently.

At her touch, my body hums. Then I see Nelson coming towards us and I feel like I'm soaring. "Yeah," I mutter. "My body likes you and my soul likes him."

"What?" she asks, but I don't answer. Nelson's near us. He tries to skirt around us and to the other set of doors, but I reach out and grab him by the jacket.

"*Now* what?" He jerks his jacket out of my grasp. He looks pretty damn scary with an annoyed expression on his gory face.

"We're going to visit Sylvie in the hospital, if you wanna come with."

Nelson looks from me to Cassie to Sam.

"That's my…Sylvie's brother, Sam," I say, like I'm doing introductions at some gala. Nelson just blinks at me. "We're going now," I tell him.

"Now? But it's…" He doesn't finish his sentence. He looks down at his combat boots then back up at us. "I'll come."

When we tell him the situation, Nelson doesn't believe us. "What kind of sick joke is this? Why're you doing this to me?"

We explain everything, two, three times. At first he looks for a hidden camera, someone recording the whole thing on their phone. But then he just flares his nostrils and crosses his arms.

"It means a lot to me that you came, Nelson. Whether you believe this whole thing or not."

"I don't believe it."

I nod, but suddenly feel like crying. "Yeah," I say, my voice breaking. "I understand."

We're a motley crew at the hospital. Sam signs us in. The nurse hesitates, pointing out Nelson and Cassie's costumes. But the place is decorated with jack-o-lanterns and ghosts on string, so they're not adverse to the holiday. "Fine," she says eyeing Nelson. "But only because she's not able to see what you look like." We follow her down the hall.

"Visitors!" she announces cheerily as she leads us into the room. She walks past the hospital bed to the windows and opens the curtains wide, revealing a world shimmering in sunlight. "It's chilly, but sunny out there, Sylvie. Gorgeous blue sky." She calls this out loudly, as if speaking to someone who's half-deaf. After rounding the bed again and stopping in front of us, she leans in and whispers, "Don't be afraid to talk to her. I believe she can hear everything." She leaves the room, the door slowly gliding shut behind her.

I haven't looked in the bed. Cassie and Sam are still as statues next to me and Nelson's hanging back near the door, but all of them are staring at the mound under the blankets. I avert my eyes and drag shaking fingers over the snaps of my coat. I take it off and hang it over the back of the only chair in the room. I scan the machines, the curtains, the bedside table. On it there's a huge homemade card, covered with children's drawings. It's from the after school program and it says, "We miss you!"

Then finally, slowly, I raise my eyes and look at her. At Sylvie. At me.

It's only been a few days since I've seen that face, but it feels like an eternity. I take a deep breath and try to stop myself from trembling. I move as close to the body as the machines will let me, studying the face that is supposed to be mine.

There's a tube stuck in the mouth connected to a machine that's making a sound like a steaming iron. Other tubes and wires cover the body, like a bionic millipede. But I can still make out the girl beneath.

My breath is stuck halfway through my windpipe. *That's me? That's really me?* I blink and blink but the picture before me doesn't change. Yeah, she's pale. But her nose and chin aren't nearly as pointed as I remember. And her eyelashes they're...so long, so thick. My eyes travel downward. She's skinny, no doubt, and worse since being here. Her arms are covered in bright red patches, probably an allergic reaction to something or other used to clean her up. I swallow a base-ball sized lump that has lodged in my throat and fight back nausea. Why did I always feel so ugly in that body? It's not perfect, but it's just fine.

"That's really me?" I ask. Cassie and Sam both nod without taking their eyes off my body. Nelson squeezes his eyes shut.

*All this time I've looked okay?* I feel dizzy and grab the machine next to the bed so as not to fall.

The machine beeps out a heart rate slow enough to make me realize that she...I...am skirting death. I put my fingers to my neck, Kevin's neck, and feel the heart rate. It pounds out a quick but steady beat. So who is dying? Kevin or me or both of us?

Cassie squeezes my arm. "You okay?"

I nod, but I don't know if I'm telling the truth. *That's me. That's me lying there.*

"What should we do?" This from Sam. I glance over at him. He looks like he's going to be sick.

Nelson takes a step closer. His eyes are glistening.

I turn back to the bed and suddenly feel lightheaded with fear. "How many of these machines do you suppose are keeping me…her…alive?"

No one answers. We all know it's just a matter of time until my body gives out without its soul or gives in to the pneumonia. But how long? Two days? Two months? How long do I have before I won't have my body to go back to?

I reach out to touch my…her…cheek, but I can't do it. My hand starts trembling again and I snatch it back at the last second.

We all stand there staring for a long time. Then I shuffle backwards to the chair. "I'm gonna try getting out of Kevin now. Just give me some time," I say. The three of them leave the room. I try to relax. Try to project. I imagine myself back in my body and will my soul to do the same. I can feel a struggle going on inside me, like a thick rubber band ready to snap.

Yet I'm still Kevin.

Half an hour goes by, and Cassie, Sam and Nelson open the door to the room. "We'd better go," says Sam. "Mom and Dad won't be gone forever."

I put on my coat and start to leave, but stop at the door. *I'm coming back.* I think it as loud and forcefully as I can, hoping Kevin can hear it. "I refuse to keep being you!" I say aloud. I look all around me to the walls and ceiling. There's no sign of Kevin. Cassie, Sam, and Nelson exchange glances and usher me out of the room.

On the walk to the parking lot, my steps are heavy but sure. I look at Sam, Cassie, and Nelson, think about those kids in the after-school program. I think about Mom and Dad and know I was always loved. Know that I was better than normal. Know I was wrong. About everything.

Determination takes over. For once in my life, I'm absolutely positive about something. It may have taken turning into someone else, but I've finally realized who I want to be.

Me.

# thirty-five

## Freaky Feelings.

None of us say a word in the car on the way back to school. Sam eats his hands, Cassie swipes at her eyes a lot, and Nelson...Nelson stares at me. Like by doing so he can see which soul is housed in this body. I glance at him in the rearview mirror. He's got a strong jaw and full, but masculine lips. Underneath that horrific makeup he *is* hot. Latisha was so right. I have an urge to tell him I'm sorry and kiss him. Hard.

"I'm not going back to class today," I say as I pull up to St. Anthony's. "I'm sick of pretending to be Kevin. I need a day off."

Cassie hugs me and Sam says, "Call me later. I'll tell you what happened with Mom and Dad."

Nelson unfolds himself from the back seat of the car. He looks me in the eye. "That was really painful," he says. Then he walks into school without looking back.

I get back in the Camaro and put the car in gear. I need to get out of Kevin. But I'm so tired of trying to project, trying to get out with no results. I sigh. *What do you want, Sylvie?* What I really, really want is to be me for just a little while. What I really want is to paint. So I take off to the store and buy several tubes of acrylics and a thinning medium along with a palette, brushes, a canvas, and an easel. With a twang of satisfaction at the huge total, I use Mr. Phillips's credit card from Kevin's wallet to pay for it all.

No one is at the Phillips' when I get back. It's still too early. I go up to Kevin's room and push back his curtains. I find the vacuum and suck all the dirt off the floor. Dust motes float in the sunlight. I open the window for a bit of fresh air and when I do, I notice the room no longer smells like him.

I set up the easel and am just putting the canvas onto it when the house phone rings. I let it ring until the machine picks up, the automatic message reverberating off the walls in the hallway. I go to the doorway to listen, to make sure it's not the secretary from St. Anthony's calling to rat me out. But it's not.

"Hi Kevin, it's your mother here."

Instinct takes over. Like my body—his body—has a mind of its own. I run down the stairs at an impossible pace to pick up the phone.

She continues talking on the machine. "I hope you're doing well—"

I whip the receiver off the base. "Hi. It's me."

"Oh! Kevin," Her voice is surprised, embarrassed, and way too high-pitched for someone over the age of six. "I wasn't expecting you at home right now…"

"Then why call now? Why not later? Why not try my cell?"

"Well, I…I'll be busy later. Now was the only time I had to call. And I didn't want to disturb you."

I listen to her breathing. Little puffs in and out. Then I say, "Okay. So I'm listening."

She makes a noise in the back of her throat. "I'm calling because I'm going to have to cancel our plans this weekend. Things are busy here at work." She sighs, but continues quickly, as if she's worried about not getting a chance to explain. "I know I've missed the last two months. I know. But some things can't be helped, Kevin."

My gut tightens and the anger comes like a torrent, despite the fact that she isn't my mom. "Yeah," I say, not holding back. "Like we can't help who our parents are." Then I hang up the phone. My whole body's pumped and my breath is coming fast. Why do I care what Kevin's mom says? Why am I so ticked?

I take the plush stairs back up to Kevin's room and stand in front of the easel. The place where my ribs meet in the middle feels hollow yet tingly. *Kevin's a jerk*, I tell myself. *Don't feel sorry for him.* But I do. I imagine Kevin's face from my dream. Not the angry face. The sad one, the one I saw right before waking up. Then I think of my own body at the hospital and how I would now give anything to get back into it. The hollow feeling between my ribs gets deeper.

I pick up a brush.

Hours later, Kevin's step-mom pushes open the bedroom door. She has David in that baby carrier and some sort of reprimand on her lips. But all of a sudden she stops when she sees the clean room, sees the easel. "What's going on? What's…what's that?"

"I'm painting," I say, putting the brush down and pushing nonexistent hair from my face out of habit. I pull the desk chair over and plop down into it. "What do you think?"

She steps further into the room and stands behind me, her breath even and slow. "My goodness, Kevin. I didn't know you could paint. I thought you were failing Art. But this... it's amazing. Kind of tortured, but amazing." Her voice goes a bit flat and she says, "Here I would have thought you'd paint a baseball." She stares into the painting and I study it, too. It's not finished, but recognizable. It's me—the Sylvie me—and Kevin. Flanked by violets and blues and golds. It's us, tangled in a silver cord.

Kevin's step-mom tilts her head toward the painting. "She's pretty, isn't she? Different looking, but pretty."

My chest aches. "Yeah, I guess so."

"But this glowing rope...?" She leans over me.

"It's the silver cord," I say quietly.

Right away Kevin's step-mom stiffens. She feels blindly behind her until she touches the bed, and then she sits down. "I see it now...the picture. It's that same *feeling*. You really have left your body."

We look at each other and it's like the animosity between us—between her and Kevin—evaporates. Her eyes go soft and so does her voice. "Your conversation with your mom, it was on the answering machine. I didn't mean to listen to it, but...I heard." She glances out the window, petting David's fuzzy head, then back to me. "I'm sorry," she says.

Tears prick the back of my eyes. "Me, too. For how I've been with you."

She puts her hands over her face and pulls in a long, shaky breath. She lets it out again and wipes her eyes. Then a wide smile takes over her face, showing off a smudge of red lipstick on her front teeth. "So, did you want to talk?" She gestures toward the painting. "About all that?"

I could hug her for being so open, so easy to forgive. "Do you think you can answer some pretty wild questions?"

"I've been studying this like my life depended on it, Kevin. And after that weekend retreat…well, I'm no expert, but I can try to help."

I nod like I know what she's talking about. "Can…do you think it's possible that someone can be punished for using astral projection the wrong way? That maybe I can't project anymore because I was selfish?"

She purses her lips and moves them back and forth. "Like a moral police force? Of course there are higher beings and all that, but they're pretty busy with other things." David makes a sighing sound in his sleep. She smiles down at him, then looks at me. "But some people have a purpose. Maybe you've served yours, or learned what you needed to learn. Maybe there's no reason for you to project anymore."

"I definitely have a reason to project."

"Okay. Well, some people follow their spiritual guides when they leave their bodies. Some don't. Do you remember the movie *Pinocchio*?"

"*Pinocchio*?"

"Yeah. The puppet and the cricket? There's a song in there…" She starts singing, her voice way off key. "'And always let your conscience be your guide.' If you're a spiritual person, your conscience is your guide. Maybe it's weighing you down. Maybe it's not clean. Or clean enough." She shrugs. "No one's perfect, but some things weigh heavier on us than we think."

My whole body tingles. *Tell the truth*. Kevin wasn't just saying it to torture me.

"You know, though, Kevin, you've got to be careful with astral projection."

"What do you mean?"

"Well, it's like swimming in the lake." She smiles at me. "It can be fun, amazing. You experience sensations and a freedom you can't experience anywhere else. But it can be dangerous. If you panic, you can drown. There's currents, cold spots, drop-offs that can catch you off guard. Same thing outside of your body. There's negative energy, waves that can eat away at who you are. Feed off your fears. Get into your head."

I swallow a rough, dry pocket of air.

"But once you know to look for it, you can sense it. A shadow. A whisper. A voice or a presence you're not sure of." David lets out a weak cry and Kevin's step-mom jiggles around a bit to calm him.

"Shadows?"

She lifts her eyes from David and studies me. "You've experienced it already?"

"Not…not always. Just sometimes."

"Was it when you were feeling sad or upset or angry? When you projected at that time?"

I think about it. When it happened. "Yeah. Yeah, that's it."

She nods. "You were probably in the lower astral."

"Huh?"

She gets up, swaying back and forth, rubbing David's little head. "So, how to explain? Okay, radio waves. We know they exist, right, even if we can't see them?"

"Yeah," I say slowly.

"Well, so do different planes. They vibrate at different levels than we do. They're out there, they exist, even if we can't see them. And how we feel when we project determines what level we go to. Lower feelings result in lower vibrations. And you end up with the lower beings. The negative energy. You don't want to open yourself up to them."

I stare at her, the hair on my arms rising. "But what happens if you do?"

She shakes her head. "From what I've read, they mess with you. Create havoc. Mischief. Chaos. Which is bad enough. Some talk about possession, but that's extremely rare—"

I must look terrified because she puts a tentative hand on my shoulder. "Don't be scared. There's so much more out there, too." She gestures to my painting. "You've seen it. And you'll start to notice that you're not alone. That most of the others out there are just people projecting, like you. Those of us who are pretty healthy spiritually stick to the higher realms."

But I can't stop thinking about the shadows. About the way they seduced me, got me to trust them. About the voice in my head, telling me I could be Cassie. That I could be beautiful. That I could get the boy. That possession was the way. *What did I open myself up to?*

David starts crying in earnest now. Kevin's step mom starts to leave and is at the door when I say, "But what about getting lost? Or stuck out there? Or in someone else?"

"I wouldn't worry about that. It's quite difficult to stay out there willingly, let alone on accident. And from everything I've read, no one's ever reported going into someone else." Then she steps into the hallway, closing the door gently behind her.

The second the door clicks shut, I hear a shuddering sigh directly behind and above me. My heart starts drumming. *Other people out there.* "Kevin?" I know for sure it's him.

I swear I hear a barely audible sobbing.

"Kevin? We need to talk." I wait and listen. But he gets silent. "I'm going to tell Cassie the truth and get out of you," I say. "Just like you told me to."

Still silent. Something in the core of me wriggles, but then I feel a suffocating squeeze. Like all of a sudden someone poured concrete into my gut.

"You heard what your step-mom said, right? We've got to get you back. It could be dangerous. For both of us. You're not with the shadows, are you?"

No anwer, but I'm sure he's still there. Positive. My entire body is covered in goose bumps.

"I don't want to be you anymore."

Still nothing. I ask, "Why haven't you ever gone into my body so we could have worked this out?" But I know the answer. He wouldn't want to be Psycho Sylvie Sydell. She's the kind of girl who tries to steal her best friend's body. Even floating around in the ether is better than being her.

*But I'm no longer her*, I think, then say aloud, "I'm no longer her. Sylvie Sydell has become a new person." I narrow my eyes at the empty air around me. "And I don't mean you."

Supper doesn't go much better than the night before. Kevin's dad comes home late from work. "How was swim practice?" he asks, as he sits down at the table.

"I didn't g—" *Just lie,* I tell myself before I ruin it all. "Uh…Good," I say, not looking at him. "Wet."

The meal's fantastic: barbecue ribs and home fries. Salad with some thick, creamy dressing. At least being Kevin has *some* advantages. I rip a huge hunk of meat off a rib with my teeth and despite my mouth being full I say to Kevin's step-mom, "This is phenomenal."

She beams at me. Like I was little David, not Kevin. A fuzzy warmth spreads through me.

"Your mother called me." Mr. Phillips skewers a chunk of salad with his fork, brings it to his mouth and chews. "She said I need to teach you some manners. That you hung up on her."

"*I* need some manners? She cancelled on me. And apparently this isn't the first time."

Mr. Phillips looks at me funny. But then he shakes his head and goes on, his voice louder and more angry. "It doesn't matter what she did. You don't hang up on an adult." He wipes his mouth with his napkin and gives me a hard look. "Why do you even want to spend time with that woman? I've told you over and over she doesn't care about you. Not one bit. She never has."

It's like someone took a huge sword and just—WHOOSH—spliced through me in one quick swoop. The pain is intense enough that I look down at myself to make sure I'm still in one piece. And then a scene flashes in my head. And I see my feet—Kevin's feet—on the stairs, only they're smaller and in Spiderman tennis shoes. I'm leaning against the wall, hiding, listening to a conversation in the living room I know I shouldn't be listening to. I hear Kevin's mom's voice, disgust lowering her timbre: "You can have full custody of Kevin, for all I care. God knows I never wanted to be a mother."

I reel back and I'm in Kevin's kitchen looking at the stern face of Mr. Phillips.

And then I know these flashes aren't just weird thoughts. They're memories, stuck in this brain. They're memories that are not my own.

Kevin's step-mom reaches out to touch my forearm, but my body jerks in reflex, up and out of my chair. "I'm not hungry anymore," I say and run upstairs.

On Kevin's bed, the tears overtake me. Long sobs that make my chest hurt.

The thing is, I don't know which of us is crying—me or Kevin.

Maybe, it's both of us.

# thirty-six

## The Upside of the Downside

Later, when I've finally cried myself dry, I call Sam.

"Hi," I say. "I just wanted to know how things are. How's Mom and Dad?"

"They were at the hospital tonight holding hands." Then he sighs. "There's no kissing or anything like that, but they don't act mad anymore."

Ironically, my projecting may have brought them back together after all. I feel the first genuine smile form on this face since I've had it. "No divorce, then?"

"They haven't called it off completely, but they're not in a hurry anymore. That's what they said."

I imagine them, on the plastic hospital seats, fingers entwined, knees touching. Maybe it's enough for them to get back together. *Wouldn't that be great?* But then I hear myself saying something surprising: "Well, as long as they're okay with each other. And with us. Married or divorced."

Sam doesn't say anything. I take a breath and ask, "Did I just say that?"

"Yeah. You did."

I think it over. "Well, I mean it. Mostly."

"Fine. But maybe if you stay Kevin long enough, they *will* get back together."

I groan. "No way."

There's a silence and I hear Sam jiggling the phone. "Okay. So you're in him. It's horrible, I'm sure, but it could be worse."

"Sam, I have a penis. How on Earth could it be worse?" But I think of the shadows, the voices. Maybe I'm lucky something even more evil didn't happen.

Sam ignores my jibe and continues instead, his voice faltering, "Sylvie, I gotta tell you something. There's bad news. Things aren't getting better. The doctors actually talked to Mom and Dad about the possibility of…you…not making it. They wouldn't have told me if they weren't really worried."

I clutch the phone tighter, hoping I misunderstood his words.

"Mom won't leave the hospital room. Dad's always outside because he's smoking constantly." He pauses. "I just think you need to know that it could happen."

I can't answer. I can't say a thing. I hear Sam sob into the phone.

Sam's crying gets me. It always has. "I'll figure something out, Sam," I say to reassure him.

But I have no idea what.

I call Cassie so we can meet, so I can tell her the truth, but she doesn't answer her phone. When I call her house phone, her mom says, "Oh, she's at a meeting of some sort." Weird. Cassie isn't in a club or anything. If I weren't so terrified about my body dying, I'd be relieved. Because despite wanting to be out of Kevin, I'm in no rush to spill it all.

Just as I close my eyes, my phone rings. It's a number that comes up unknown on Kevin's phone. "Hello?"

"Cassie gave me this number." It's Nelson's voice. I bolt upright like a rocket.

"So, you know it's me? You know I'm not Kevin?" The words rush out. Then I stop and take a breath. "You believe me."

"No," he says. "I just...you said Sylvie needed a friend. I just wanted to know how you think I can help her."

A happy ache bobs inside me like a buoy on water. "You just did, Nelson."

I'm about to go to sleep when the phone buzzes. I pick it up, hoping it's Nelson again because it says UNKNOWN caller. But it's not. I don't think. The phone buzzes. And buzzes. It's a message. And another one. And another one. And another one:

*"rd sum mor"*
*"red som mre"*
*"read sm mr"*

I stare down at it, wondering what the hell is going on. But I can feel Kevin. In the room. Like a breath on a sigh on the wind. A shiver runs down my spine. It's got to be him.

But what's he saying? The phone buzzes again:

*"READ SOME MORE"*

I stare down at the screen, swearing. Then it hits me: the notebook. He's trying to tell me something.

I page through it and stop on a long passage. His writing slants to the left, and the blue ink is thick and smudged in some places. I read:

*October 27: Bryce won't let me go back on the bet. Like everything else with him, the damn thing has taken on mega proportions. Why did I even agree to it? But he knows where and when and how to strike with me. And I was wasted. Too wasted.*

*But I like her. A lot. Yeah, she's hot. But it's more than that. Sometimes, when I look in her eyes, it's like I get lost there, she's so deep. And she knows what it's like to have parents who want you for what you can do, not who you are. I'm actually kind of glad I didn't hook up with her for the bet. She's delicate. Breakable. I want to take it slow. And I want her to decide.*

*So I told Bryce off. Fuck him. Fuck everyone. He can still take the Camaro if he has to. I came home early from his place. Couldn't stand looking at his face anymore. I'm gonna AP a bit, and then tomorrow I meet her for lunch. I have to tell her the truth, or she'll hear it through Bryce, and that would be BAD. He'll give her all the details, and then make more up, that's for sure. I've typed up a sort of confession/apology to text to her. Because I know I won't be able to say it out loud. She might hate me. She will hate me. But I have to let her know. And maybe I'll figure out how to win her back.*

I stop reading and look again at the date. October 27th. Whoa. That was when I projected. Into him. In the middle of the night, sometime between the 27th and the 28th. He was going to tell Cassie the truth. But he never got a chance.

I page through some more and can't believe my eyes. The guy's a closet poet. He's written tons of poems, from haiku to free verse. And a lot are about a copper-haired girl with green eyes and a sad smile. *How the hell did I miss that?* My spying skills suck.

So Kevin is a complete cretin for even taking part in the bet, but I can't say he's all bad. He genuinely likes Cassie. For the right reasons.

"All right, Kevin, I won't judge you anymore," I say out loud. Then I laugh a bitter laugh. "Like I can."

"Tomorrow I'm getting out of you. And we take care of things on our own."

# thirty-seven

## Or Not So Psychotic

I dream again of Kevin. He's standing before my painting, tracing the lines of my brushstrokes with his finger. "You're really good," he says.

I don't move or say a thing, but I can feel my heartbeat in my throat.

He glances at the door of his room, then keeps his gaze there, like he can see beyond it to where the rest of his family is sleeping. When he turns back to me, his eyes are full of a sad sort of humor. "I saw you with Amanda. Seems like you're a better me than I am. Maybe—"

"Kevin, I—"

But he disappears. When I open my eyes there's faint glow in front of my easel. It dissipates until the room is completely dark and I feel I'm all alone.

# thirty-eight

## Collateral Damage

After tossing and turning, I finally fall asleep again near dawn, when I'm woken up by Mr. Phillips's knock on the bedroom door. He comes in and stands in front of my painting while I wipe crusty sleep from my eyes. "If you can do this," he says, "why the hell are you failing Art?"

"I'm not failing anymore. I've actually gotten nothing but decent grades this week in Art and everything else."

"Can you keep it up?"

I think of Kevin. He's a jerk at times. But not dumb. "If I hang around the right crowd, yeah."

He turns around, nodding. "Then see fit to hang with the 'right crowd'. I don't want anything interfering with your success." He glances at his watch. "I'll be at the meet tonight. To see you win."

I open my mouth to say I'm not so sure about the meet, but Kevin's dad silences me by holding his hand up. "Swimming's what you're good at. It's what will take you places. Like it or not. Later," he pauses, looking at me meaningfully, a small, tight smile on his face. "Champ."

I know something important just happened, yet I'm still too groggy to figure out what. Besides, any good feelings Mr. Phillips has about me now will be long gone if I don't get out of Kevin before the meet.

At school, I find Cassie before first hour. "Hey, where were you last night?"

She looks around us, her cheeks suddenly burning pink. "I went to a meeting. For teens with alcoholic parents." She shrugs and gives me an embarrassed smile. "I guess I'm finally angry enough to do something other than complain."

I gently rub her back. "Good idea, Cass. Did it help?"

She shrugs again. "Didn't hurt. I'll keep going, anyways."

The bell for first hour rings. Crowds of kids run past us, banging into our shoulders and schoolbags. "I need to talk to you," I say. "I have something to tell you." My voice sounds like broken glass.

"At lunch?"

I think of how what I say might cause a scene. "Yeah, but downstairs. In Mrs. Stilke's room."

The warning bell goes off. And Cassie smiles widely at me. "Okay. See you later."

I nod and watch her walk off. I think she'll probably never smile at me again.

The rest of the morning I feel on the verge of puking. I think of all the winters Cassie and I spent building lopsided snow forts to take refuge in from the snowball attacks of the older boys down the street. Or how in the summers, we would draw pictures all over the sidewalk with giant-sized chalk, our clothes covered in pastel-colored dust. Or, more recently, how we would giggle over yearbook pictures, or surf

YouTube for the stupidest videos, or lie on the grass under the moonlight and share our secrets.

I'm going to lose all that. I'm going to lose my best friend. And while I'll still remember things fondly, all her memories of me will be tarnished with anger. She'll look at me and see deception.

When the bell for my lunch hour rings, I head down to the basement which I know will be deserted. Mrs. Stilke's not there, and the supply room is locked, but the classroom itself is wide open. I sit down and pick at a dried mound of red paint on the table until I hear the shuffle of feet in the hallway. Then Cassie comes in. Nausea clutches my insides. I breathe in through my nose and out through my mouth, hoping it will pass. It doesn't.

"So, what's up?" Cassie tosses her hair over her shoulder and sits down next to me. "You look awful. Are you okay?"

I take another intake of breath and let it out slowly. It doesn't help that Cassie's hair and skin look so touchable to these hands. I shove them in my pockets. "I'll survive."

"You need to shave, you know that? I don't know if Kevin would approve of the Cro-Magnon look." She raises one eyebrow. That's another thing I'll miss. The one eyebrow trick.

"I can't shave my legs without nicking them all to pieces, Cass. There's no way I'm going to try dragging a razor across my face."

"You've got a point there."

"Look," I say, forcing myself back to the subject. "I need to tell you something. But before I do, just know that I've changed since then. Maybe it was temporary insanity, or some evil force, I don't know. But now, I would never...I think you're the most wonderful person there is. I always have

-- despite being angry, despite what I told myself at times. If there was anyone in the world I would ever want to be besides me, it's you. For lots of reasons. I hope you can see that that's flattering in a way."

"Uh…okay."

"I've learned a lot in the past few days and I'm a better person. Really." I let out a huge breath. "I hope you can forgive me."

"Sylvie, I'm not following."

I can't look at her. I stare at the silver barrette above her right ear. "The whole projecting thing? I never wanted to end up in Kevin's body."

Cassie lightly smacks her forehead with her hand. "Duh? I know, Sylvie. You—"

"I wanted to end up in yours."

"What?" Cassie says, her voice thin.

"My plan was to get you out of your body so I could be you. So I could be with Kevin. So I could be normal and pretty and smart and have parents who stuck together. And you…you were supposed to end up in me."

It's like all the air is sucked out of the room. I glide my eyes from Cassie's barrette to her face. She's staring at me, her eyebrows shoved together.

"Be me? You mean like…possess me? Or steal me?" She adds a nervous laugh.

"Yeah. Exactly."

"Is this supposed to be funny?"

"No." My voice is hoarse. "No. It's the truth."

She just continues to stare, her head shaking back and forth like she can't believe it.

"It's the truth," I say again. "I know it's hard to swallow."     .

The green of her eyes turns fiery. "Hard to swallow? We've been best friends forever. Blood sisters. And you tell me your wanting to *possess* me might be 'hard to swallow'? What the hell, Sylvie? What the fucking hell? First, Kevin spies on me and then you try to…to…become me? I never should have gotten in between you two. You deserve each other." She stands up and shoves a strap of her backpack onto her shoulder with shaky hands. "Serves you right. Ending up in him. I hope you never get out." She runs out of the room.

I sit for a minute while my stomach churns, then sprint over to the large garbage can next to the door, letting my nausea finally get the best of me.

# thirty-nine

## If at First You Don't Succeed...Get Drastic

I imagined that the second I told Cassie the truth there'd be a flash of light and I'd pop free of Kevin's body. That he'd be yanked back into his own, just like that. But it doesn't happen that way. I'm still him, heaving and sweating over the garbage can in the art room, when Nelson comes in.

"Kevin?"

I wipe a hand across my forehead and lean against the wall. I slide down it and hold back tears. "Nelson. What're you doing here?"

His eyes are enormous and startled. "Got study hall this hour. I told Mrs. Stilke I'd carry some stuff in instead of sitting in the library."

I only notice now that he's holding a huge box. I see some white material sticking out of the flap on the top.

"What's in there?" I point to the box.

He sets it down on a table and pulls a T-shirt out of it. A T-shirt with my design—the lacy looking one with the St. Anthony's icons in the details—printed on the front and *St. Anthony's High School* in bold letters underneath it.

"Fundraising for the yearbook," he says, setting the T-shirt back in the box. "Sylvie's design." His voice is low, sad. Then he looks at me again. "Why are you upchucking in the art room?"

I put my forehead on my knees and let huge sobs rip through me. They're loud and messy. I wipe my nose on my sleeve. "I'm a horrible person, Nelson. Really horrible. You wouldn't like me anymore if you knew."

"Um...Kevin, I've never liked you."

And all of a sudden my sobs turn to laughter—I'm deranged enough to find Nelson's comment extremely funny. But I stop laughing almost as soon as I start. "No, Nelson. Not Kevin. Me. Sylvie. If you only knew what I did. When I ended up in Kevin, I was really trying to end up in Cassie. To see what it would be like to be beautiful, you know? How sick is that? Talk about shallow."

"Maybe you'd better see the nurse." Nelson's pupils are pinpricks in the dark turquoise of his eyes.

"You say that a lot." I try giving him a smile. "Go with me, please? Just...walk me there?"

He looks like he'd much rather bolt. But he says, "Okay," and helps me up off the floor.

We walk the halls in silence until I knock on Nurse Carey's door. I turn to Nelson. "This is the second time this year you've walked me to the nurse's office, you know? Remember when I bumped my head? I wasn't there, Nelson. I was projecting. Out of my body."

He just stares at me.

"Same thing when you kissed me. I was so shocked, I just—" I snap my fingers.

His face reddens then pales.

Nurse Carey opens the door. Nelson takes off back down the hallway so fast you'd think I was contagious.

Nurse Carey pokes and prods me a bit, asking some questions, but I tell her that I just need a little rest. She nods, gives me a blanket and tucks me into what looks like a dentist's chair. Then she turns out the light and closes the door between her office and the sick room.

Dull light comes in through the windows and there's a long line of clouds in the sky, their bottoms silvery-grey. The silver lining. Every cloud has one. My silver lining after telling Cassie and even Nelson the truth will be to get out of Kevin.

I take a deep, deep breath and let it fill my lungs. Then I exhale slowly. *Relax. Relax your toes. Relax your feet. Relax your ankles.* Eventually, I'm able to get to that state where I feel light and heavy at the same time. I imagine a rope above me that I pull myself up on, inch by inch. I feel a slight release and then a clamping down.

"Not yet," says his voice, light as butterfly wings. "Can't happen…can't…don't…please…hurry."

And the moment is gone. My body feels solid again. Still his body.

*What!?!?* Was he right about telling the truth? Or is he messing with me? Maybe he doesn't even want to come back. Maybe he's not ready! *Don't hurry?* You've got to be kidding me!

I pound the chair with my fists. "*You* might not be ready, but I am! You can't hold me here forever! My body will die, you asshole! I told Cassie! That's the first step and you know it!" I sit glaring at the air around me hoping looks can kill—or at least scare a soul back into its body—when the door to the room opens.

"—clean it off," I hear the nurse saying. Behind her is an overweight freshman boy with a bloody hand. They shuffle in, and she apologizes to me about the disturbance. He sits awkwardly on the table in the middle of the room listening while Nurse Carey blabbers on about safety in biology classes. The freshman slipped up with a dissecting knife.

I wait for them to finish and leave so I can try to relax again, try to leave Kevin again, but then the interphone in the room rings and Nurse Carey's saying, "My goodness, what's with the kids today? Of course, bring her up."

At this rate, I'll never get out of Kevin. And right now I'm so mad at him I could strangle myself.

I sit up. "Nurse Carey? I think I want to go home."

"All right. Just sit tight and we'll call your parents for you."

"No," I shake my head. "No, I've got my car. I can take myself home."

She wags her finger at me. "Uh-uh. School policy. I call your parents or you stay."

"Fine. Call."

Kevin's step-mom isn't at home and isn't answering her cell. So the nurse calls his dad. She explains things to him, then is quiet a bit and beckons me over to the phone. "He wants to talk to you." I take the century-old yellow thing with the curly cord and put it to my ear.

"Hello?"

"You're not coming home, Kevin. You have a meet to-night."

"But Dad, I'm sick. I threw up." *Out of guilt and despair. But I threw up all the same.*

"You're trying to get out of the meet."

"No. I'm sick. Besides, there are other guys on the team, you know."

"How many times are you going to try to pull this?"

"What?"

"Until you become good enough at something else, sports is what you focus on, young man. Like it or not, that's the only thing you excel in. Poetry won't get you into college on a scholarship. So suck it up. I'll be there tonight. And you'd better damn well be suited up and ready to go."

I hang up and look at Nurse Carey and the freshman, reeling from the fact that Kevin's tried to get out of meets before. I blink at them a couple times then say, "Guess I'm hanging around here."

My mind is racing. I try in vain to relax while sick or hurt kids parade through the office. My mom always uses the expression "No rest for the wicked." For me it seems a perfect fit.

Once the final bell rings, I try to leave school unnoticed and take all the deserted corridors to get to the parking lot. But I can feel Kevin's presence the way you can feel a storm coming with the change in the air. I know he's there and won't let me leave his body. Not yet.

"What kind of baby are you, anyways? Need me to fight your battles for you? What, can't you face Daddy on your own?" I spit it out it under my breath but I know he can hear it. I know he can. "I can't swim, you idiot. There's no way I'm going to that meet."

But when I slip through a side door that leads to the dumpsters and eventually the parking lot, I think maybe that's what Kevin's counting on. That I won't participate in the meet. That I'll lose his spot on the swim team. That I'll take the heat from his dad and bring his grades up until it's safe for him to come back.

"Coward," I whisper.

I get into the Camaro when a thought hits me. A crazy thought. I get out of the car.

Some guys on the swim team are crossing the lot and I find myself calling after them and walking to the pool building with them.

As we're opening the door, I hear Sam yell from across the parking lot, "Hey!"

"It's okay, Sam!"

"Mom called! She wants me to come to the hospital." He runs up to me. His face is white. "Sylvie...she's worse. Mom and Dad are worried she won't last the night."

I feel like I'm sinking, sinking into the ground. Everything around me spins. "God. Now what, Sam?"

"I don't know!"

I can't seem to breathe. Can't seem to focus on anything. Then Tyrone and Ryan smack my shoulders, bringing me back to reality. "Come on, Phillips!"

*Do this, Sylvie. Do something.*

"Okay, okay. I've got an idea. To get out," I say to Sam. I know he's worried, but I wave him off and follow the guys inside. All's fine until we get into the building and Ryan pushes open the door marked *Boys Locker Room*. "Whoa!" I say, unsure I can handle a room full of naked guys snapping wet towels at each other.

Maybe I can keep my eyes on their feet.

Ryan says, "What's your problem, Kev?"

"Nothing." We walk in, the humid air already causing beads of sweat to form on my brow. My eyes sweep over the dozens of hairy legs, the hairy toes, and scan the lockers. *Oh, no.* I have no idea which one is Kevin's.

I scan the lockers, looking for one that no one's using, but there are tons. My heart jumps around in my chest.

"Hey," I say, looking at the curly hair on Tyrone Dickson's knees. "I know this sounds completely ridiculous, but I'm drawing a blank. I can't remember my locker number."

There's silence, so I quickly bring my eyes up to his face. He's looking at me like I just grew two heads. "You *forgot* your locker number?"

Then Bryce gets up from the bench he was sitting on. "I effing knew you banged your head on something, man. Either that or you've been smoking too much."

"Hey, Phillips! How many fingers I got up?" a voice calls out and everybody laughs. But Bryce narrows his eyes at me and says, "Locker seventeen."

I squeeze past some guys to stand in front of the tan locker. I try the combination I know Kevin uses for his locker in school, but it doesn't work. I fiddle with the numbers on the dial some more then say, "You don't happen to know the combination, do you?"

Even though he'd said it before, Bryce sounds surprised. "You really are high!"

I say nothing.

"After the attitude you've been giving me lately, why should I help?"

I stay quiet.

He comes over and turns the dial, right, left, right, then yanks open the door with a clang. "Just don't lose your head out there. Or we're screwed."

I nod and undress. When I start to suit up, Bryce says, "It's not effing pantyhose, dude. What's *wrong* with you?"

I notice my pointed toe, the way I'm holding one leg in the air as I slip the suit over my knees. The guys around me are all gaping.

Luckily, Coach comes round and starts riling everybody up. He gives some sort of motivational speech, talking some foreign swim language: district preliminaries, medley relays, and things like freestyle and dual meets. I've come to see Kevin race tons of times, but all I ever knew was that he got in the water and moved fast. I try to look like I understand what is going on.

"Phillips!" Coach yells. All eyes are on me. I look up and catch Bryce's gaze. He looks both amused and confused.

"Yeah?"

Coach points to his own chin. "What the hell is living on your face? Go shave it off. Now."

"I...uh...don't have a razor."

Coach rolls his eyes. "Hensley, give Phillips a razor."

And so Bryce and I go over to the sinks together while Coach rambles on about qualifying for regionals.

"I really think you're losing it, man. For real. Going insane." Bryce watches me closely in the mirror.

I shrug. "I'd say I'm finally going sane."

Bryce puts a can of shaving cream and a razor on the edge of the sink. The razor is a cheap disposable one. I use enough shaving cream to make me look like Santa, and then bring the blade up to my right cheek and drag it slowly down. All's fine until I hit the chin line, nicking the skin. "Ow!"

Bryce just raises his eyebrows.

I keep shaving, and keep grazing the skin. By the time I'm done, there's a good amount of blood trickling down my neck.

Bryce goes into a toilet stall and comes out with a roll of toilet paper. "Here," he says.

I know what to do. I've seen my dad blot his cuts with toilet paper plenty of times. I end up looking like I'm covered in polka-dots.

"News is you and Cassie broke up. That she spent all afternoon crying."

Now I study him in the mirror, his cool blue eyes, the cocky set of his mouth. "I told her the truth," I say. "She didn't appreciate it."

Bryce snickers at this. "You can always get a new girlfriend, Phillips."

"What I need," I say to his reflection, "are new friends."


I'm apparently supposed to compete in the 200 yard medley relay, the 400 yard freestyle, the 200 yard individual medley and another relay. Whatever. I walk out into the pool area behind the rest of the team, the humid air even warmer out here. There are dozens of people in the bleachers. I feel odd in a Speedo and swim cap, being stared at by half the school. Mr. Phillips in the first row is watching me like a hawk, and further back is Sam. He looks frantic at the sight of me suited up. He knows I can't swim.

But I don't intend to. What I do intend to do is play a game of chicken with Kevin. *Release me or I'll make a fool of you in front of the whole school. Release me or drown.* But so far he isn't biting. I look over at Mr. Phillips again, who nods at me and gives a thumbs up. *Come on, Kevin. You don't want to disappoint Daddy, do you? Not like this.*

It all starts with the 200 yard relay medley. I'm third in my relay team. After Tyrone and Bryce. I follow them to the platform or block or whatever it's called. Men in maroon T-shirts with TIMER written in white across the back crowd the empty spaces between lanes.

Then I hear Kevin, his voice weak and scared in my ear. "Hurry...the truth!"

"I already told her the truth!" I say it out loud. One of the Timers glares. Tyrone and Bryce share a look.

*Come on, Kevin. Let me go. You can do it. You can let me go and get into your body on time to save face. On time to save us both. Now!*

But a cold breath ruffles my hair and goose bumps pop up all over my body. "Truth."

And then I realize it. What he's been trying to tell me all along. Oh my God! *Tell the truth!* He has to tell Cassie, too! Here I'm playing chicken with him and he's been trying to get me to do the right thing all along!

I whip around and run, my feet slipping on the wet floor. I land on my side with a loud thud, pain like the slash of a whip in my bones.

"Phillips!" It's the coach.

I get up and shove open the door to the locker room. I've got to get to Kevin's phone. Locker seventeen. Seventeen...I yank on the padlock, but it's locked. *Crap!* It was Bryce who opened the damn thing before! *What was the combination?*

But then Kevin's fingers seem to move all on their own. 22-6-98 The lock snaps open.

I whip Kevin's jeans out, feeling for his iPhone. I go into *Messages*. Then I find the ones that haven't been sent.

*Come on. Come on.*

But Bryce and Tyrone are suddenly next to me. "Phillips, you get out there. Now." Bryce sounds pissed.

Suddenly, I realize how buff they are. How scary. "Just… on…minute," I say as I scroll through the messages, trying to find the right one.

Tyrone reaches for the phone. I pull away before he can grab it. Then both he and Bryce are trying to snatch it from me.

There it is: a message to Cassie, titled *SORRY*. I swipe my thumb across the screen to send it. And that's when Bryce grabs the phone and throws it across the locker room. It smashes into locker 42. Glass from the screen falls onto the floor.

I feel weak all of a sudden. I almost collapse, but Tyrone and Bryce are holding me in a vice grip.

*Please let it have sent. Please let her get it. Let her read it. Now.*

*I don't know if we can make it otherwise.*

Bryce and Tyrone drag me back out towards the pool. As we enter the area, my eyes flick up to Kevin's dad. His face is dark and angry. I can tell he's barely holding it together.

Coach swears at me under his breath and threatens to cut off my balls if I pull anything else.

*Nice guy.*

Tyrone finally loosens his grip on me so that he can get up on the platform. There's a splash as he dives in.

*Come on, Cassie. Read it. Read the thing.*
*Come on, Kevin. Come and take your body back.*

Bryce narrows his eyes at me then steps onto the platform. I look at the fake blue water, breathe in the scent of chlorine and feel fear tugging at my insides.

A whistle blows and Bryce, sleek as an eel, is in the water. I stand watching for a second until coach yells at me to get onto the platform. I step up, totter, stand still. Bryce is already on his way back.

*Come on.*

The shiny black surface of Bryce's swim cap makes its way towards me. My blood stops flowing, I'm sure of it. My whole body's petrified.

Bryce is right underneath me. I can't breathe. I can't move. All around me is a wave of sound. MOVE! GO! COME ON! Furious shouting over splashing. But I stay, staring into the water, at the tiny blue tiles lining the bottom of the pool.

MOVE IT, PHILLIPS! NOW! I imagine the coach turning purple, Kevin's dad standing up, screaming himself hoarse. My breath is coming quickly now, too quick. I can't catch it, each inhalation too fast, too shallow.

And then there's something wet and strong around my ankle, yanking me forward and down. As I catapult towards the water, I see Bryce's disgusted face. See him release his hand from my leg.

The water is cool, and it startles me. I thrash around. Sink quickly. Panic strangles my brain, takes over my thoughts. I know I can't take a breath, but I open my mouth and gulp water anyways. It burns going in.

*Kevin's body knows how to swim. Let it. Let it take over.* But the thoughts don't dampen the terror. And so I can't let go.

*You can't drown at a swim meet*, I try telling myself, but it doesn't matter. I'm twelve again and in Lake Michigan. I'm twelve again and drowning. The fear is more than memory. Everything is blurry and I try to find the way out of the water. I see wavy faces staring down at me, hear a dull echo as someone jumps in.

Right then I see Kevin, his face contorted in confusion. I see a silver cord float between us. A black stain in the water.

And I feel a tug.

# forty

## Millisecond Memory

In the space of a millisecond, in the time it takes me to feel a tug and a jolt, Kevin and I share a memory.

It's the memory of a fifth-grade girl who was looking for a hero and found one. It's also the memory of a fifth-grade David who brought down a hairy Goliath with one good bite and felt like a hero, even sitting in the principal's office. It's one positive memory we have together. Only it was a long time ago.

The millisecond is over.

Pool water fills my lungs. I know I am drowning.

But I feel a release. Then a yank.

I see Kevin. A flash of gold.

And the next thing I see is my mother's face, her eyes ringed with dark circles. I hear her voice, tinny and ragged, as she sobs, "Oh, thank God, Sylvie. You're awake."

# forty-one

## Where I Belong

The first thing I do is hug my mom. We navigate our arms through all the tubes and wires connected to me, wrap them around each other like we're afraid to let go, and bawl like babies. Mom's wearing her turquoise velour sweat suit. In it, her shoulder is soft and welcoming.

I want to tell her I've missed her, but a tube is stuck in my throat.

Mom's whole body heaves as she starts a new set of sobs. "Oh, Sylvie. I love you so much."

My movement must have set off something at the nurses' station, because suddenly one is at the door, gasping, her eyes bulging like marbles. Then there are other nurses and a doctor, all shocked but happy and I'm prodded and poked and petted. They take out tubes and stickers and needles, and put others in. "How are you feeling? Do you know where you are? Can you tell me your name? Who's this woman?" The doctor pelts questions at me as he rotates my head, checks my eyes. "Any nausea? Lightheadedness? What about pain? This is so unusual. No one ever comes out of a coma so alert."

I cough and cough, my lungs aching, but answer everything he throws at me until he says, "What do you remember?"

I shrink back into my pillow and squeak out of my sore throat, "Actually, I'm pretty wiped. Can we...can we talk about this some other time?"

My mom shoots up like a firework. "If she's tired, I'd rather she rest, doctor." The doctor, flabbergasted that I'm so with it, seems to want to study me, but he agrees not to tire me out. So, finally, the whole medical team leaves with stunned smiles on their faces and I'm alone with Mom again.

"Rest, sweetie."

But I think of the meet. Of Kevin's confused face. Of the water rushing into my lungs. Oh, my God. He released me, but did they save him? I sit up straight. "Where's Kevin?"

"Kevin?" My mom's face clouds over with anger. "You mean that horrible Phillips boy?"

"He's not horrible, Mom. That was me. That was me in him."

Her eyes widen, then she says, "Shush, Sylvie. You're tired. You don't know what you're talking about."

I close my eyes and breathe in the scent of antiseptic. I'm about to tell her more when I hear the whoosh of the door. My eyes fly open to see Sam standing there panting. He looks at me, his lashes wet behind his glasses, his chin quivering. "Sylvie?"

I nod and he runs over, throwing his arms around me. I feel a sharp tug on my hand as he accidentally pulls at my IV.

"Ow!" I say, but give him a smile to let him know it's no big deal.

He pulls back and stands by the side of the bed shifting from one foot to the other. "I was worried. With what happened in the pool—"

"Where's Kevin?"

His eyes water over. "Here. At the hospital, I think. But…" He puts a thumb to his mouth and bites down as he talks. "They gave him mouth to mouth, the whole works. He…I don't know if he's alive. When they put him in the ambulance, it didn't seem like it. But how can someone drown so quickly?"

*No. No, no. He can't be dead.*

"I need to know how he is." My voice is trembling. *This is all my fault.* I suddenly start coughing like crazy, pain sawing through my throat.

"Sylvie, I don't want to leave your side. You've still got pneumonia." Mom's face is grey.

"Please? Please, Mom."

She hesitates. Looks from me to Sam. "You stay here," she tells him, and goes out into the hall.

All I'd wanted to do was get out of him. I was sure he'd come back if he were forced. Sure it would work if Cassie read the message. But what if…what if instead of saving us both…what if I killed him? What if I'm a murderer?

"Oh God, Sam," I say, feeling woozy. "He has to be okay. He just has to."

Sam gives me another hug, carefully this time. We stay like that until my mom comes through the door again. "We can't get any information on Kevin. Hospital policy." She sits in the one chair in the room, pulling it as closely as possible to the bed. "I called your father. He's on his way here."

"Okay."

"I'm so happy, Sylvie." Mom strokes my arm. I know I should be euphoric, but there's an anxious gnawing in my gut, cutting into my happiness. *Where is Kevin?*

"Sylvie," Sam says. "Nelson gave me a ride over here. He's out in the waiting area…"

"Get him." I say without hesitation.

Mom grabs Sam's arm to stop him leaving. "It's too soon for visitors, Sylvie."

"Just for one minute, Mom. It's important."

When Sam brings Nelson into the room, Mom's too concentrated on me to even notice his blue hair. He stands at the foot of my bed, looking nervous.

"Nelson." My voice is still rough from the tube. "I thought after what I told you in the Art room today you wouldn't like me anymore."

He shakes his head, then looks up to the ceiling and blinks a bunch of times. "It's true?"

I wait until he looks at me and then I say, "I know it's nuts, but, yeah, everything's true."

He doesn't leave. He just stands there staring at me, like he's not sure what to think. My mom and Sam silently slip out of the room.

"I should have gone to that bonfire that time you asked me. And I should have kissed you back," I whisper to Nelson. "Thing is, I only wanted Kevin. I couldn't see that there were better people out there."

"Guess you got Kevin after all," Nelson says bitterly, looking down at his feet.

I laugh, but it hurts my chest. Nelson comes over to the side of the bed and briefly touches my hand.

His warmth is like a little fire. It warms all of me. Especially my heart.

The door to the room flies open and my dad rushes in, looking like a rumpled Clark Kent. He sits on my bed and crushes me in a hug. His shoulders shake as he cries. "I was so worried we'd lose you," he says. I glance towards the edge of the bed.

Nelson's gone.

My whole family stays well past visiting hours that day and the next two. They pull in chairs from a neighboring room then take turns accompanying me while I'm forced out of the room for a whole set of tests I don't know the names of. From an MRI to a 40 question survey to making me smell stuff one nostril at a time, the experience is both terrifying and strangely surreal.

I don't bring up being Kevin again, but every once in a while I ask one of my parents to see if they can find out what's happened to him. They do it grudgingly. No one tells them anything.

Near 11 pm, the head nurse kicks everyone out. "Sylvie needs rest and so do you. Go home. You can come back tomorrow morning." At my parents' hesitation she insists, "She'll still be here."

I nod. "Believe me, I'm not going anywhere."

When they leave, my room is quiet except for the faint bustle of the nurses in the hall. It's lonely and chilly, so I pull my blanket up to my chin but keep my eyes open in the semi-darkness. I stare out the window to the brightness of the parking lot, and beyond that to the dim glow of the moon behind clouds. I wonder if Nelson's lying awake in the moonlight. I wonder where Kevin is, if he can see the moon.

I wonder if Cassie's looking at that same moon right now and I suddenly wish I were with her. That we were in my backyard staring at it together.

Three nights later, when I get the green light to take a walk with my mom in the hospital halls, I decide to search Kevin out.

Mom holds my arm like I'm weak, but I'm not. I feel fine. Great, in fact, apart from the bruising and itching in the spots where there were stickers for the EKG or whatever it was. But, hey, I'll take minor allergies over a penis and facial hair any day. I shuffle along the shiny Linoleum floors in paper hospital slippers eyeing the names on the outside of each room: Conroy, Harper, Adams, Schmidt, Krusinsky, Sanchez...We do the entire second floor but I don't see a Phillips anywhere.

"Let's get you back to your room," my mom says, steering me that way.

"No. I want to keep walking. Third floor."

"I really think—"

"I need to find Kevin, Mom," I say softly.

"Sylvie!"

"Mom." Apparently something in my voice gets to her, because she blinks at me then sighs and heads towards the elevator.

We walk the whole third floor, then my mom forces me to sit and rest for five minutes in one of the lounges. We watch the doctors and nurses bustle past, along with other patients trailing IV's hanging from a pole on wheels. Visitors in winter coats carry stuffed bears and flowers wrapped in cellophane. I time five minutes exactly, then I tug my mom's sleeve. We board the elevator for the fourth floor.

When the doors open, I feel my insides jump. There in front of me is Kevin's dad and step-mom, both looking tired and disheveled. They get in as we get off. I turn around as Mr. Phillips presses the button for the restaurant level. Kevin's step-mom and I cross gazes, and I see sudden shock in her eyes right before the elevator door closes. My painting. She recognized me.

"He's here," I whisper to Mom as we try to walk casually down the hall. Now there seems to be a lot more hospital staff in the hallway. Two nurses chat at the nurses' station, pointing to something on the computer. A doctor stands rubbing her temples then writing something down on a chart. An orderly pushes a cart around the corner. Suddenly, Mom's grip on my arm tightens. I look at the room we're passing. Room 404. K. Phillips. A big laminated sign stating NO VISITORS hangs on the closed door.

"I've got to see him." I move towards the room.

"No visitors," Mom says between clenched teeth as she smiles at a nurse walking by. The same nurse who was on duty those mornings I snuck in to see my body.

"I don't care."

"Sylvie, you are not going in there." Mom whispers it with force.

I turn around. All the staff seem busy, their backs to us for the moment. It's now or never.

"I'll meet you by the elevator," I say, prying Mom's hand from my arm and slipping into room 404 before she can do anything about it.

Inside, it's déjà vu. The machines, the tubes. Just like me, just a few days ago.

I stand next to the bed, looking down at the thick lace of Kevin's eyelashes and suddenly feel like crying. Yes, Kevin's been a jerk. And no, I definitely don't have a crush on him anymore. But I do care about him. A lot. I just hope he's learned as much as I have throughout this whole mess.

I can't feel his presence like I could when I was in his body. "Kevin?" I whisper. "Are you here?"

Dread trickles through me when I hear nothing. *Please, please be here.* I glance at the window and see something shimmery over my left shoulder. I blink and concentrate and there is his reflection, his copper hair brilliant under the light, his shoulders strong. My body goes weak with relief that he's still here, still nearby. "I'm sorry about all this. I didn't mean…" But I stop, swallow and say, "Why don't you come back?"

He doesn't answer. I think about how his mom doesn't spend time with him and how his dad forces him to compete. How his best friend is a prick and his grades are in the toilet. How Cassie now knows what he did.

"You're strong enough to deal with it all, Kevin. Despite what you think."

The only sound in the room is the beeping of machines.

I think of the memory I experienced just before I left his body. "Heroes don't run away. Maybe it doesn't mean much to you anymore, but you were a hero to me back in fifth grade." I swallow and blink back tears. "You could still be."

I turn away from his reflection and take another look at his body covered in wires and tubes. "Come back, Kevin. Before it's too late."

Suddenly, the body on the bed convulses and there's one huge gasp for air. The machines go wild, beeping and screaming. Kevin's eyes open and he looks at me. There's no anger there, no hatred. Just the feeling of something shameful shared.

I hear footsteps running down the hall on the other side of the door. I cover my face with my arms and slip out of the room, fast as I can.

"Hey!" that same nurse yells. But she goes into Kevin's room instead of following me.

When I get near the elevator my mom's pacing furiously and looks ready to kill me. She sees me running and knows instantly to punch the DOWN button. I reach her just as the bell dings. I push her inside, and she pulls at the sleeve of my gown. "I cannot believe you!"

I catch my breath and give her a wide smile. "It's okay, Mom. Kevin's gonna be okay."

The hospital gives me my discharge papers the next afternoon. But before I leave, Dr. Hong comes to visit. "Sylvie," he says, smiling.

"Dr. Hong. What are you doing here?"

"I wanted to wish you a good trip home. And let you know that if you want to talk, I'll listen."

My voice is sharp. "I already did talk to you, Dr. Hong. But you never listened."

He nods. "Fair enough." He holds out his hand for me to shake. I hesitate, but take it. "I'm very glad you're back."

"Me, too."

When Dad comes to take me home, there's a light dusting of snow melting on his shoulders.

"Snow? Already?"

"It's Wisconsin," he shrugs. He wraps my winter coat and scarf around me and, because of hospital policy, rolls me in a wheelchair out to the parking lot. On the passenger seat of his car is a paper bag filled with Twix and Nestle Crunch bars. I pick it up with a lump in my throat.

"I have a feeling you won't need to hide them anymore," Dad says when I set the bag gently on my lap. "Your mom will cut you some slack for a while."

I smile at him and then he takes me back to the house he no longer lives in. When I open the door I breathe in the scent of the place. It smells like potpourri and charred vegetables. It smells like home. Mom and Sam have decorated the place with purple and green crepe paper, long streamers hanging from the light fixtures and the doorways. They've gone all out—there's even a cake, a fancy bakery one, one that's full of trans-fats. Mom beams at me while I shovel in forkful after forkful.

The four of us sit around the kitchen table eating cake and playing Dad's beat-up Parcheesi game. I feel a strange settling in my stomach when I look at my parents and my brother licking frosting off their lips and moving their colored pawns around the board. It's like we're a family. A real family. That is, until Dad says, "I'd better get going."

"Now?" A thin needle of pain pierces my chest.

Dad grins and pats my head like I'm a Labrador. "It's midnight. I don't want to turn into a pumpkin."

"What about the snow?"

"It's light, Sylvie. Don't worry." He hugs me. I squeeze him back hard.

Mom walks Dad to the door. "Thanks, Nicole." Dad's voice is soft as velour. Mom touches his upper arm briefly before he leaves. Sam and I exchange hopeful glances that they might still work it out yet.

"We should all get to bed; especially you, Sylvie," Mom says.

"You guys go on ahead. I kind of want to sit here by myself for a bit."

They both hesitate. Mom can't seem to make her feet move. But they eventually go upstairs and leave me to my own devices. I listen to the water running in the bathroom, the floorboards creaking above my head. This house is noisier than Kevin's. But better. So much better.

After a bit, I go up to my room and bite down on my tongue to stop from crying. I love this place. Love the art-work on the walls, the desk stained with ink.

I sit at my desk chair and take in the fact that I'll be sleeping in my own room tonight. My cell phone rests in its charger. On the screen it says *1 message*.

I open it and see the text. It's from Nelson:

*"Offr 4 bnfire still stnds. We cn talk. bout evrything. And mybe try anothr kiss?"*

The tears take over, but there's a smile underneath.

# forty-two

## Two Girls on Either Side of the Hedge

I can't sleep. I go downstairs into the living room and sit down on the couch. There's a dim light shining in the driveway between my house and Cassie's. I get up and lean against the window, stretching my neck to try and see if Cassie's bedroom lights are on. They are.

I wonder if she's already painted over her butterfly mural. Already thrown out everything I've ever given her.

I'm about to go back upstairs when I hear the squeak of Cassie's storm door. I move into the kitchen to see out the window and hold my breath as I watch her trek across her backyard and stand at the hedge. She looks up at the moon, then at my house.

I rush to the back hall. My boots are on the floor. I stuff my feet into them and pull my down coat from its peg on the wall. I open the door and step into the backyard, sensing the quiet that comes with snowfall. With the layer of white on the ground and trees, the night is dark, but faintly glowing.

Snow squeaks under my boots. I make a trail of footprints to the hedge, now just straggly branches in the bitter cold.

Cassie stands on the other side, her arms wrapped around her middle, staring at me with her lips pressed together.

It's like the first time we met. In the winter. Across this same hedge. I try to say something, anything, but I can't decide on the words. My breath comes out as smoky puffs with no sound. Finally, Cassie says, "So you're out of Kevin."

"Yep." Crisp air sidles down my jacket collar. I lift my shoulders and punch my hands into my pockets.

Cassie looks off into the dark corner of her yard. "I heard about the swim meet. Is Kevin okay?"

"He's in the hospital. But he's him," I say.

"You're sure?"

"Positive."

"I read…I read the message," Cassie says. "Why did you send it?"

"It wasn't from me. I sent it, yeah. But it was from Kevin. He wanted to tell you the truth."

"He made a bet about –"

"Yeah. I know." I dig the toe of my boot into the snow. "I don't know what was in the message he wrote you. But he likes you. For real."

Cassie shrugs. "I'm not sure how I feel anymore. About anything." A tiny smile tugs at her lips but it doesn't reach her eyes. They're sad, sad eyes.

I can't hold back. The words tumble out of me: "Oh, God, Cass. I'm sorry. I miss you so much. And I know you can't forgive me but—"

"Blood sisters always forgive." Her voice is barely audible.

"What?"

"Our oath: 'Blood sisters, blood sisters as long as we live. Always together, we always forgive.'"

I stare at her, mouth open. "I thought you hated me. That you'd never forgive me. But you forgive me?"

"I took the oath didn't I?"

I feel light as air. "You mean it? You mean things can go back to the way they were?"

But Cassie shakes her head and her voice hardens. "I said that I'd forgive, Sylvie. Not that I'd forget. Things will *never* be the way they were. Never."

My throat is raw. I swallow down the pain.

Suddenly, the light goes on upstairs in my mom's bedroom.

Cassie gives me a little shove. "You'd better go. Your mom'll probably start checking in on you twenty times a night until she's sure you're all right." She starts walking back across her yard.

I do the same, listening to the crunch under my boots.

I hear her storm door squeal. She goes inside, letting the door bang shut behind her.

I put my hand on my own doorknob. At that moment, something changes. The cold air on my neck gets warmer and the chill in the air loses its crispness. The shadows in the yard seem to pull back. They've lost the power to influence me.

I know it'll take time. Almost forever. But that Cassie and I will be friends again. That I'll learn how to keep the shadows at bay. And that I'll be able to see myself for who I really am.

It's like a stopper is pulled from me. Like the emotion I've been bottling up is suddenly let loose. I feel like I can breathe again.

I go inside and pull my usual trick of pouring a glass of juice to fake a midnight thirst. Mom rushes into the kitchen as I set down the container. Her hair is a mess and her bathrobe is on inside out. "Are you okay, Sylvie? You weren't in your room…"

"I'm fine, Mom. I'm home." *And I'm me.*

And I can live with that.

# forty-three

## Life is Never Usual

I sit on the examining table in the lab, the paper gown crackling with every move I make. Machines line the walls. A handful of wires hangs from one, ready to attach to the little sticky pads all over my body.

There's a quiet knock on the door. Dr. Hong comes in, a questioning look on his face. "So, Sylvie. More tests?"

"That's your thing, isn't it?"

He chuckles and opens his arms wide, palms up. "Not this time."

He pulls over a high stool on wheels and sits on it. His lips purse up as he studies me. "You realize, Sylvie, if this is for real, if you can prove it, it will have consequences. First, I'll have to reconsider everything I believe. And you...well, I think you'll have to get used to being tested."

"This is me you're talking to, Dr. Hong. Little miss lab rat. I think I'm actually starting to grow a tail."

He throws his head back and laughs. I notice he's trimmed his nose hairs.

When he's stopped laughing, he looks at me. "Like I said, I'm here to listen. Just tell me what to do."

"Okay. So, I've got a test for you." I smile. "Take a piece of paper and write anything you want on it. Something I won't guess. Then go put it on your desk. When you leave your office, lock the door behind you..."

## THE END

# acknowledgements

There are so many people I want to thank that it is impossible to list them all here. From friends to neighbors to other writers who have given me your support or advice in one way or another—be it a shoulder to cry on, babysitting time, or just a kind word—I appreciate all you have done.

Thank you to all my beta readers. You know who you are. Those of you who read the earliest versions of this book and were still able to encourage me to keep writing, despite the mess the manuscript was back then. You all deserve medals for wading through the thing and finding ways to give me constructive criticism.

Thank you to Jane Dystel and Miriam Goderich at DGLM for believing this book had potential.

To Susan Tiberghien and everyone in the Geneva Writers' Group. I doubt there are many places as welcoming and nurturing to writers as the GWG. You all have made the group my home away from home.

To my brothers and sisters—Mary Kay, Terry, Julie, Stephen, and Matt. The only reason I can write about sibling relationships is because I have you! And special thanks to

Julie, who called up with plot ideas and twists and who told me that freaky story about the boy in her high school who claimed he could astral project.

To my sister-in-law, Elaine, for being my cheerleader, but also for being honest about what needed work. And to Celine and Paul for the whole wasabi on the cereal bit.

A big hug to Mom and Dad. You are the best.

A high-five to Robbie Loewith for the title. Two words: love it.

And another high five to Nathalia Suellen for the fantastic cover!

To Yassine Belkacemi for the formatting and for answering all my questions.

To Mslexia magazine. I still can't believe my book was a finalist in your children's novel competition!

To my husband, Laurent, for not complaining about all the nights I left him with tuck-in duty to go write at the university. *Merci, et je t'aime. Je ne te le dis pas assez.* And to my daughters, Emma and Elodie, who talk about their mother being a writer like it's akin to being a superhero. I hope I'll make you proud.

To the Queens of Awesomeness: The Birks—past and present. You ladies rock. You have changed the way I write and the way I feel about myself, all for the better. A hug to those of you who helped out with this book and the writer that came with it: Paula Read, Jawahara Saidullah, Daniela Norris, Tima Mujezinovic, Sharon Pollack, Sher Gordon, Moyette Gibbons, Christine Hendricks, and Melissa Miller.

And, finally, to you, reader, for picking up my book. I sincerely hope you enjoyed it.

# about the author

K atie Hayoz was born in Racine, WI, but ended up in Geneva, Switzerland, where she lives with her husband, two daughters, and a very fuzzy cat. She loves to read and devours YA novels like she does popcorn and black licorice: quickly and in large quantities.

Connect with her on her website:
http://www.katiehayoz.com